Finding Linda

Finding Linda

(with WPC Janice Morton)

Julie Harris
February 2022

JULIE HARRIS

© Julie Harris, 2021

Published by J H Harris

A CIP catalogue record for this book is available from the British Library.

ISBN 978-1-9989954-0-0

Book layout and design by Clare Brayshaw

Prepared and printed by:

York Publishing Services Ltd
64 Hallfield Road
Layerthorpe
York YO31 7ZQ

Tel: 01904 431213

Website: www.yps-publishing.co.uk

For Steve

Contents

Prologue

How uncomfortable could this be? It was the third week of my police officer training at Ryton and I was sitting in the Criminal Investigations class, one Friday afternoon during an unusually hot English summer. But it wasn't the heat making me squirm. And it wasn't the prospect of having to sit in the stuffy atmosphere either.

I was used to the format by now. Our friendly instructor, Sergeant Jim Phillips, stood at the front of the classroom, neat as a pin in his uniform and ready to introduce the speaker for the next ninety minutes. Ninety minutes of acute discomfort for me as it turned out.

The man I had known as Detective Inspector Francis Jarvis stood before me, smartly dressed in his silver-buttoned uniform and black peaked hat. He was Detective Superintendent Jarvis now and deserved the respect of his student audience who were expected to stand to attention and salute him before he nodded for us to sit.

Tall and slim he wore his uniform with a familiar ease. His short hairstyle hadn't changed since I'd first met him. His hair had been chestnut, and it had faded into a dark auburn colour with a sprinkling of grey at the side of his ears.

I knew it wasn't my imagination when he spent most of the time staring in my direction while he spoke. Maybe it was because I was one of the few who sat upright, shoulders back. It had been pointless to slump in my seat on the third row hoping he wouldn't see or, worse, recognise me.

You don't get promoted to superintendent for turning up to work on time or having shiny shoes. I would find that out during my own career, but I realised as soon as Jarvis spoke that the friendly man talking to a nine-year-old girl, ten years earlier, was sharp and focused. He knew the job of a successful criminal investigator and throughout the ninety minutes we were all hanging on his every word.

Instead of inviting questions at the end he asked his own. His Mancunian accent hadn't changed during the ten years since we'd first met in Birmingham.

'After a twenty-year career in the force are there cases I didn't solve with criminals still at large, possibly laughing at me?' He didn't wait for an answer. 'Yes. Less than 5%, but that's too many.'

'Let me give you an example ...' He pursed his lips and gazed up at the ceiling as though searching through the files in his head. 'In 1964, when I was a DI, I had a missing persons case ...'

The blood drained from my face, crystallising into ice cold shards as it seeped through my body. The sweltering heat, causing sweat to leak from the weight of my standard issue shirt, dropped to freezing point. I felt sick from the heavy perfume of Sure and Hai Karate deodorant disguising the dreaded BO that threatened ostracism for any sufferers.

'It was a little girl.' Jarvis was determined to tell the story. 'She was only ten years old and disappeared one night while she was staying with her sister and brother-in-law.'

My shoulders drooped and I dropped my chin onto my chest, wishing I could make myself invisible.

'No one heard her leave the house and we had to suspect the brother-in-law – a young man who could have lured her away and dumped her body. There was even a freshly dug, grave-sized hole in his garden.'

Jarvis nonchalantly walked up and down each of the rows of desks, pausing now and then to make eye contact with an eager student. We ignored each other and he continued with his story.

'But it wasn't him. I knew that as soon as I met him. You'll get to know the body language of genuinely guilty criminals over time … Yes?'

A hand had shot up and smarty-pants Richard Day had a question. 'Sir, did you have a real suspect?'

Detective Inspector Jarvis stared straight at me and rubbed his chin as though trying to recall something. 'Not a suspect exactly, but you can never be sure … There was someone I was certain knew more than they were letting on …

'The sister, sir?'

'No, not the sister …' He answered PC Day again but continued staring directly at me. 'Unfortunately, there was a serious case of arson a few weeks later and someone else took over the case while I dealt with the murder of three people who had lived above an Indian restaurant.'

He beamed at the class as the clock showed it was time for the day to end.

'I'm pleased to say that I did solve that crime and the offenders are still locked up.'

Jim was on his feet with his hands pressed together, but Jarvis raised his voice above the enthusiastic applause.

'But you never forget the ones you don't solve … We never found the missing girl, but I've never forgotten her. I will find her – one day.'

A curt nod acknowledged our salutes and, with his peaked hat placed firmly on his head, Jarvis strode from the room. I hoped he had left my life as well but after that I was fated to bump into him at every turn during my first posting at the station where he headed up CID. Whenever we passed each other, he would always say with exaggerated politeness, 'Good morning' or 'Good afternoon, WPC Janice Morton.' There was no doubt in my mind that he remembered me from 1964 and made sure I knew it.

1

1964

Lonnie was digging. Linda was talking. Baby Rosie was crying. I was hiding.

I sat on my bed in semi-darkness re-reading *The Four Marys* in the *Bunty Annual 1964* I'd had for Christmas. I'd found it behind my bed after tugging the sheets off for Mum to wash. It was just what I needed. A good excuse not to go outside.

The warm morning's July sunshine dappled through my thin curtains, making the large pink roses on my new carpet appear to sway. Dressed in a thin, pale pink short summer dress I enjoyed feeling the heat on my shoulders and the top of my head. I bowed over the book trying to make out the comic strip dialogue in the gloom. If I snapped the light on to see better Mum would hear it and want to know what I was doing.

The sash windows were open top and bottom and from the garden next door voices floated over the fence and into the bedroom, disturbing my intention to keep away from Linda for as long as possible. The thud and thump of Lonnie's spade disturbed the earth and I knew he was digging up the grass to prepare a vegetable plot ready for the autumn planting. He'd talked about it to Mum last week while he bounced on the balls of his feet, cradling his new daughter, hoping she would stop crying and sleep.

'Are you sure you told Janice I'd be here today? Sometimes you forget things, Lonnie, or you don't listen to a word anyone says.' My heart sank and I screwed my eyes shut as though that would drown out the sound of Linda's voice mimicking her sister's favourite complaint about her husband.

The spade paused and I heard the scratch of a match in the still air. It wouldn't be long before the smell of Lonnie's Player's cigarette wafted through the window. When he answered Linda, I pictured him standing up tall in his white vest and black trousers with the bottoms rolled up to reach his knees.

'Don't you worry yourself darlin'. That lazy friend of yours will be down before you know it. Trust me.'

'Janice, what are you doing sitting here in the dark?'

My time was up. Mum was through my bedroom door clutching a laundry basket and standing in the pile of cotton sheets flung from the bed. With one hand she reached up and parted the pink satin curtains, letting in the dazzling sunshine and even more heat. She plonked the wicker basket on my stripped mattress and stuck her head out of the gaping window space.

'Hello Linda, you're back with us then.'

Mum sounded harassed and spoke quickly.

'Yes, Mrs Morton. It's my first day and I'm here for six weeks this time. When's Janice …?'

I heard the digging resume and faint grunts from Lonnie.

'She'll be down in a minute, Linda.' She turned her head towards me as she withdrew it. 'Won't you, Janice?'

'I'm reading, Mum.' I flicked the annual over to show her the hardcover with Bunty riding a white horse with her little black terrier. 'I like *The Four Marys* …'

'Put that away and read it later. That girl's waiting for

you – and you read that annual about five times before the end of Boxing Day. You must know it by heart.'

It was spooky how Mum was so right, so often.

Reluctantly, I pushed the book under my bed, meaning to read it again later. I stood at my window, which was narrow and reached almost from ceiling to floor. When I was younger, I liked to kneel beside it on the lino floor, before we had carpet, and watch the outside world with my head on the window ledge. I was too tall to do that at nine years old but sometimes, when I was anxious or unhappy, I knelt on the floor and leaned my forehead against the glass.

On the other side of the gardens the tops of the orchard apple trees were visible. Their trunks were hidden by wooden fencing running along the twenty terraced houses bordering the private land. At that time of year, in summer, the thick leaves and branches obscured everything in the orchard. On closer scrutiny I could make out tiny apples starting to grow on the top branches.

It was the closest I ever came to seeing inside the orchard and I could stare at it for hours, wondering what it must be like to run in and out of the trees and pick the fruit. I'd never forgotten *The Faraway Tree* in a book I'd read when I was younger. Although the orchard was small it wasn't easy to see deep into the middle of it.

I tried to work out if there had been any progress or changes in the growth of the apples since the morning before, studiously ignoring Linda who I sensed was looking up from her garden waiting for me to wave to her. Mum panted as she quickly stretched a crisp new sheet over my single mattress.

'Janice, you can either go out and play or you can help me in the house.'

'Linda wants me to play with her,' I answered with a sudden desire to wave furiously to my school-holiday friend who was indeed staring up at our house. I could see the creased frown between her blue eyes.

I breathed softly with irritation. There she was. Chubby Linda Bateman, slightly taller than she had been at Easter. She wore a bright yellow sun dress with large white spots. It fitted her perfectly and I could tell it was new. She was looking up at my bedroom window, chewing the end of her fingers. I fidgeted with the armholes of my faded cotton dress which were already digging into my skin.

'I need a new dress, Mum.'

'Yes, I know. Wear that one for this week and we'll go shopping next Saturday. I'll buy you some sandals as well.'

I tried to look excited about the promise of a rare shopping trip, but I was distracted by Linda in her garden. She'd seen me watching her and held each of her arms in the air, waving two Sindy dolls in her hands. We were both crazy about Sindy and her wardrobe of clothes.

'We've got one each, Janice. Hazel and Lonnie bought me a new one.'

As I turned away from the window, I glanced at my own doll. I'd had Susan since I was two years old. She was my best friend and I felt disloyal at preferring the cute little Sindy doll.

Eager now to be outside in the garden, I heard the new baby screaming louder. Hazel, Linda's sister, appeared with two glasses of lemonade and placed them hurriedly on the cement path before running back into the house.

A daring plan was forming in my head and as much as I wanted to explore the orchard on my own, I was too much of a coward. But Linda was here for the next six weeks and she might be persuaded to join me. Why hadn't I thought of this before? I chuckled out loud.

It was the start of the summer holidays and I didn't feel in the least bit guilty that I could look forward to days and days of being spoilt like Linda with lemonade, chocolate biscuits, shop-bought cakes and threepenny bits from Lonnie to buy sweets.

'We're having lemonade, Mum,' I shrieked and ran from the bedroom.

'Don't drink too much sweet stuff,' Mum called after me. She rarely let me drink any kind of pop, scaring me about the effects of too much sugar on my teeth.

'I won't,' I lied and skipped down the stairs, holding the rail with one hand and sliding the other along the thin wallpaper on the opposite wall. Linda could be a real nuisance but there were advantages to having to be her friend. And I was ready to enjoy every one of them.

Linda Bateman was a year older than me. I didn't know her very well and she wasn't really a friend. She just happened to enter my life each school holiday while she stayed in the house next door with her sister Hazel, Hazel's husband Lonnie and their squealing new baby. Her Mum and Dad worked on a market stall every day. Lonnie had recently become an apprentice to the local butcher in the parade of shops around the corner.

'Did you pass the 11 Plus?'

I asked the question as I gulped down the cold lemonade, loving the way tiny bubbles popped inside my mouth and nose. If I drank it quickly enough, I knew the gassy drink would force me to burp out air and in the past Lonnie had laughed and called me a 'little eejit'.

Today, though, he was too busy measuring the patch of earth he'd revealed beneath the discarded grass and pegging green string along the edges. When Lonnie set his mind to something, he did a thorough job, measuring with a steel tape and scratching his unruly black hair when things didn't look right.

'I didn't take it.' Linda's pale cheeks were flushed pink from standing in the sun for too long waiting for me to join her. She spoke between mouthfuls of lemonade, used to drinking all flavours of pop. It wasn't an unusual treat for her.

She studied each of the Sindy dolls, turning her head from the new one and then back to the old one she'd had at Easter. 'There wasn't any point because I'm not very clever. And anyway, Mum said if I did go to the grammar school it would cost a fortune with the posh uniform and paying for trips and everything.'

The two Sindy dolls, one with stiff blonde hair and the other with artfully coiffed nylon chestnut hair, bobbed along the grass where we were sitting on an old woollen blanket. I watched as Linda walked the two dolls in their tiny plastic heeled shoes, itching to snatch them both out of her hands.

'I'm going to the comprehensive in September. The uniform isn't very dear, and I won't need to get there on a bus because I can walk there. Mum said it won't take long and I'll have a new mac if it rains.' She sounded very grown up until she said, 'Here Janice, you have the new Sindy. She looks a bit like you.'

I couldn't disagree and grabbed the new Sindy who wore a shiny black mac and carried a newspaper and a bag with three oranges inside. Her knee-length red plastic boots would be a challenge to take off – but it wouldn't stop me from trying.

Lonnie had stopped digging and measuring and disappeared into the house for a 'cuppa'. He watched us from the doorstep, smoking another cigarette. He was a good-looking man with milk-white skin and thick hair that hung in curls around his shoulders. Up close, I noticed his eyes were a deep blue with long, black eyelashes.

'Girls,' he called between puffs and slurps, 'I'll be having to come through with the wheelbarrow to shift all the dirt. You'll have to play in Janice's garden. I'll fetch the box.'

At Easter Lonnie had made a sturdy wooden box for Linda to stand on next to the fence. It saved her walking around the houses from her garden into mine. With a bit of effort and tugging I could help her to climb over the privet hedge while Lonnie held her above it as high as he could. The spiky branches must have pricked her soft skin, but Linda never complained.

'Come on then, the pair of you,' he said when he finished his tea. 'Janice first.'

With his Irish sense of humour, the simple task took longer than it should have done. He picked me up and pretended to throw me backwards over his broad shoulders, asking Linda if she knew 'where the devil has Janice gone?'

We shrieked with laughter until he put me down on my feet, after two attempts to 'get it roit' and then it was Linda's turn. With his sister-in-law he held her over the hedge and then kept changing his mind, deciding she could help him wheel the barrow when it was full of dirt. Linda wriggled and kicked her feet until he announced it was obvious, she preferred her Sindy doll to him.

Rosie was still crying in the house, but now it was a softer and quieter sobbing while Hazel sang to her. With us both standing in my garden surrounded by Sindy dolls, Sindy clothes and Sindy hairbrushes I saw Lonnie stare at the back door, his forehead furrowed with worry.

'If this keeps up, I'll call the doctor meself,' I heard him mutter and he left us to play while he returned his empty mug.

I stared at the dolls scattered over the grass and then looked at Linda. We giggled and straightened up clothes and other items, ready to begin our games. The summer holidays had begun, but neither of us had any idea our time together would be shorter than we could ever have expected.

2

Secrets

A week later we decided to play a game that ended in disaster.

It had started with Linda trying to make out she had a 'big secret' she couldn't tell anyone. I tried not to care but before I could help myself, I whispered into her ear that if she told me her secret then I would tell her mine.

'You've got a secret, Janice?' Linda's lips pouted with doubt and the usual frown between her eyebrows deepened. 'It can't be anything like mine.'

'It'll be better,' I boasted. I knew I had the best secret ever, but it wasn't much fun knowing something and not being able to share it with anyone else. Worse still, I had a plan and I couldn't carry it out on my own.

We were sitting on a tartan blanket in my garden with damp from the grass seeping into the material. It had rained the night before and the strong smell of the earth in Lonnie's ditch mingled with hollyhocks and tickled my nose.

Linda chewed her middle finger, opening the sore-looking skin until spots of blood appeared. She sucked it and stared at me with distrust. I'd cheated at her daft Magic Robot game the day before and hidden the principal piece, persuading her that next door's dog had run off with it when she wasn't looking.

'Lonnie said your neighbour doesn't have a dog – and, if she did, "even I'm not that stupid I wouldn't see it running around your garden".'

I came clean and admitted I'd found the Magic Robot, still holding his wand, amongst a patch of tall grass after she'd gone home. Linda wasn't impressed and needed to be convinced that we would swap secrets when she'd told me what she knew.

'You'll never be able to guess in a million years.'

Thinking hard about Linda's life and what I knew about it, she was probably right. Unless she was really a fairy there wasn't anything that sprang into my mind that I couldn't know about. Our Sindy dolls lay untouched on the tartan blanket, their arms and legs sticking out at painful angles.

'You're right – I can't guess.' What was the point in trying to work out the secret? She'd never guess my secret and I couldn't be bothered to play twenty questions.

Linda beamed in triumph. 'You're giving up, Janice?' she squeaked in triumph.

'Yes. I'm giving up. Tell me yours and I promise I'll tell you mine. But you have to promise never to tell anyone – EVER.'

She promised and crossed her heart with her bloodied finger, hoping to die if she betrayed me. I did the same and I meant it too. I liked secrets and this couldn't be anything that important.

Satisfied with the new arrangement, we paused for a lunch of fish finger sandwiches and tomato sauce which Hazel passed to us over the hedge. Rosie was balanced on her shoulder, red-cheeked and with her eyes squeezed tight in exhausted sleep.

'Don't make too much noise, girls. She needs her rest – and God knows, so do I.'

We murmured our thanks and sat on the blanket to eat in silence. This was the perfect excuse to talk quietly and not be overheard by any curious adults.

'Go on then. You first.' I licked my fingers and picked up an orange Club biscuit, peeling off its wrapper with exaggerated care, glancing over my shoulder to make sure I was being quiet.

'OK.' Linda's Club biscuit was already in her hands and she bit it in half, chewing thoughtfully. 'It's Hazel. She's not really my sister. She's really my mum.' She sighed heavily as though this was too incomprehensible to even try to understand. 'Don't ask me how it works because I don't know.'

I didn't know how it worked either but a few years later I worked out the truth. Would it have been a big problem for Linda – if she'd been found?

'How do you know?'

Linda shrugged and finished off the biscuit, smudging melted chocolate into a pencil line around her top lip. 'I heard my mum and dad at home talking about her being my mum and that she's got to "step up now I'm older, even if she is a disgrace". I can't have two mums, can I?' She sighed again and I noticed her eyes glistened as she twisted her closed mouth into tight shapes that mostly curved downwards.

When I didn't say anything and sat fiddling with the soft, frayed strap on my red Clarks sandal, she grabbed my arm tightly. 'You mustn't tell anyone Janice. You mustn't. Promise me you won't.'

She was hurting me and I was startled into agreeing. 'Of course, I won't.'

Linda didn't smile with relief. 'Everyone likes Hazel. I don't want anyone to know she's a "disgrace".'

'OK,' I nodded seriously, going along with her concern. 'I'll never tell anyone.'

'Trouble is, Janice, Lonnie said he'd never trust you as far as he could throw you and you're a "right little liar, and no mistake".' She folded her chubby arms and her face reddened.

Lonnie's words stung. I liked Lonnie and didn't want him thinking I was a liar and not to be trusted. I held up my right hand like I'd seen witnesses do in court on TV. 'I, Janice Morton, promise never to reveal Linda Bateman's secret about Hazel for as long as I live.'

It was silly, but Linda's relief, relaxing her mouth into a happy smile, made me determined that I wouldn't let her or Lonnie down.

'Even under torture ...' Linda encouraged, not giving up.

'Especially under torture,' I drew my fingers across my closed lips. 'My lips are sealed. So help me God.' I finished the oath, not quite understanding what on earth I was talking about.

Thank goodness she giggled and flopped her body on the blanket. The moment had passed, and it seemed I had passed as well. I wasn't sure what all the fuss was about. It was an intriguing secret, but it was rubbish compared to my own. Did I really want to tell Linda after all?

'I don't think I should tell you my secret when we don't understand what yours means ...' I began. Linda stopped giggling and sat up. I had to admit Lonnie was right – I wasn't to be trusted.

She whined, 'Tell me.' Then she reached over to pick up her Sindy doll from where she sat next to the empty plate, a morsel of bread in her tiny hand. 'Come on Janice. I won't tell anyone. I promise I won't tell.'

It was tempting to brush off the pact of exchanging secrets and go back to sitting on the yellowing grass in my garden, combing the hair on each of our Sindy dolls.

Linda was taller than me, her body chubby and her face flabby. Her parents and sister – mother (?) – gave her sweets and cakes whenever she asked for them. She was spoilt while I didn't expect anything from my mum, who worked in the school kitchen in term time.

She had everything – two Sindy dolls, when I didn't even have one and always new clothes for every holiday. I was only friends with her so I could enjoy extra sweets and cakes, play with her vast collection of dolls and try on her shoes.

I struggled with my conscience. It was easy to bully Linda, but I had to be careful I didn't go too far. It could all end badly – for me. Plus there was now the added suspicion that Lonnie had rumbled the underhand intentions behind my being Linda's friend.

Linda scrambled across the overgrown grass without getting up, reaching yet again for the small plastic hairbrush that had flown out of her fat fingers. She still moaned as she carried on brushing Sindy's hair. 'If you don't tell me the secret then I won't play with you anymore and I won't let you dress Sindy One in her duffle coat.'

That was a low shot. She knew I liked fastening the teeny toggles.

It was a tough calculation for my young scheming mind. We were only one week into the school holidays and it was ages before we were due back at school. Ahead of me lay days and weeks of free pop, chocolate biscuits and shop-bought cake. I'd be a fool to give all that up.

My shoulders slumped and I pressed a finger to my lips, pointedly staring into Linda's sky-blue eyes urging her silence. 'OK,' I whispered. She nodded her head, unable to hide the broad smile beaming across her face.

I stood up and gestured for her to stay where she sat. With the stealth of a wartime spy I tiptoed across the lawn, over the kitchen step and into the living room. Just as I expected, Mum's head snuggled the sofa cushion, toffee-coloured curly hair hiding her face as she slept. *Mrs Dale's Diary* droned in the background from the radio.

I tiptoed out as dramatically as I could to convey the seriousness of what was to become *our* secret and beckoned Linda to follow me. We stood side by side at the garden fence which separated us from the orchard behind. Wooden fence panels ensured its privacy.

'You can't tell anyone. Promise.'

'Promise.' Linda forgot to whisper, and I nearly had a heart attack, guiltily looking beyond the discarded Sindy dolls, clothes and pathetic plastic hairbrushes on the grass. Mum didn't appear but I still whacked Linda's shoulder with my hand. I shouldn't have done that. She had the fair skin that bruises easily. If questions were asked would she blurt out the secret?

Breathing hard with defeat, I decided to chance it. From Linda's house I could hear Rosie crying so I knew Hazel would be busy with her. Lonnie had already popped home from his job in the butcher's shop. He always ate a quick sandwich for his lunch and then rushed back around the corner.

I clawed at the overhanging ivy which obscured our fence. Lonnie always clipped their ivy back each year and painted the wood an attractive white colour which Linda's sister-mum said reminded her of the Mediterranean.

'Look,' I commanded Linda, still staring at the gaping kitchen door. I parted more of the ivy behind me and let my fingers search for the outline. I had to chance it and swivelled around to examine the area.

'What is it? It looks like the door in *Alice in Wonderland*.' Linda read more books than I did but I still knew what she meant. 'It's not very big is it?'

The door wasn't high or wide. An adult would find it difficult to climb through, but two small girls or a medium sized dog would manage it easily.

'It's big enough,' I whispered. 'We could get through it – if you want, I'll let you come with me to see if there's any treasure hiding in the trees. It'll have to be when everyone's asleep though.'

A puzzled frown creased Linda's forehead. 'Can't we look now?'

She had a point, but I'd heard Mum and her friend Mrs Chant talking about the owner who had put up signs on his property saying 'Trespassers Will Be Prosecuted' which meant sent to jail. I shook my head.

'We can't risk being seen. It's OK if you don't want to come – I'll go on my own. Just don't tell anyone.' I hissed the last instruction with the fierceness of a bank robber giving orders to his gang.

'No, I want to come,' Linda said in a frantic rush of words. 'I want to find the treasure as well.'

And so, our plan was hatched. At midnight we were going through the secret door to the orchard, and nothing was going to stop us from exploring the forbidden territory we could only see from the back-bedroom windows. If we came back with a chest full of stolen treasure, we'd be rich for the rest of our lives.

If only Mum – or Hazel – had shouted to us at that moment, asked us what we were doing, marched over, and told us in no uncertain terms what would happen to us if we even thought about trespassing. If Mum had woken up during those plotting moments, then nothing would have gone wrong and Linda would still be at both of her homes with her real and pretend mums.

3

Midnight

I didn't sleep that Tuesday night, and lay in bed wearing my navy rain mac over my pyjamas, thick winter socks on my feet, ready to jump into wellingtons as soon as my Timex watch told me it was midnight.

It wasn't a well-lit night. The *Secret Seven* would never have ventured out unless there was a full moon or a cloudless sky. I couldn't cancel the adventure and worried Linda would back out at the last minute. If she did, I wasn't sure I had enough courage to wander around the orchard on my own.

I crept down the stairs, holding my breath. She was there, standing on the wooden box Lonnie had set up to help us climb over the small hedge. We performed the usual clumsy scramble as quietly as we could until she was safely standing next to me.

Linda looked cosy and warm in her suede winter boots, with a knitted sock peeking over the top, a woollen hat perched on top of her blonde hair, which was divided into tight pigtails. Her plaid dressing gown belt was tied tightly so that her whole front was covered, with the hem reaching the tops of her boots.

My thin mac was too big for me, so I left it buttoned up but unbelted to keep out the chill. I was consumed with a growing resentment that Linda had everything I didn't have.

The secret door had been something that was mine – for a short while. Why had I shown it to her?

Determined to appear more superior I parted the ivy slowly, heart thumping now that we were really going to carry out the plan. If I'd only been brave enough to do this on my own, I could have dangled my secret over Linda for the rest of the holiday.

There it was. The secret door. Linda stepped from side to side, either from the chilly air or excitement. The long sleeves of my mac fell over my hands and it was hard to hold the torch, slide back my sleeve and push against the door.

'Why won't it open?' Linda whispered my own thought.

I bit my lip. I had tried it the first time I saw the secret door at Whitsun and it had moved slightly, but Mum called me in for my tea and I'd felt too guilty to try again after that. Too late, I realised I had no idea if the door would even open.

'You try it. My hands are cold.'

Linda's hands were tucked into the warm woollen pockets of her dressing gown. My hands were small and weak, freezing in the cold night air.

With two strong pushes, two muffled grunts and one tongue poking between her lips, Linda did it. Yippee, we were through. We both squealed into our hands with delight.

It was only fair I went first. Linda politely stood aside to let me pass and discover if there was a deathly trap on the other side or an armed guard gleefully waiting to capture us.

What had we expected from an orchard? We walked through rows of trees packed tightly into the dark space in front of us and stumbled over fallen unripe apples. Finally, we were on the other side of the door, but we had no idea what to do.

I flicked the torch on and off to help us see the ground. The summer night was dry. I could smell fruit and earth mingled with the scent of Lux soap whenever I brushed against Linda. Even the soap she used was better than the Palmolive mum always bought.

Was it my disappointment at the anti-climax that brought out the worst in me? I've never understood why I behaved so badly but discovering how tame the orchard turned out I became even more aggrieved with Linda at my side. I imagined how different the secret would have been if I'd found all this by myself.

Having made the effort to be there we trudged on, breathing more easily, confident we were alone. The regiment of trees thinned out to a small, cleared space to reveal just one tree standing alone. Could this be the fabled *Faraway Tree*?

Linda and I faced each other, eyes widened with the unspoken question. What was this? Here was something different after all. A small grassy patch had been cleared into a picnic area using a silver-barked tree trunk lying on the ground for seating. We peered up into the gloom of the branches. I couldn't flash the torch skywards in case the light was spotted by someone nearby, but our eyes were gradually becoming used to the dark.

Linda prowled around its base. We'd been bumping into low hanging apple trees with some of the fruit scattered on the ground. This fruit though was somehow different.

'Do you know what?' she asked in a half whisper. We were bolder now we were sure there was no magical mystery to an orchard of apple trees, and we weren't going to encounter fairies ready to reveal a treasure chest. 'If you climb on my shoulders, you'll be able to grab one.'

After five minutes of collapsing into giggling heaps on the damp grass we worked out I could stand on the log, while Linda crouched in front of me, and scramble onto her shoulders. She then staggered across to the tree with me waving my hands.

Peaches. Furry on the outside. The one I grabbed felt as hard as a Granny Smith. Not ripe, we decided, and took it in turns to fondle the rough surface.

'I should take it home,' Linda declared in her spoilt, hoity-toity voice.

'Why you?'

'I can hide it better than you can. No one comes into my bedroom so I can keep it somewhere safe until it's ripe.'

I was cold and tired and just hearing Linda's words made me cross. She always had more than me and now I'd shared my secret with her she was taking the one thing I could have. I snatched the peach from her hands and pushed her.

'No, I'm having it.'

It was one of those silly arguments and, being girls, we just shoved each other around. Linda easily snatched the peach from my little hand, holding it behind her back. I didn't stand a chance so with both hands I bounced them off her chest, feeling the soft wool brush my numbed fingers.

She back-pedalled, her boots brushing the grass, then slid until she hit the tree trunk, twisted and toppled over, banging her head as she fell.

'Now look what you've done.' She rubbed the back of her head.

I thought she would cry louder but she didn't.

I decided I'd had enough, ran off and left her to make her own way back home.

It took a while to find the secret door which we'd left ajar, hidden as it was by the ivy on the other side. I stumbled a few times and was certain I'd break an ankle or something. Just in time I avoided tripping on a pile of old wooden panels piled against a fence which turned out to be two gardens along from mine.

I started to feel guilty and before I slipped through the doorway, I sat on the cold, sloping ground and waited for Linda. I thought I heard some shuffling footsteps, but she didn't appear. I played with the torch, switching it on and off, not caring now if anyone saw us.

What had we done really? Pinched a peach in someone's orchard. Big deal.

The cold finalised my decision. At least I had the grace and fondness for our friendship to leave the secret door open for Linda to find. Good luck to her. I realised too late that she still had the stolen peach.

Back in my bedroom, I couldn't go to bed without waiting to see her stumble through the doorway, so I knelt on the itchy woollen carpet and leaned on the window ledge, resting my forehead against the glass. The darkness lightened as the morning dragged slowly towards dawn. I thought I saw the ivy shudder, but it wasn't light enough to see clearly, and no one appeared.

I woke at 7am with my cheek stuck to the ice-cold glass and ran down to the fence. With shaking hands, I parted the ivy to check if she'd closed the door.

The secret door had disappeared, leaving only plain old fence panels.

Linda was never seen again.

4

Two Days Later

'Janice, come down love, there's someone to see you.'

Mum's voice trembled, sounding thin and high pitched. It wasn't often, never even, that the police came to our house. I'd been standing at my bedroom window all morning, just like the day before, staring at the ivy-clad fence, chewing my thumbnail and asking myself over and over 'where has it gone?' I didn't know it then, but I must have sounded like a Buddhist monk chanting a mantra. In my case though, it wasn't so comforting.

Two days after I'd abandoned Linda, I'd crept outside again, desperately trying to find the door. It had to be there but after I'd climbed back through it alone it had melted away with the fence panels closed over it. It wasn't the only exit from the orchard. Linda could easily have walked around to the owners' house and waited for them to unlock the main gate. Thank goodness she didn't though, or I'd be in a whole load of trouble for leaving her.

'Janice!' Mum shouted louder this time and I heard her slippered feet starting to climb the stairs. She stopped when she saw me on the landing. 'It's OK, love, you know why they're here.'

Of course I knew. I'd heard the police car stop at the kerb a few minutes before the knock on the door. And I'd watched two men in uniform, even wearing their helmets in the sweltering heat, moving around the garden, opening the shed door and peering inside.

A big part of me hoped they'd find Linda in there, huddled up asleep. I'd looked myself the morning after our adventure but there were no footprints in the dust, so I knew she wasn't hiding in there. Mum and I had never been inside the shed since Dad died before I was two. With all the carpentry equipment it was nearly a death trap.

But if the policemen found Linda there then finally my nightmare would be over.

A tall, thin man and a uniformed woman stood in the middle of the living room, making it look even more cluttered among the pouffe, newspaper-strewn coffee table and wide wooden sideboard overloaded with framed black and white photographs.

The man wearing a neat grey suit and grey tie introduced himself and his companion while we sat down.

'Hello Janice, this is Policewoman Alison Harper and I'm Detective Inspector Jarvis. You know why we're here, don't you?'

I did know why they were there but there was something I didn't know.

'What's your name?' I asked trying hard not to sound cheeky.

'Jarvis. Detective Inspector. I'm part of the criminal investigation department searching for …'

'I mean your first name. You said she's *Alison* Harper. So, what's your first name?'

Mum grunted my own name with as much warning as she could convey to behave myself. She looked tired and worried and sat on the edge of the sofa cushion, smoothing her hair away from her pale face.

Detective Inspector Jarvis puckered his lips. Alison Harper gazed at a blurry photo of Dad standing outside his shed, shirt sleeves rolled up to his elbows, cigarette in his mouth. Her slender fingers pinched her nose and she licked her lips with the tip of her tongue.

'It's an unusual name these days – Francis.'

It wasn't that unusual. 'Like Francis Drake.'

He only muttered 'Mmm' and gestured to Alison to sit and take notes. She had a small black notebook perched on her knee and licked the end of her pencil. Her white-blonde hair was scraped back from her face into a tight bun that made her eyes open wider.

I had prepared myself for hours for this moment, ever since Lonnie's frantic visit on Wednesday morning desperately hoping that Linda was sleeping at ours.

'I'll have to call the police,' he'd said when he left.

It had been two days since then and I'd had plenty of time to rehearse my story. Standing here in the living room wasn't like *Dixon of Dock Green*, though. Francis Jarvis was a slippery detective, trying to catch me out.

'We just have a few questions to ask you about your friend Linda,' Jarvis said and I noticed he didn't speak with the familiar Birmingham accent.

'Aren't you from Birmingham?' I asked, keen to delay what was to come.

'No, Manchester.' It was an effort for Jarvis to reply when he had his own questions to ask. 'WPC Harper is from Solihull, though.' He breathed deeply and smiled without opening his mouth or crinkling the skin around his eyes.

Jarvis was around six feet tall and had the familiar leanness I recognised from young men who had lived during the last war. His pale cheeks were hollow, and he stroked his razor-like cheekbone as he glanced at Alison Harper. She was much younger than him, with round curves and sparkling blue eyes. She held her small black notebook – ready for action.

I braced myself and remembered my rehearsed responses.

What did I do yesterday? (Unexpected start.)

Answer – I had to think about that one. I looked at Mum and stumbled a little over my words ... 'Umm, I went to Wrenson's for broken biscuits and a small tin of peaches – and Stork.'

I scratched my head and nodded to confirm that was about right. Mum smiled.

Is that all? – I had to think about that as well. Popping down to the shops for errands was something I could do two or three times a day.

Answer – 'I think so. I played in the garden for a bit – on my own.'

What about the day before?

There it was – the crunch question. I looked down at my scuffed red Clarks sandals. My straight brown hair dropped forwards as I knew it would.

Answer – 'I kept hoping Linda would turn up – but she didn't.' All true.

When was the last time you saw Linda?

Answer – 'Tuesday. She let me brush Sindy's hair.' Also true.

Is this another friend?

Stupid man.

'Sindy is a doll, sir.' Looking back, I'd like to think Alison took great pleasure in saying those words to her boss. I would have done.

Detective Inspector Francis Jarvis dropped his voice and sounded very severe, warning me that Linda's disappearance was a serious matter, and I must think very hard about my answers.

'She's been ever so upset,' Mum said, and Alison wrote in her notebook.

'When you and Linda were sitting in the garden playing with your dolls, what did you talk about?'

Answer – I bent my head again just like I'd rehearsed. 'I pretended I had a secret to annoy her. It was a terrible thing to do. She just kept asking me over and over until I told her.'

I could never be certain Linda hadn't said something to her sister-mum or Lonnie.

The secret?

Answer – 'There wasn't a secret. It was just a trick to play with her Sindy doll – and it worked.'

I looked up to see if my part-truth had worked but Jarvis was looking to his right watching the two policemen poking around the garden, having abandoned the shed. I breathed in with a startled gasp. One of them was parting the ivy and should have found the little door if it had reappeared.

The detective's head turned towards me, but I kept my eyes on the policeman outside, my mouth open with curiosity.

'Is that a truncheon?' The weapon was being used to part the tangled plant. 'I've seen the police get their truncheons out on *Dixon of Dock Green*.

'Yes, it is,' Jarvis was distracted but beckoned a smiling Alison to stand with him, thanking Mum and me for our time. 'This Francis Drake, is he a boy in your school or a man you've seen hanging around you and your friend?'

I couldn't help it. I ran upstairs, laughing loudly, thinking the so-called detective inspector was an idiot.

But as I stood by Mum's open bedroom window watching Alison and Jarvis leave the house, I heard him say in a low voice, 'What do you think, Harper? She knows more than she's saying, doesn't she?' I didn't hear her reply, only him again: 'Yes, we'll keep an eye on her.'

5

Mrs Chant

'Lonnie was soon back. My old man was sure he'd be gone for hours – near certain he was, the lad's guilty. If anyone knows how to chop up a body, it's a butcher.'

Mrs Chant from two doors away had a loud, coughing voice. She wheezed her way through endless cigarettes which she was happy to share with anyone who gossiped with her.

Mum was battling with the twin tub, while I folded wet laundry for her to hang on the line. Mrs Chant sat at our kitchen table smoking and drinking cups of tea. She always wore a flower-patterned apron covering her skirt and bosom and wrapped a scarf over the curlers in her hair. I never saw her look any different in all the time I knew her.

'He thinks the world of Linda. Anyone can see that.' Mum's hands were red from the boiling water and I knew she'd already had this conversation twice before with Mrs Chant. It didn't stop her going on though. 'He's always ever so kind to both the girls.' I deliberately didn't meet her eyes when she dipped her chin in my direction.

'That can mean two things – we all know that.' When Mrs Chant sucked on her cigarette deep lines crinkled around her lips and her round eyes bulged in her slightly grubby face. 'But I grant you, he likes being a family man.

And Tarrant was ready to stick up for him when he heard the lad was on his way to the station with that Jarvis copper. But there's never any smoke without fire.'

Mum caught my eye, even though I was trying hard to show I was concentrating on neatly folding the single sheet from my bed. She knew me too well, I decided.

'Take the washing basket out for me. I'll be out in a minute to peg it.'

It was hard to hear much after that ... just whispers.

But it wasn't long before I found out what had been happening. Lonnie was taken to the police station just because he knew Linda.

'Shame,' I heard Mrs Chant say, in a tone that seemed to convey, 'Serves him right.'

I crept along the kitchen wall like Cathy Gale in *The Avengers* when she was eavesdropping. Mum seemed to have forgotten me.

'He's a nice lad.' Mum defended Lonnie. Everyone liked him and I hoped he wouldn't get into trouble for something I knew he hadn't done. 'He loves Linda as much as he loves Hazel – he loves having a family and a home. He wouldn't do anything daft like ...'

It was so frustrating when adults never finished a sentence. Like what? That's what I wanted to know.

Lonnie's real name was Leonard Donnegan. As a child he'd been called Lenny which changed to Lonnie after the singer became well known. We'd only ever called him Lonnie.

Later I found out he was suspected of treating Linda like a girlfriend and that when she threatened to tell someone, he'd killed her and buried the body. The police had dug an even bigger hole in the garden, widening the patch where Lonnie had carefully measured out the string. Nothing was found apart from empty old rusty Spam tins.

How could the police believe something that was never true? I wasn't sure if I should tell them there was once a secret door behind the ivy and I'd left Linda alive in the orchard. Would they laugh at me? Even I wondered if it hadn't been a dreadful nightmare.

The Taylors, who owned the orchard, had been on their way to Spain when Linda disappeared, oblivious to the whole mystery of her disappearance. The police arranged to speak to them at their villa and obtain permission to search every inch of the orchard. I found this out a week later and was again only partly relieved when they found no trace of my friend.

They never found any signs of a grave either.

The big buzz around the street really grew in strength when Lonnie was dropped back home in a shiny black police car. Detective Inspector Jarvis opened the door for him and curtly nodded, saying nothing. Hazel had walked towards him, looking scared but Lonnie kissed her cheek and they held hands as they slowly walked inside their house.

Lonnie told Hazel what had happened at the police station. Hazel told Mum when Mrs Chant just happened to pop in and soon everyone – even I – knew what had happened.

A few hours after Lonnie was taken away to answer some questions a very posh solicitor from London turned up. The detective inspector was heard bellowing to anyone who would listen that he'd never heard of the man.

An unknown friend of Mr Thornton-Lea had asked him to make sure Lonnie was treated fairly. No one ever found out who the friend was – except for me. But I didn't make that discovery for another twelve years.

Hazel told us the interview had gone like this:

'Had Lonnie left the house on the night Linda disappeared?'

No. The baby was teething and even though Hazel tried to nurse her, Lonnie was in bed next to her the whole time. Eventually they'd both fallen asleep, knocked out with exhaustion.'

'Was there any evidence of digging a grave on any of Lonnie's clothes?'

Only on the clothes he'd worn when digging the vegetable patch. Hazel had sponged them afterwards, ready to wear for second-best in the future.

'Were any of Lonnie's clothes missing?'

No. Hazel confirmed Lonnie's best suit was clean and hanging up in the wardrobe. His work clothes were laid out on the chair for the next day and hadn't moved. His weekend trousers were in the wardrobe and his two other shirts were in the dressing table drawer.

'What about any missing clothes?'

Those were the only clothes Lonnie owned.

'Had Linda ever complained to her family that Lonnie ill-treated her?'

No. Lonnie spoiled her. He spoiled Hazel and their baby.

'If there is nothing you can charge this man with, Detective Inspector, then you really have to let him leave here now. He wants to go home and be with his family.' The cultured voice must have irked Jarvis, who was not only from up North but eager to make an arrest and obtain a confession.

Lonnie went home.

The police spent the rest of the year trying to find Linda. They arrived at people's houses unexpectedly and asked the same questions, trying to catch them out. I knew how that game was played and genuinely answered that I couldn't remember what I'd been doing but I think we were playing with our dolls. It wasn't a good idea to remember everything exactly.

Inside my head, I re-played every minute of Linda's last day and night and never stopped wondering what had happened. I leaned the brunette Sindy, which I'd kept, still wearing her shiny black mac, against my bedroom window frame. The bag with the newspaper and oranges had disappeared but I wanted her to face the orchard, ready to greet Linda if she ever reappeared. Her right arm was pushed up as far as it would reach, seeming to wave to her.

Every night I dreamed about us in the orchard, except we always arrived back in my garden together. The dreams were short and woke me up. I squeezed my eyes shut and willed my mind to re-write events: Linda was home with her family. It was always hard to get back to sleep and I was plagued with insomnia for many years. Rather than lie in bed I'd fall asleep with my head against the window frame, searching the darkness for signs of her in the garden.

I wanted to roam around the orchard and all the other gardens, looking for any clues that could solve the mystery of her disappearance. That was impossible – and scary. What if I was taken away as well? How could I begin to find her when the police had no idea what had happened?

At grammar school I was distant from the girls in my class. I couldn't be bothered to try to have a 'best friend' or latch on to a clique whom I could sit and giggle with at break time. The fear of speaking about Linda and our night in the orchard always held me back from any situation calling for shared secrets. Fortunately, I was good at sports which was an easy way to be popular and I grinned proudly when I collected medals and cups for athletics and tennis, enjoying the thunderous applause from the whole school.

Academically I wasn't bad either. Not being preoccupied with The Osmonds or Marc Bolan meant I focused on homework, determined to achieve high grades which would help my future. The *Encyclopaedia Britannia* saved me from thinking about Linda too much. I could lose myself for hours in the volumes Mum had bought from a salesman at the door, researching every tiny subject in minute detail.

Linda haunted my dreams and turned me into a self-sufficient loner but if I allowed my life to be different, I was scared I'd forget her. I avoided Hazel and Lonnie, afraid they would ask me questions I didn't want to answer. I was more scared of them than of the detective, Inspector Francis Jarvis. I watched them from my bedroom window, sitting alone next to the green beans and raspberry bushes, playing with Rosie or staring into space, smoking.

I was desperate to find her, but years passed without any news. There was only one way I could search for her myself. I needed every tool known to the police to do it and the solution was simple. I would have to become a police officer. Maybe even one day become a detective inspector. To begin the journey, though, I had to start with being WPC Janice Morton.

Nightmare #1

'Wait for me.'

I rushed away but I could hear her hurrying footsteps swooshing through the wet grass. The panting breathless groans of frustration whispered on the air behind me.

The top of the small doorway separating us from the orchard and my garden reached my waist but as I lowered myself to step through it began to shrink.

'Hurry Linda, hurry,' I wailed, no longer caring if we were heard. We needed help – grown-up help.

The night, though receding into early dawn, blackened and I couldn't see the house at all. It was just me and Linda struggling to bundle arms and legs through the shrinking doorway. My thin mac had ballooned around my body worsening the problem as I thrust my way through the gap.

I felt Linda's warm breath on my neck as she pushed and pushed against my back.

Finally, I stood on the grass in my garden.

'Wait for me.'

To add to our problems the ivy on the fence had fallen back into place, hiding the doorway. Linda's arm, thickly covered by her dressing gown, stuck out with her tiny hand flailing through the leaves.

My own small hand, below my heavy macintosh, reached out for hers and I grasped the smooth skin but immediately my grip loosened. I tried again and caught the heavy woollen sleeve. Both hands now were pulling her arm.

Nothing moved. The small doorway had shrunk until the hole was only the size of Linda's arm. Still, I pulled. And pulled.

'Come on,' I grunted, angry that Linda was doing nothing to help herself.

Her pleading words, 'Wait for me,' faded as I pulled, but I knew if I kept on tugging then eventually the soft wooden fence must give way and she would be free. We would be together again. We would be friends again.

Then the black night folded around me. I was alone. I tried to scream Linda's name. There had to be another way into the orchard, and I could run round to find her.

If only my feet would move. But the rubber wellingtons were sunk into the wet grass and it was an effort to lift them out – one step at a time.

I woke with a sobbing gasp, knowing that all I needed to do to find Linda was to run from my garden, along the empty street to the big house at the top where the owners of the orchard lived. If I slipped through a gap in their garden, I could search through the trees to find Linda ...

Screwing my eyes tightly shut, I was desperate to fall asleep again and re-dream a new ending where Linda left the orchard with me and the nightmare would end.

If only the nightmare could end.

If only the nightmare had never begun.

6

Jarvis

After the first encounter with the superintendent at training school I struggled with my conscience, knowing I should finally confess what had happened that night with Linda. I wasn't a scared nine-year-old anymore and after the first shock of hearing my story there was a chance he would understand.

What was my excuse ten years later? I was scared again – scared of Jarvis exposing my past and telling my station inspector so that I wouldn't complete my two-year probationary period. He'd instantly make the decision I wasn't the right kind of person to be a police officer. It was common knowledge that females were only tolerated in the police force, accepted for their usefulness in doing jobs the men hated. Very few wanted to work with us on a shift.

Linda's mysterious disappearance had been my reason for joining the force: to learn the skills to find her. But skills hadn't helped Jarvis and since joining I'd loved being a policewoman, despite the blatant sexism. More than once some cocky male colleague had taken all the glory of an arrest, distorting facts to make himself look good.

After twelve weeks at Ryton I was paired up with various constables and sergeants to mentor me through my shifts.

From some, I learned a lot about how to be a good police officer. From others I learned a lot about how to be a lazy and uncaring police officer. I avoided or ignored those men as much as I could.

My judgemental opinions of colleagues changed dramatically after the terrible night of Thursday 21st November when bombs planted in two Birmingham city centre pubs exploded. Over a hundred people including teenagers enjoying drinks with friends, were killed or maimed. I'd arrived for my night shift early as usual and walked in to Edgington Road police station to find the late shift, manning phones and doing their best to keep things running. Most of the officers had been posted to airport duty and were hurriedly being bussed into the city centre.

PC Nick Watson, looking shocked and tired, asked me to make tea for everyone and for once I didn't mind at all. 'I can't imagine what the bobbies in town must be going through,' he said after relating some of the events to me. 'All they've got on them is a small first aid kit and a whistle.'

It was a horrible start to my career and a lesson that I never forgot; in a crisis, everyone does whatever they can to help the situation. Lonnie's butcher shop window had a brick thrown through it by an unknown attacker one night. Hazel was frightened their house would be targeted and I promised to arrange a patrol to pass by at night. Unfortunately, without success. I could understand the high emotions against the Irish community, but it didn't make sense, when they were as outraged as everyone else. Lonnie wouldn't even tread on a worm, let alone harm a human being.

Nearly a year went by after that first encounter with the CID superintendent and I kept quiet. Strangely, so did

Jarvis – never once challenging me with his suspicion of my part in Linda's disappearance. Perhaps he had given up trying to find her after all.

It was a hot June evening, and I was in no hurry to go home after my shift ended. The main office was quiet at night; the duty shift was out on patrol. CID lights were off since most of the detectives left to carry on celebrating their latest successful arrest in the police social club.

I was still working at 10.30pm, writing up my intelligence report for the tray. I'd run it past my sergeant and he'd reluctantly grunted that my sighting of the Tally twins by the canal could be of interest to CID. He'd had to agree it was strange to see the usually nocturnal brothers in daylight, idling their time away sunbathing in long trousers, sleeved shirts and striped, woollen tank tops.

He hadn't noticed Tally #1 furtively stuffing a pair of battered binoculars beneath the parka jacket he sat on, as we approached them for a pleasant chat. They'd probably have lied about bird-watching or something stupid if we'd mentioned it, but I'd deliberately kept quiet.

'Alright lads,' Sergeant Fraser began.

'Keep walking, copper,' the furtive twin snarled, screwing his freckled features into an unpleasant grimace. 'We've got nothing to say to you.'

Fraser hesitated for a deliberate second before moving on. 'You want to watch you don't get sunburnt,' he advised with undisguised malevolence.

'What's that building over there?' I asked Sergeant Fraser after we left the lads to enjoy their leisured rest. He was a year and ten days away from retirement and already winding down from his 24 years in the force, cynical of changes. He hadn't liked being saddled with me from the beginning and it wasn't long before I realised this was mainly due to having to give up his freebie snacks and meals in the local cafes.

The black stagnant canal water was the foreground to an even blacker and bleaker windowless building on the opposite bank. It appeared to be derelict, with half-hearted attempts at mis-spelt graffiti scrawled across the side in faded pinks and blues.

It was a mixture of Victorian brick and a rotted wooden roof. I knew from riding along on patrols in the early hours of the morning that at the front yellow warning notices were plastered everywhere. Only the brave or the stupid would venture inside without a hard hat and a particularly good reason to be there.

Fraser kicked dusty pebbles with his shiny size nines and squinted into the sun. 'It used to be a paper storage place when the canal boats were around before the war. There was a paper mill nearby but that closed as well – moved closer to the railway line. Made more sense.'

'Tally boys seem to be interested in it.' I observed.

Fraser picked up a large pebble and tossed it into the water, whistling when it bounced past a floating tennis racquet a couple of times. It had been an excuse to look at the building with fresh interest. We walked on in silence, the sergeant's hands in his pockets.

'Might be worth writing up for the Intelligence Notes when we get back to the station – if you don't mind staying late after shift.'

I didn't mind. It was after 8 o'clock and still light with two weeks to go before Midsummer's Eve. The next two hours were busy with a petty theft at the new corner shop near the town centre so it was after shift ended before I could start my notes about the Tally twins.

'Writing a book, are you?' The eraser pencil flew into the air when I looked up and heard his voice. CID weren't sometimes called the rubber-soled lot for nothing.

Around the corner, unseen, was Jarvis's office and I was startled when he suddenly appeared in the doorway. How long had he been there watching me type, curse, erase and type again? I could only hope my tongue hadn't been sticking out while I concentrated on finding the right words for the report.

Even at the end of the day heat lingered in the room. I'd removed my tie but was still sweating over my report, which I wanted to sound interesting but factual when it was read by the higher ranks the following morning.

To add to my embarrassed irritation, Jarvis sauntered over to my desk.

Where was everyone? I wondered. The place was like a morgue. I prayed for a cleaner at least to walk in and start hoovering.

I'd shot up to acknowledge Jarvis' senior rank, but he waved me back into my seat. 'We're both off duty, Constable; no need for all of that.' He stood beside my desk and shuffled the first draft of my report towards him to read it. I bit my lip, furious with all the mistakes.

After glancing at it, Jarvis became interested and held it up to read more closely.

'Tally twins eh?' he said and brushed his fingers backwards and forwards across his mouth. 'Not like them to leave the crypt until after midnight – at the earliest. Binoculars? Is that what that word is?'

I swivelled my chair to face him. He seemed genuinely interested.

'Can't be certain – one of them was pushing something under the coat he lay on as we approached. It looked like one half of binoculars – you know, the fat end. But I was wondering about that building – patrol stop around there sometimes to check nothing's going on. But we never go inside the place.'

Jarvis tapped his fingers against the flimsy paper. 'Safer not to – for more than one reason.' I frowned, unsure what he meant. 'First, you could break your neck and second if there's something going on in there that interests the Tallys then you could face all kinds of danger.'

His vivid blue eyes surveyed the darkened CID office where an hour before there had been whisky-fuelled celebrations after a known local pimp was finally sentenced. He'd battered a few prostitutes in his time and that never sat well with any of the officers and detectives.

'Are you in a hurry to go home?'

I shook my head, 'I told Mum I was staying late. She'll be in bed with the latest Jilly Cooper.'

Jarvis tipped his head, indicating I should follow him out of the office. 'How is your mum?'

'She's fine, thanks … sir …' Blast the man. He couldn't resist reminding me, he hadn't forgotten how he knew me.

7

Tally Twins

Downstairs in the night shift inspector's office Jarvis proposed a little visit to the old paper warehouse with a couple of patrol cars. Inspector Paulson, who was responsible for my welfare during my probationary period, greeted us with a wary frown. He read through my carefully typed report and nodded slowly at Jarvis.

'You want to go along for a look? I've got two men on patrol who can meet you there. How dangerous do you think it will be, though?' Both men turned in my direction. 'She's a probationer – and off duty.'

Jarvis folded his arms and leaned back against the closed door. 'I'm thinking a patrol car can do the usual drive-by. Maybe stop for a crafty fag. Then we'll drive up and stop for a chat and see if anything's unusual. Carter's doing AA so he went home this afternoon.'

The two men met each other's eyes, and the inspector lifted his head higher when Jarvis mentioned DC Carter. I'd never spoken to him, but I knew he was a well-respected detective in his late thirties.

'How's he doing?' Paulson asked in a low voice.

Jarvis dipped his head towards his shoulders and looked uncomfortable. 'Good. Took him a while after what he saw in the *Tavern in the Town* pub that night. But he's back on track now. I'll see if I can pick him up on the way. He loves the Tally boys.'

The inspector made a few calls and then radioed the patrol officers with the plan. He stared directly at me and, if I'd had a father, I guessed his expression was what paternal concern looked like.

'I'm not sure you should get involved, Constable Morton, but I can see you're itching to go too. Make sure you follow orders from all the officers. Do you understand?'

I waited outside while Jarvis checked the radios were working and signed out two firearms. I was in full uniform with my jacket buttoned and belted, ready for action. Hopefully, none of the other guys, especially Jarvis, would hear my heart thumping like a beating drum.

He'd been right about DC Carter. Sober and single, he'd welcomed the opportunity to leave his police flat for some extra time on the job – especially if it could lead to outwitting the Tally twins.

He ignored my presence in the back of the black sedan when Jarvis collected him from his flat in the police accommodation. The two men talked together quietly in their own private slang, peppered with 'F' words and agreed on a plan for our arrival at the warehouse.

'What do you know about the Tally's?' Jarvis questioned me while keeping his eyes on the road.

'Not much, sir. Local thieves from a thieving family.' What else did I need to know. Their distinctive red hair made them easy to spot, which was one of the reasons they stayed inside during daytime.

DC Carter shuffled round in the passenger seat and I stretched my body to hear him better.

'That's about right. The mum's always been a handful – different men and husbands – three of them so far. The first one was a Scot from Glasgow. Ran off to Spain with her sister, leaving the eldest son behind. We don't see much of him – tends to live out in Spain.'

'Don't blame him,' Jarvis chipped in as he peered out at empty streets which I knew led to the canal area. Recent newly built high-rise flats loomed above us on both sides.

'Tally twins … Frank … second dad, yeah?'

'Yep. He's in Wakefield for life. Cannabis deal went wrong up in Liverpool at the docks. He was in the thick of it and caught by Customs with a bloody knife and a dead body. Even he couldn't talk his way out of that one.'

Carter tried to look into my eyes through the flickering light, alternating with the night shadows. 'Tally twins give out the impression they're petty thieves … but we've always wondered if they're carrying on their dad's game – drugs.'

Did that explain the firearms precaution, I wondered? I hadn't encountered any arrests for drugs since leaving Ryton, but I'd heard drug-dealing confrontations were becoming more violent. A flicker of excitement rippled through my chest and my heart beat a little quicker. Finally, I might be involved in something more exciting than checking MOT certificates on old bangers.

It was almost midnight when the car slowed to five miles per hour approaching the desolate industrial area. As we reached the dirt track, Jarvis stopped the car and Carter stepped silently out of the vehicle. I lifted my head to watch him, but he disappeared in front of the bonnet. Only a faint breeze stirred the air and fragranced the musty interior of the car which reeked of stale cigarette smoke.

'Might not mean anything,' Carter explained as he sat back in the passenger seat. 'There's a lot of tyre tracks – could just be courting couples though.'

He'd barely finished speaking when the silent wind wafted sounds of alarmed shouting from ahead. At lightning speed Carter slammed the passenger door and barked into the radio. Jarvis revved up the running engine.

With one hand on the wheel, still driving slowly, he reached into his jacket and in seconds held a gun in his other hand. Carter too, I realised, was armed. Both their windows were lowered so we could hear everything going on around the warehouse. From the raised voices they decided it was the two duty officers and possibly two more men.

As we drew nearer to the warehouse, Jarvis swerved the car across the track at a slight angle to block any vehicle driving in either direction. He and Carter spoke in lowered tones into their jacket cuffs and fumbled with earpieces before stepping from the car.

'Janice, jump into the front then lock the doors and stay low.' Jarvis didn't even look at me as he spoke, intent on the blackness ahead. 'Stay on the radio and let Control know what's going on. I've asked for back-up. Wind up the windows just enough to hear any sounds.'

I did as he said. One vital thing I'd learned after training was to always listen and do everything my experienced colleagues ordered. One of my fellow recruits, smarty-pants PC Day, failed to do that in his first week and was swiftly booted off the force, never to return. I was determined that would never happen to me.

Jarvis and Carter disappeared quickly into the shadowed gloom and I listened to the rising voices of my colleagues and the unknown ones. There was an argument of some kind, with one voice at least trying to pacify the situation. Then an ugly laugh followed and with my blood freezing at the sound I knew something bad was going to happen.

Police radio in my trembling hand, and the thumping of my heart echoing inside my head, I did my best across the static to articulate the distorted sounds floating through the window to Control. 'Back-up is on its way,' the calm voice informed me. I strained to listen for any other noise from outside and quietly opened the passenger door a few inches to enhance the sounds. A shot was fired, and I lay low across passenger and driving seats.

I didn't wait long before the shouts grew louder and I heard tyres scrunching on gritty tarmac, driving towards me. My mind calculated what could happen next. In a flash I reached for the key in the ignition and pressed the lock down on the driver's side door.

A pair of headlights lit up the interior of the car. There was dense shrubland and thistles along the track and with the police sedan blocking the escape route the oncoming car halted within inches of the bonnet. I heard rather than saw the other car door flung open. Within seconds I heard the heavy panting of the driver as he leapt from his vehicle.

With his exit blocked the escaping person had to run past the sedan's passenger side first. Still lying flat on the seats, I braced myself. I'd only seen this tactic used once by a six-foot-two, muscled instructor and prayed that my own five-foot-six frame could achieve the same result he had.

The crunching gravel told me the person was in reach of the passenger door. With a strength I hadn't known I possessed I pushed my whole weight behind my feet and slammed the door open as far as it would go. Sure enough, the technique I'd been shown at Training School came in useful. A body – I wasn't sure at the time whose body – was flung to the ground grunting in pain and yelping like a kicked dog.

Ignoring the pains shooting up my legs I leapt from the car and wished the force issued WPCs with handcuffs.

Lying face down on the ground was a young boy, Tally twin 1 or Tally twin 2? I had no idea, but I was relieved I hadn't just knocked out one of the patrol officers.

He was winded and clutched his chest, but I had little sympathy. I ground my knee into the middle of his spine and twisted his arms to hold his wrists. His hands were hot and slimy with sweat. My own hands didn't feel much different, but I still gripped onto him. Without handcuffs I had never felt so ridiculous.

The Tally twin, face stuck in the gravel, was still yelping and swearing when Jarvis, Carter and a PC I vaguely recognised, rushed into the glare of headlights. The PC took handcuffs from his pocket and passed them to me. He watched my shaking hands as I clicked them onto the Tally twin. He'd tired himself out and given in when he saw the three men.

With only a perfunctory glance in my direction to check I was unharmed Jarvis leaned down to pull the twin's head back by his hair, eyes searching his face to identify him.

'That's the both of you. We've got your brother,' he yelled into the grazed face.

'That pig's broken my ribs.' Saliva shot from the contorted mouth, but Jarvis ducked sideways just in time. He probably expected it.

Staring at the ground he shouted, 'Carter – weapon.' Jarvis picked up a gun lying a few inches from where the Tally twin had fallen. Standing up he passed it to Carter who placed it in a clear plastic bag. 'Looks like a service revolver – probably from the last war.'

Breathing heavily from the struggle of handcuffing the Tally, I looked up at the three officers, silently questioning what should happen next. I was aware that I must have looked a poor sight, with my hair straggling from my plait and black tights ripped from the rough stones. The young man groaned under my weight but didn't try to escape.

'He's your collar, Morton,' Jarvis said. The men still watched me, not moving. In the background I could hear the radio crackling with an exchange between Control and the other officer at the warehouse.

Finally, Carter placed a hand lightly on my shoulder. 'Caution him Morton, there's a good girl.'

Trying to keep my voice from shaking I was going through the '… I'm arresting you …' when I heard two more police cars hurtle along the track, stopping behind us.

When I finished the caution, Jarvis hauled the Tally twin to his feet and shoved him towards the officers. He gestured to me and Carter to join him and jumped into the driver's seat of the sedan. I passed him the car key I'd taken from the ignition. The other officer, whom I realised was the handsome PC Nick Watson, reversed the Tallys' vehicle back up the track while we followed at a fast pace. 'Nice driving,' Jarvis muttered, and I too admired the skilled manoeuvre of the vehicle into pitch black nothing, dimly lit by our headlights.

Somehow, I was disappointed when we arrived at the warehouse. An identical twin of our prisoner sat in the back of the patrol car, screaming and stamping his feet in frustration. Another officer assigned to the patrol leaned against the car smoking while he mumbled into his hand-held radio. PC Watson joined him and lit up a cigarette, taking over the radio.

A shadowy Carter shone his torch onto an open doorway and a tentative hand pushed it wider. There were no other vehicles parked nearby so he must have been certain no one else was on site.

Jarvis watched him and positioned the car where its headlights lit up the entrance. 'I expect you'd like to see what's inside, wouldn't you?'

He asked the question without taking his eyes from Carter, who waited at the open doorway.

I didn't need to be asked twice and was on my feet almost running after him. As I passed the patrol car I saw PC Watson, leaning against the vehicle's passenger door. He paused on his radio and, still with a cigarette between his fingers, gave me a mock salute. It was enough acknowledgment, and I was stupidly pleased.

Three single torches gave poor light inside the vast warehouse, but they were enough to reveal the sacking-covered packing chests stacked in the nearest corner. I peered between the shoulders of the two men, wondering why we weren't venturing closer.

Jarvis held his arm in front of me, palm facing inwards. Carter too, stepping sideways grabbed my shoulder to prevent me from proceeding.

Each of them shone their torches downwards, searching the dusty floor. A trail of shoe prints, clear and smudged in both directions between the door and the chests showed up in the torchlight. The two men exchanged triumphant grins.

'What d'you reckon are in those?' Carter said.

'Hard to say. I'd like to think it's smuggled booze. But I've a horrible feeling it's something far worse.' Jarvis moved slowly around the side wall to the closest chest and felt around it with his fingertips. 'Not worth it. We'll wait until we've checked every one of them for prints.'

Carter waved his torch at the boxes where empty crisp packets and a metal jemmy were scattered around them.

'Plenty of footprints and fingerprints ... what more could we want, sir?'

This was bigger than I had thought, despite Jarvis and Carter revealing their firearms and the shots that had been fired. All this had happened because I'd spotted a pair of binoculars and the Tally twins behaving in a dodgy manner. There was a chill air in the warehouse and my body trembled. I thought about the revolver, knocked from the twin's hand, and tried to ignore a faint buzzing started up inside my ears. I felt my legs buckle.

'Catch her, Mick,' I heard Jarvis say.

Carter moved to stand behind me and grabbed each of my arms to stop me from falling backwards. We remained in the warehouse until my dizziness passed.

'Happens to the best of us,' he said to me while Jarvis pretended nothing was happening and shone his torch around the warehouse again. 'You'll get used to it. Not the same as arresting drunks when the pubs close, is it?'

As the arresting officer for Tally #1 or David Charles Talbot as he later gave his full name, when we were safely in the bright lights of the police station, I was involved in processing the prisoners. He wasn't my first arrest in ten months, but he was my most notorious and most wanted. Uniformed and plain clothes officers appeared from nowhere down in the Custody Suite while I filled in forms, coughing from the thickening cigarette smoke.

They took great delight emphasising to the twins they had been taken down by a mere policewoman. It was a humiliation they could never forget. A drug squad superintendent with Jason King sideburns threw the worst and most demeaning insults, determined to knock the cockiness out of them.

The Tally twins, identical brothers, distinguishable only by their different clothes were almost impossible to tell apart. They used the confusion to their advantage, changing their names whenever they were addressed. Charles became David and vice versa.

'What kind of mother just transposes the names of their kids – twin kids at that?' the weary desk sergeant complained as he tried to fill out the arrest sheets for them and assign each a cell number.

'One with limited imagination,' Jarvis grinned, pumped with adrenaline after the night's unexpected arrests. The officers around us laughed as though he was Ken Dodd.

The one we were sure was David Charles Talbot sneered at the superintendent and screwed his mouth into a suspicious-looking ball. Carter pulled me towards him, and the other officers also took a step backwards.

'Watch it, Sir,' PC Watson called.

Jarvis, not wanting a repeat of the brother's earlier actions, thumped the twin on his back.

'Go on Tally, just try it why don't you?'

'Watch yourself, Chaz, just go along with it.' Wise words from David and I studied the two young men.

PC Watson and I stood side by side at the desk, answering questions thrown at us by the custody sergeant trying to complete the forms, but the noise increased, and it was difficult to hear his soft voice. Finally, exasperated, he called for quiet after my third 'Pardon, Sarge'.

He'd asked if I agreed to have my name on the arrest sheet for Tally #1.

'I do.'

He asked the same question of Nick Watson.

'I do.'

Some bright spark in the crowd shouted, 'Blimey, it's like I'm at a wedding. Ever fancied yourself as a vicar, Sarge?'

The three of us ignored the lewd remarks that followed until Jarvis, with just one word, '*Gentlemen*!', shut them up.

I waited quietly to add my signature to Charles Talbot's arrest sheet. I watched each of the twins in turn: unwashed ginger hair stuck up on their heads in sweaty spikes and their faces were sprinkled with dark freckles. They should have kept out of the sun while they sat by the canal.

The twins were sullen and un-cooperative, reluctant to give any other details except to confirm the names already known to us. They were of average height and although they looked around fourteen years old, we knew from their records they were born in March 1950, making them twenty-four. They had used their youthful looks and twin status to create a two-man crime spree since they were in junior school.

'Chaz, watch out,' I called suddenly and Jarvis's head snapped in my direction. So did the head of Tally #1. 'Hello, Charles. Did you forget your name when we asked you earlier?'

There was a low grumble around the room, and we watched the real Charles snarl at me while the sergeant switched the forms around. All the details were the same after all.

Carter and Jarvis nodded at me, impressed with my intuitive action. I stepped closer towards Jarvis and he inclined his head to hear me speak quietly.

'Charles has a small freckle at the side of his left eye – almost looks like a 4-leaf clover. David doesn't have one.'

Jarvis signalled to attract the sergeant's attention and stepped beside him, examining the two near-completed forms on the desk-top. With his own pen, he bent and wrote a sentence on the form and I didn't need to look myself to know he'd made the entry in the 'Distinguishing Features' box.

The drug squad superintendent appeared at his side. 'Frank, a quick word.' He glanced at my scuffed uniform and ripped tights but seemed to look straight through me.

'Doug, this is WPC Janice Morton, one of the arresting officers.'

'Yeh, I know who she is.'

The two men moved away and in mirror images leaned against the wall. The conversation started easily, but quickly turned into a disagreement. The superintendent who Jarvis had called Doug pointed in my direction and they both watched the Tally twins being led away to the cells.

I heard Jarvis say, 'It's too late now. Her name's on the arrest sheet.'

'Big mistake, Frank.'

For a few days afterwards both Tallys were questioned at length by drug squad officers, but I wasn't involved in any of that. Jarvis knew they were just the small fish swimming in a big sea and wanted as much information as they could give him about men and women further up the chain.

They wouldn't say a word at first but after their home and a nearby lock-up garage were searched it was pointless for them to stay silent, especially when both their mother, Red, and her latest husband were also arrested. There wasn't enough evidence to take them to court but after a long period preparing the case, the twins were not so lucky: they were sentenced to three years for handling stolen goods and selling illegal drugs. They were assigned to separate prisons and were bounced from the courtroom, yelling threats and protests.

For a few weeks after the arrest my path didn't cross with Jarvis's. I'd learned not to expect praise from my colleagues other than a grudging 'Well done'. It stopped bothering me that he never mentioned the incident with Linda whenever we passed in the corridor.

It was only when Inspector Paulson asked me if I wanted a temporary attachment to CID that I realised there were many ways of showing appreciation. Paulson wasn't expecting to wait for an answer so I agreed to the proposal with just the right amount of enthusiasm and left his office before I could throw up my lunchtime shepherd's pie.

If I were to work with Jarvis, though, I knew the time had come to be straight with him. I'd rehearsed my confession a thousand times since he'd given his lecture at training school. My brain swirled with the possible outcomes and my biggest fear was dismissal from the force. I prayed that my part in the Tally twins' arrest would outweigh his contempt of my silence.

8

Confession

It was rumoured – and distinctly possible – that Detective Superintendent Jarvis never went home until the small hours. No one had told me whether there was any reason for this, but it meant I was certain he'd be in his office when I finished my late shift. Sure enough, his office light was on when I approached like a prisoner on death row, dragging my feet, knowing I was about to experience the meaning of 'career suicide'.

After changing my mind twice and turning back to the main office, I decided it was now or never. My stomach flipped over and over with each step and I forgot everything I'd rehearsed. The only thought in my head was the reminder that this could be the last time I would wear my uniform and walk the corridor of the police station. Despite this dread and expectancy, I had to do it. I had to speak to Jarvis.

He'd heard my reluctant footsteps approach and was staring at his open door when I appeared, with just a hint of distraction in his eyes. In one hand he held up a flimsy, closely typed sheet of paper, but his head tilted towards a crackling radio commentary. When he saw I was his visitor he waved to me to sit down. Placing the paper on his desk he listened intently to hear the outcome of the bowl of an Indian cricketer with an unrepeatable name. He grinned with some satisfaction after the commentator announced the result and fiddled with the volume knob until the sound was so low it was impossible to hear anything.

'Test Match in India,' he said. 'My wife hates cricket so she's happy for me to listen to it here and then head home.'

That was all I was getting to know about his personal life. It was more than I needed to know. I smiled and straightened my uniform tie with shaking hands.

Jarvis's initial friendliness changed to a more professional position. His features hardened and his grey, tired eyes frowned at me. 'You've got something to tell me?' he asked with a trace of anticipation.

'I do,' I replied, wishing that what I had to say would be as interesting as my last report on the Tally twins. 'It's not about the job, sir … it's more personal. It's something I should have told you years ago.'

The radio was abruptly switched off and the superintendent leaned forward on the desk-top, pushing scattered paperwork aside. He breathed deeply and I took that as a bad sign. This was not going to be easy.

'Go on.'

If I were a bank robber sitting opposite him in an interview room, I'd plead guilty just from hearing that stern tone of voice. Goosebumps rippled across my skin.

'It's about the night Linda Bateman disappeared. I was with her.'

Raised eyebrows told me he was surprised, and his face creased into deeper lines around his eyes. This wasn't a good sign.

Even my endless rehearsals of explaining how Linda and I had ended up in the orchard couldn't prepare me for this moment and the dryness in my mouth as I faced those piercing eyes.

I spoke quickly and concisely as I'd been trained to do for giving evidence in court. Jarvis nodded slowly every now and then after giving me sharp looks at intervals. When I finished speaking, I sat upright in the uncomfortable plastic chair and twisted my police hat round and round in my hands.

Jarvis scratched the back of his neck and I guessed he was torn between finally listening to the result of the cricket and considering this new evidence about Linda's disappearance.

'So, let me get this straight, Janice. You and Linda planned to explore the orchard that night and climbed into it from a small door in your garden fence ...' I nodded. 'You had a falling-out ... you left her in the orchard but the next morning the door had disappeared, and you never saw Linda again.'

This time I drew in a deep, deep breath. After all these years I was still perplexed about that door and how it could have closed over after I'd climbed through it, leaving Linda on the other side. Somehow, I was sure that if the door had still been there, I could have told Mum and we would have searched for her together, found her and brought her back home.

'That's right. I didn't realise at the time that if I'd told Mum – or you – about the door you could have found Linda and it wouldn't have mattered about us being out late ...'

'And when you were older ... knowing Linda's bod ... that Linda was still missing – you didn't think that information would have been helpful?'

I'd asked myself the same question many times. 'It was the door, sir ... I couldn't get my head past the door not being there. It made it all seem like a dream; I wondered if I'd imagined everything and someone had taken Linda away from her home in the night.'

'You know that isn't true, Morton, don't you? Door or no door, both of you were in that orchard at midnight – not at home sleeping in your own beds.' His voice was stern, and I noticed he hadn't called me Janice. He stood up to pace around the office, disconcerting me each time he walked behind my chair. It was a good intimidating technique and I stored it up to use next time I had to interview a suspect.

Please, please let there be a 'next time', I silently prayed.

'I feel bad for keeping the secret, but I still can't understand how Linda disappeared. She wasn't dead when I left her so what happened? I know it sounds crazy but for years I almost believed in fairies.' How lame was that? But almost true. 'After a week I climbed into the orchard through an opening near the owners' garage to look for her – just in case she was lying there – but I never found her.'

'Yes, I know you did. Tell me, Janice, now that you're a police constable don't you think the orchard was one of the first places we searched at the time?'

My hair fell across my face as I hung my head, embarrassed. I hadn't considered that possibility. 'How do you know I searched the orchard as soon as I could?'

They'd been watching me from the moment Jarvis left my house, convinced I knew more than I was telling him. One of his constables watched me squeeze through a gap in the fence, usually used by trespassers scrumping for apples and pears in autumn. I'd scratched every inch of my skin pushing through stinging nettles on the other side of the fence seeking the peach tree in the centre.

When I'd emerged, filthy dirty, empty-handed and looking more puzzled, the constable had reported the incident and Jarvis was satisfied that whatever I was hiding it couldn't help them.

'I thought you must have searched the orchard,' I admitted. 'Finding Linda was one of the reasons why I joined the force. Every time I learned something useful in training, I tried my best to work out how she went missing and how I could find her.'

Something like a club hammer seemed to hit me between my shoulder blades as I finished my confession. Jarvis was back in his chair and watched me exhale every breath from my body. I remembered something my sergeant had told me in the early days of our graveyard shifts. He'd been showing off bits of knowledge from his time in CID and all the years he'd spent as a police officer on the beat.

'Sir,' my voice sounded thin and a little scared, 'did you find her but decide not to tell anyone?' Sometimes the police made decisions to spare family excess pain when there was no point in making them suffer if a death was accidental or stupid.

The superintendent shut his eyes and I realised he'd probably been in the station since five or six o'clock in the morning. The dark stubble covering his chin was tinged with grey, like the tufts of hair around his ears. At the same time, though, he had that look on his face I'd seen when he'd read through my badly typed report on the Tally twins. Something I'd said had irritated him.

'Janice, Constable Morton, don't believe everything any officer tells you when he's a few months short of his retirement. No, we didn't find the body and that case has haunted me for years. You should have told me about the door in the fence – I do think it's important …'

I leaned forward in my seat as though I'd been scalded by hot water. 'No, no. It was just a door …'

'... a door that disappeared overnight – the same night a little girl disappeared. Don't you think that whoever took Linda out of that orchard is the same person who somehow replaced the fence?'

I froze like a stiff board and my mind worked furiously to process his words. No, it hadn't occurred to me that the fence panels had been replaced – it should have done, especially when I was old enough not to believe in a disappearing door. I leaned my right arm on the desk and scratched my forehead.

'I'm an idiot,' I said, no doubt confirming Jarvis's opinion of me.

'It won't be the first time you're blinded by a thought you can't see around. Just make sure there aren't too many of them in the future.'

I looked up, hopeful he meant I still had a future in the force and especially in CID.

'It's my fault the orchard wasn't searched straight away – Linda could have been found alive and well ...'

'The orchard was searched as soon as we started looking for her,' Jarvis snapped, incredulous that I could have thought otherwise. I spluttered something about the owners being away in Spain when Linda went missing but he just snorted.

'As if that would have stopped the search. One of my men went in straight away – one I could trust not to trample over any evidence. All he found was a half-eaten peach.'

I had to say it but muttered rather than spoke in a normal voice, 'What about a ... warrant ...?'

Jarvis waved the word away with a derisory dismissal. 'We couldn't find a number for their villa in Spain for two days – and yes, we did apply for a warrant.' I breathed in, satisfied that I'd shown some evidence of my training. He sniffed, 'Eventually.'

'I'm sorry,' I said. 'I was stupid and now the trail will have gone cold. Do you have any idea where Linda could have gone – or been taken?'

His tongue peeked through his tight lips for an instant and then he chewed his lip. With a sigh he mentally decided to tell me more.

'Five years ago, a sixty-year-old paedophile, Len Ward, was arrested in Warwickshire. He'd never been known to us, but when he was picked up the officers quickly saw him as a suspect for child abduction. They were able to solve a number of abductions going back to the end of the war.'

Noisy boots tramping along the corridor told us it was break time and some of the duty officers were returning for hot coffee and sandwiches. I hadn't realised we'd been talking for so long.

'Carter and I went over and questioned him about Linda Bateman but all he said was he couldn't remember if she'd been one of his victims or not. He was a vile man who revelled in being caught and put away for life. He died last year – heart attack brought on by a scuffle in the canteen.'

This was a blow to me, and I slumped back in my seat, tears pricking the back of my eyes. I'd always hoped that Linda was alive somewhere despite knowing it was unrealistic to think that way.

'You think he took her ... killed her?

'I never said that. He was a suspect, but he never admitted anything. Scum like Ward enjoy dangling you on a string, pretending they know something when all the details they're giving you are all over the newspapers.'

Jarvis patted his pockets for car keys.

'Janice, if you're going to join us in CID, you'll be too busy to worry about someone missing in the past. You'll be crushed under the amount of work we've got on our plates. You'll be doing the boring stuff at first.'

He stooped down and rummaged in the bottom drawer of his desk. I could tell he was shuffling files and sure enough a pale green, medium-sized bound file was extracted and dumped on the desk.

'This is Linda Bateman's file: statements, evidence, photographs – it's all there.' Scrambling for paper and pen he scribbled on two sheets and pushed them towards me. 'Sign both and keep one for yourself. The file stays at the station but when you do have time, look through it – maybe you'll spot something we missed.'

My mouth opened and closed like a confused fish thrown onto a riverbank. After all these years I could finally start my own investigation into Linda's disappearance. I owed it to her to find out what had happened.

Before I could say anything, Jarvis yelled at a passing bobby: 'Watson, when you've finished your break, drive Constable Morton home – I've kept her here long enough.'

9

Death by Contract

Everyone called her Red. Had done since she was at junior school and her stupid mother had dressed her in a knitted scarlet woollen dress to match her thick curly auburn hair. Poor Mrs Hawkins thought it looked lovely – co-ordination she called it. She'd read about it in a magazine while she sat under the dryer at the hairdressers.

Her daughter's unkind school friends fell about laughing at the ensemble. It hadn't helped that dropped stitches and a wonky appliqued rose completely changed the look from the original picture on the pattern. Red, not a stranger to embarrassment at the hands of her well-intentioned mother, spent the day scratching her skin raw from the itchy wool and wishing she could disappear into a hole.

The experience toughened up a little girl into a strong, spirited young lady and later a feisty woman, married twice to known criminals and mother of three boys who preferred the inside of a prison to being home with their tea on the table. Red could knock teeth from a patronising grin and black the eye of an aspiring boxer – if she were riled, insulted or had too much rum and coke at the weekend, or at parties, Christmas, or almost any social gathering.

Charles David Talbot waited impatiently at the assigned table in the visiting room, scratching at his fingernails with the side of an empty matchbox. He watched his mother enter the room and shouted 'Oi' at the inmates' wolf whistling as she followed the warder to his table.

'What d'you wanna wear that for? You look a right tart.'

Red glanced down at the tight, sequinned mini dress, stretched around her chest and backside. She pretended to act surprised, as though she'd dressed in the dark and this was the first time she was aware of her outfit. Red had perfected the naïve and sympathetic expression since she was sixteen and an ex-boyfriend told her she shouldn't look so surly.

'Don't be daft, Chaz. What do you think your cell mates are gonna think of you now? They'll be asking you to set them up with me. Then they'll treat you right – make sure you're looked after.'

'S'pose so.' Chaz grunted and cast aside his makeshift nail file. 'You look like a pale, freckled Donna Summer. Where are you living now?'

'Same place. After the cops messed everything up and ratted Graham out to the council, we pleaded poverty and promised to get rid of the mattresses and fridge in the front garden if they let us stay.'

'And they did?' Chaz was constantly surprised by his mother. She could charm curdled milk out of the bottle.

'Course they did. Two things helped. Graham knows when to turn a blind eye and the man from the council had just broken up with his bit on the side. Perfect timing for your old mum.'

Chaz puffed out a disgusted 'Euw' and looked around to check if anyone was listening. Red's voice was soft and low. To hear her properly the listener had to lean closer to her, smelling her Madame Rocha perfume and if so inclined enjoy a long, hard look at her barely covered 38DD chest.

Her 18-carat gold, diamond-cut bangles clinked when she lifted her arm and patted her hair, loosely piled into a bun so that the style resembled a soft, floating cottage loaf. Red tendrils waved around her face when she moved. She openly scanned the room, her gaze lingering on anyone who turned their head to lock eyes with her.

'Grey-haired guy two tables from the left at the back.'

'What about him?'

'I'll have him.'

'No you won't. Barney Brooks. Shady bastard. He's the hardest bloke in here. And he's bent – can't you tell?'

Red smiled with a hint of triumph playing around her lips. 'They're the best ones. They like a trophy to boast about. You mark my words. Anyway, we haven't got long. Why d'you want to see me? I can't make this a habit.'

Both pairs of grey eyes checked the wall clock and Chaz felt sure the hands were moving quicker than any other timekeeper. Why did Red always have to be so late? He leaned forward two inches and waited for the warder to complain. Nothing was said.

Red examined her fingernails while he talked and frowned as she nibbled a tag of skin on her middle finger, sucking the tip between her richly rouged lips. Chaz heard the sighs and shuffles murmur through the room and raised his eyes to the ceiling.

'OK. You need to get a message out to Golden Boy's dad.'

'Which one?'

'The one in Spain, living with Aunty Heather and pretending there's nothing going on between them. Not the soppy git you live with.'

'The one who paid for the solicitor for you and David and never asks you for money even though you've sponged off him for years. Is that the soppy git?' Red never raised her voice or stopped smiling. She was a hard nut – but fair. Graham couldn't help being weak and only had her to stand up for him.

'Alright,' Chaz conceded with ill grace. 'I've got a job for our step-brother.'

'He's got a job and it pays well.'

Chaz sniggered. 'D'you think I don't know what he's up to. We're in the same game, mother. But I can't get hold of him – not from in here. The only person I trust is you.'

'Always.' Red wiggled her fingers in the direction of the inmate with the bouffant grey hair – Barney Brooks. He smirked back at her, ignoring the petulant skinny lad facing him.

'Tell him I want him to take out that woman copper who dobbed us in and got us into this mess.'

'Which one?'

'There was only one and her name was in the papers. Janice Morton – dark, poker-straight hair and a stinking attitude like she was head girl at school giving out detentions. I knew she'd clocked us that day we were watching the warehouse by the canal. I told … never mind. I knew it was a stupid mistake and no one ever went near it, night or day.'

Pretending to be distracted, Red made a mental note of the name. Janice like the cleaner's name at the social club and Morton, like … court'n. Courting.' She grinned. Might help her to remember. If not, the name was in the papers so Cam could check for himself.

'You don't want him to kill her?' She wasn't shocked. Why should she be bothered? She didn't know the woman and Cam was always careful. One thing with Chaz, whenever he asked her for a favour – he paid well.

'I don't care what he does to her – just tell him to make sure she never works again. No one wants someone like her as a copper. I can tell the type. Keen and clever.'

Red screwed up her mouth and nodded. Keen and stupid in a copper was fine. Keen and clever was a threat to all criminals.

'What about the other men who arrested you and made sure you both went down – and sent to different prisons? Davey can't expect me to travel all the way up to Yorkshire to see him. This place is bad enough. It sounds close but it's two buses.'

A short sharp whistle blast let everyone know they only had another ten minutes for their friendly chat with loved ones.

'Listen, Mother. At the back of my bed you need to peel the wallpaper off – carefully mind. There's cash behind it – a lot of cash. Tell Cam there's five grand for him when he's done the job. Buy yourself a car with the rest – an old banger mind. Don't raise any suspicions.'

Red was impressed with her son's ingenuity. 'The coppers tore your bedroom apart – and the rest of the house. They found the two hundred and fifty quid you'd hidden behind the boiler and Davey's five hundred in the toilet cistern.'

'They were meant to.'

The whistle blew again with a chorus of groans accompanying the shrill noise. Chairs scraped on the hard, wooden floor and Chaz suspected that a couple of the tear-streaked faces were genuinely upset. He didn't bother kissing Red goodbye. Why start something they'd never done before in their lives.

'You'll do it when you get back, eh Red?'

'Straight away. There's only an hour time difference and he'll be in the kitchen cooking that foreign muck I expect.'

She gave him an affectionate pat on his shoulder as though it was his first day at school rather than seeing him return to his prison term in the grimmest of surroundings. 'How d'you know you can trust me – with all that money?'

Barney Brooks waited by the door, standing next to the warder, politely letting his fellow prisoners pass by. Chaz's heart sank. Red had succeeded with her plan. 'You and Davey are the only people I trust.'

'And Cam?'

'Not much. Also, Mum,' he turned away from her, ignoring her silly wave to Barney, 'you don't know where I've hidden the rest of the money.'

With just the faintest twinge of maternal instinct Red turned back to watch Chaz disappear with the other prisoners. He reached Barney and smiled grimly when his new friend's arm hugged his thin shoulders.

She chewed her red lips. 'Ah well,' she thought. 'He'll be alright.'

10

Cassandra's Nightclub

If there was anything I hated more than being on my own with nothing to do on a Saturday night, it was sitting in a crowded nightclub on my own with no one to talk to on a Saturday night. The evening hadn't started off that way. It had been planned for weeks with my grammar school friend Pat Green insisting that we celebrate her birthday with cocktails at the Holiday Inn before we went on to Cassandra's Nightclub in the town centre.

When I breezed through the revolving door, trying to look as though I always spent my evenings in a posh hotel, I was surprised to see Pat on her own studying the cocktail menu. Surely it wasn't going to be just the two of us. I remembered, too late, Pat hadn't been all that popular in school. I should never have let her bully me into joining her for a 'crazy night out'.

'Liz and Annabelle cancelled,' she explained when I lifted my head high on purpose and looked for the 'crowd' she'd been going on about in her daily phone calls to me 'just checking you're still on for Saturday'.

'They're both shattered after working in Rackhams all day.'

Her explanation didn't ring true to me. The girls I knew who worked in shops on a Saturday couldn't wait to party all night and sleep all the next day. Liz and Annabelle, if

I remembered right, worked in the accounts office, not on the shop floor. I grinned and tried not to let my face betray any signs of pity for Pat.

'Let's try a cocktail then,' I suggested. 'A couple of the lads at work said if we were coming here, we should try the cocktails.' My eyes widened when I skimmed the printed list and saw the prices. Pat, reading over my shoulder, muttered 'Ooh' every now and then but I realised she wasn't looking at the prices.

She worked in a dressmaking factory all week and earned a small fortune compared to my wage, even with shift allowance. Using a few of my newly learned CID techniques I'd checked if she were telling the truth and was amazed at the money she was making.

'I'll have a pina colander,' she announced after squinting at the menu.

I laughed, 'Colada. It's a *pina colada*.' Pat laughed too. 'I'll have the Singapore sling. I've always wanted to go to Singapore. This'll be the nearest I get.'

Pat gently tapped on the shoulders of a couple of suited men and flashed a knockout smile at them, pointing to the bar area. They stepped aside immediately and even pushed through the crowd themselves to let her through. I watched, amazed at her natural ability. She was tall and willowy in red 5-inch stiletto sandals and wore a very short black satin strapless dress. In that outfit a mountain would step aside for her.

Why didn't I check with her before deciding what to wear? My own pleated black peasant skirt sparkled with tiny sequins. I'd initially felt good in a near-matching black fitted jacket that reached midway between my waist and knees. But in comparison with Pat I felt dowdy and definitely not sexy.

After the first cocktail we agreed to order two different ones before heading next door to the club and the mixed alcohol quickly had us laughing inanely at daft stories from school. It was beginning to be fun with Pat even though we had little in common. She gossiped brazenly about the people in the factory and blurted out a few details about the owners' side deals.

'Pat,' I started to caution her, 'don't forget I work in CID. You should be careful about what you say ...' But it was no use. She was too busy cackling and squawking to listen to me. I tucked away the information she was spilling out, storing it for future reference.

When I could get a word in edgeways there was something I needed to impress on her and I hoped she wasn't too drunk to remember what I had to say.

'I don't want anyone to know I'm a policewoman, so if anyone asks, I'm a secretary.'

'Secretary? Yes, secretary.' She ran her pink tongue over her lips, tasting the last of the Harvey Wallbanger. 'I don't blame you. And watch out if I do anything stupid. I can't see a thing without my glasses but I'm not wearing them here.'

It seemed like a good deal, although I doubted any male within a five-mile distance of Pat would care whether she could see or not. What must it be like, I wondered, to look so gorgeous?

'Come on, Jan, it's after 11. Let's get going next door and start the boo – oo – gee – ee – ing.'

Jan? No one called me Jan. I didn't like it and I was about to tell her not to either. Then I decided it would be another way of disguising my identity. I followed Pat through the dense crowd in the hotel bar and with very little fuss we were past the bouncers and in the club.

As soon as we'd slipped through the rope at Cassandra's and popped into the ladies', giggling about a good-looking bouncer, I watched her change from an attractive young woman into a predatory panther on a mission. She frowned at my reflection in the mirror as I swirled the pleated skirt around my ankles.

'Take it off.'

'What?' I was horrified but couldn't stop her from dragging down the elasticated material, until it floated around my Mary Jane shoes. The black jacket now looked like a short mini dress, just skimming my thighs. My thin, long legs stuck out from it like a dressed-up stork.

'Much better, Jan. Squash the skirt up and hide it in your handbag. It's big enough.'

My bag was too big, compared to Pat's miniscule purse which just about held a £5 note, tampon, lipstick and a comb. Next time, I'd learn a few tricks from Pat and buy a bag the same as hers. In fact, we could go shopping together before the next night out. What was this? Me, planning to go out shopping with someone other than Mum? Oh well, there was always a first time!

Pleased with my new look and tidily arranging the skirt so that it didn't bulge out of my bag, I turned back to the mirror for another look and to check my lipstick. I was just in time to see Pat disappear through the door into the club with barely a backwards glance.

After searching for her in the heaving crowd of bodies and threading my way back and forth across the dancefloor I gave up on finding her. Later I discovered I could have saved time and headed for the entrance, where she'd spent most of the night behaving like a star-struck groupie distracting the handsome bouncer. He'd adopted the outdated Jason King, bushy hair and moustache look and I remembered the drug squad officer from the Tally twins' arrest. I hadn't liked him and immediately disliked the leering club bouncer.

Despite our shared reminiscences over cocktails, I'd never known Pat very well at school. She was in my form and I'd never considered her as one of the bright girls like myself. My guilt from playing a part in Linda's disappearance stopped me from making close friendships. I had to avoid those close, shared girly secrets where I might have blurted something out about the orchard and the secret door. Left to be a loner, there was ample time to study for exams.

Trying to avoid being overly jostled at the bar I managed finally to buy myself a Cherry B, wishing I had the courage to show my police ID card. My fellow officers assured me that drinks appeared like lightning when they did it and most times the barman waved away any attempts to pay.

Still nursing the Cherry B a couple of hours later I knew I was well and truly abandoned. It was nearly 1am and the club was heaving, noise levels were high as couples tried to ask each other stupid questions above the soul music booming from the speakers. I'd given up on Pat and decided to finish my drink and then try to find a taxi home.

With the sparse seats already taken by couples smooching each other's faces, I leaned back against the wall, wishing my feet didn't hurt in my cramped heeled shoes. Nightclubs, I realised, were tawdry and not at all fun when you were on your own. Looking around at everyone else shrieking and dancing I knew I was in the minority.

'Where's your mate?'

It was a simple question but yelled into my right ear by someone wearing just the right amount of Paco Rabanne to smell interesting. I turned to face an expensive pale grey shirt, still fresh and with no sweat patches under the arms.

Unlike the other men in the club the tall guy wasn't wearing a ridiculous patterned shirt with wide lapels. This one fitted tightly to a lean body and he'd added a thin tie, loosened to a narrow gap at his neck. Even his smart black trousers tapered at the bottom rather than billowing out like a bell. He reeked of the West End and I remembered seeing outfits like it in the window of a men's clothes shop when I did a day trip to London last year. Paul Smith – that was it. A trendy designer with his own shop and a range of men's clothes. This guy must have a good job to dress like that.

I peered at my watch in the muted lighting. The club would be closing soon. Already the men were lining themselves around the dancefloor, mentally choosing their target to press their sweaty bodies against in the last dance. The mood was slowing down with a medley of slow Barry White songs and even my hormones were feeling the beat and the heat. Exactly where was my so-called mate?

'No – I – dea.' I mouthed as loudly as I could as the booming speakers drowned out conversation.

It was impossible to talk and with the crowd increasing around the dancefloor my handsome companion and I were squeezed closer together against the wall. I held my half-empty glass between us like a shield. Despite the feeble attempt, the right side of our heated bodies brushed together. My stomach flipped and instinctively I looked up at the cause. His smile showed even white teeth and the whites of his crinkled eyes shone from his tanned face.

He seemed less bothered about Pat, or should I say, my 'mate', and stayed with me, holding out a protective arm each time a drunken male threatened to squash us both. My body tensed with the familiar professional reaction when three men in front of us started to throw drunken punches.

I should intervene and defuse the situation. Before I could move, he gently held my elbow and led me away to a far corner where it was marginally quieter. Two bouncers raced from nowhere towards the fight and the men were hustled out of the exit with one of them protesting about wanting to dance before he went home.

'That's better,' he said and sipped his pint of untouched pale liquid. 'I've been watching you all night and like an idiot I decide to speak to you at the last minute – almost.'

I braced myself for the inevitable 'You're beautiful you are', 'How are you getting home?', 'Where do you live? We could share a taxi.' Nothing any man said at a club would be intelligent or meaningful.

'I'm Rob by the way.' He didn't exactly hold out his hand for me to shake but picked up mine and pretended to wave it as introduction. I laughed and thought he was probably nicer than most of the men in the room.

'I'm Jan.' Well, it was half true. I didn't waver from my decision not to tell anyone outside the job my full name or what I did for a living. Most men expected females to be secretaries so why should I disillusion them. If I was really pressed, then I could admit I was a secretary at the police station. That might shut them up.

Rob didn't ask me about my job or say anything about his own. The DJ's muffled voice announced that Marvin Gaye would end the night and a hundred or so bodies clung to each other swaying to 'Let's Get It On'. He leaned in close to my ear and asked if I wanted to dance.

'I know it's corny, but we can dance right here.' Before I could answer he'd taken my hand, empty glass still held tightly and with a respectable distance between us he weaved around me. It was sexier than anything going on in the darkened club. With an imperceptible casual move, he took the glass from my hand and drew me slightly closer to him. I relaxed, prepared for four minutes of bliss – and Paco Rabanne.

'Jan, we're going. Come on.' My arm was wrenched from the warm clasp and Rob was pushed aside, frowning and bewildered at the interruption. Instead of his dark blond hair and smiling face gazing at me I was dragged away by Pat, her skirt rumpled with smudges of white plaster on the back of it. Her mascara had clumped under her lashes and she was in no mood for any resistance.

'That bloody bouncer's married. The other one – with the spots – just told me after I've been talking to them all night. Don't know why either of them couldn't have mentioned it before … 25, duck.' She pushed a pink raffle ticket at the cloakroom girl and before I knew it I was out on the cold street, struggling into my thin coat and with no sign of Rob anywhere. Even if he had followed us, there were too many people leaving the club in search of taxis and night buses for me to find him.

At least we were near the front of the taxi queue and it wasn't long before I was in bed trying to sleep and not think about my mystery Rob – tall, blond and handsome Rob with the kind smile and his sexy dancing. If it wasn't for my dedication to my job and determination to have a good career, I could cheerfully have killed Pat. Instead, I finally fell asleep plotting her unsolvable murder.

11

CID

The excitement of having Linda's file in my possession was overshadowed by everything going on around me inside and outside work. I'd flicked through it after taking it from Jarvis, certain I would find the vital clue to bring me closer to finding out what could have happened to her. After day shifts ended and I should have gone home, I spent an hour reading the reports and statements, including my own. There were a few photographs and press cuttings but other than that the file was thin, with little in it. How could I be surprised. Linda only had a small family and few friends.

Nothing had prompted me to raise new questions apart from Jarvis's suspicion of the dead paedophile. I made a note of his name and squiggled three question marks after it. It couldn't be difficult to find the names of his cell mates while he'd been in prison. Maybe he'd said something to one of them.

After a long day cataloguing names and addresses collected from beat bobbies in a run-down area notorious for drug dealing, I wanted to go home. I locked the file in the bottom drawer of my desk, never expecting that it would be almost six months before I looked at it again.

Jarvis had advised me never to take the file home.

'Cold cases are resurrected all the time,' he'd explained, 'especially if a suspect from the crime raises their ugly head again in later years, or a prison con hears a confession from a cell mate and rats him out. You don't want the file at your house when a chief super starts looking for it – especially if a likely suspect is sitting in the interview room.'

Wise words. During my time in the job so far, I'd seen exactly that same thing happen after a straightforward arrest and fingerprints matched a burglary or worse, from ten or fifteen years before. On these occasions a palpable buzz filtered through the station and officers, sometimes retired, would quickly be on the spot for the moment of the arrest.

Jarvis had taken note of my observations of the Tally twins' features while waiting for the arrests to be completed. One of my first duties in CID was to match descriptions with e-fits and then with existing mug shots. I quickly developed a keen eye for facial recognition and had an almost 80% success rate for matching photo-fit images to real photographs. Studying faces almost became an obsession, especially after Jarvis and even one or two CID colleagues agreed I had a 'knack' for it. It helped that I had some skill at drawing. It hadn't been enough to distinguish myself at school but sketching the face of a suspect from even the vaguest details helped to speed up investigations.

Jarvis never referred to it, but DC Carter sat down at my desk one morning and watched me while I was working until I looked up, my hand shaking. He was the same age as the superintendent but his lack of looks and years of alcohol abuse had left him with a bloated red face, spider-webbed with blue veins across his cheeks, and a bulbous nose. I knew the two men had trained together at Ryton and it was Jarvis who had made sure he stopped wrecking his career and committed himself to AA.

'Don't underestimate what you're doing there,' he said and nodded his jowly chin at the photograph of Don Anderson, leaving an illegal nightclub in the early hours. His head was bent slightly over a striking match and the camera had managed to capture the moment when the flame lit up a small scar puckering the skin between his nose and top lip.

'Cleft palate,' I said and again Carter nodded. 'Not a very good op but better than leaving it as it was.'

'What's he done?'

'Nothing yet – but I can confirm that this e-fit is 92% Don Anderson. The bobbies can watch out for him now and next time he decides to mug an old lady – especially if she isn't as observant as the last one ...'

Carter chuckled without smiling and slid the photo back onto the pile. 'Another big mistake people make. Old ladies are not as daft as everyone thinks they are. Some of them were in top-notch jobs in the war – usually because they were clever, not stupid. Never underestimate anyone, Janice.'

I agreed with him.

'But I meant what I said. Don't underestimate what you're doing here, either. You've got an innate skill with facial recognition. It's invaluable – do everything you can to improve it.'

The short exchange was enough to boost my fragile confidence in my abilities. My size-5s were used to walking on imaginary eggshells whenever I stepped through the door of the CID office. I loved being part of the department even though I was still in uniform and my time was mostly spent in administrative work or answering the phone. If I continued to do a good job, I hoped I was safe from any possible disciplinary action or dismissal.

As one of only two women in the male-dominated department I put up with the lewd and crude remarks flung around the office or peppering conversation in an unmarked car while on hours of observations. Mum would have been mortified if I'd used the same language at home and I didn't want to risk it slipping out when I bashed my knee on the wooden bed or burnt myself with the iron.

Like many of the officers I worked with, I tried hard to maintain a distance between my working life and my home life. It wasn't always easy, but I was more fortunate than many of the married officers who rarely had anyone at home who understood the pressures they faced every time they were on duty.

At least I could sound off to Mum and wind down from a bad day which might have involved a good arrest but in sad circumstances. Not all criminals were like the Tally twins, belligerent and certain they had the right to break the law. Some were sad cases where the only way to eat or keep warm was to resort to petty theft, which nearly always escalated and ended in disaster.

'Janice, if you're going to keep feeling sorry for every person you arrest and who gets locked up in prison then you should seriously think of becoming a social worker.'

This advice was given to me more than once and often in different tones of voices. Some officers empathised with how I felt and meant the advice as a positive move. Others almost spat out the words. Too many encounters with low life made them cynical and they warned me to think more about the victims.

Every day I learned so much about the job, improved my skills and increased my experience. But there were days when I felt I knew nothing, when I worked with detectives like Jarvis and Carter. I was meant to study for my sergeant's exams if I wanted to progress in my career, but the demands of my job overwhelmed me and I was often too tired to do anything on my days off but lie in bed or on the sofa watching TV.

One of the things I enjoyed after work was recalling the few moments I'd spent with Rob at Cassandra's nightclub. To me, he represented a normal kind of life and I wondered what work he did to afford expensive clothes. He hadn't spoken with a Birmingham accent, but I couldn't detect any of the London dialects either. Somehow, smart, sharp clothes like the ones he'd worn instantly made me think of Chelsea or the Kings Road.

After Pat's birthday celebration I'd dragged her back to the club every Saturday night when I was off duty, hoping to find him there. She'd been keen at first, eager to re-connect with the married bouncer, but after lame excuses from him she gave up hanging around the door while he was working.

Looking over my shoulder, pretending I was searching the room for friends, became embarrassing when I failed to see Rob's handsome face and ended up catching the eye of an unwanted, leering drunk. Pat's long jacket idea appealed to me, especially if it had attracted Rob to watch me for most of the night. Together, we shopped for similar-looking clothes and I made it my own style. Although I wore a uniform to work, I looked very different when I was out so whenever I spotted the occasional petty or die-hard offender, I was confident I'd never be recognised.

Pat's experience with the lying, philandering bouncer taught me a lesson. Even though I hoped to see Rob again and dressed with great care, I prepared myself to see him with another girl in the club. Maybe even overhear him repeating the same words he'd spoken to me. After too many abortive attempts to see Rob again I decided to give up the effort and use my time and money in better ways. There were other men in the city beside him.

Work consumed me and I would sometimes be asked to do a shift at another police station in the county, using my developing facial recognition skills when they were needed. My reputation grew slowly and with it, unexpected respect from colleagues in CID and uniformed officers. Occasionally I bumped into PC Nick Watson, who always managed to say something in connection with the Tally twins.

'Have you tracked down Mr Big yet, Morton? We're all relying on you.'

Nick was popular wherever he worked but general gossip was certain he didn't have a regular girlfriend. For social occasions he would always turn up with a different attractive woman and be very attentive. He was on the graduate entry scheme, destined to fast track through the ranks to a senior position in a short time.

'We'll all be saluting him before he's thirty – that's what a university degree in Law does for you,' Carter grumbled one day when we sat in the canteen watching Nick charming two new women probationers.

A good detective misses nothing and the good detective Carter could hardly miss my eyes fixed on Nick's flirting. He leaned towards me and looked serious as he chewed the last bite of his cheese and salad cream sandwich.

'Seriously, Janice, avoid ever being alone with that man. Some of us call him the Handyman and it's not because he can bang a nail in a piece of four by two.'

It took me a moment to work that one out. Why were good-looking men such a disappointment?

'I'm hardly his type, Mick.'

No reply from Carter. It was like he rationed himself to so much conversation per day and now he'd used up all his allocation. I ate my own cheese and salad cream sandwich in silence. Was I destined to like unobtainable men, I wondered? I told myself to settle for being a career woman and maybe one day colleagues like Carter would be saluting me before I was thirty – if I behaved myself.

With this thought in mind it was a shock when Jarvis and Inspector Paulson called me into Jarvis's office. As I entered the room, the inspector, stern-faced, closed the white blinds so that we weren't observed by the rest of the team. Surely they knew everyone in the main office would now be certain I was in some kind of trouble.

Although both men were standing, we all sat after Jarvis closed the door. He stayed behind his desk and the inspector sat in a chair next to me. Frantically my mind played over events from the last few weeks for anything I might have done or said that could be cause for disciplinary action. My stomach gambolled like the spin cycle on Mum's new washing machine.

Jarvis spoke. 'Janice, we've had some intelligence from more than one officer, and we can't ignore it any longer. The Tally twin with the freckle ...'

'Chaz?' I recalled.

'Him. He sounded his mouth off in his cell to a man we've planted in there for more information about the drugs ring. He's been in contact with someone – we don't know who, to ...' he glanced at the inspector. '... well, cause you harm for your part in their conviction.'

I waited calmly to hear what he would say next. Threats like this were thrown at policemen and women every day; shouted during an arrest, screamed from a locked cell, and even yelled across a court room: 'I know where you live, copper.' It had disturbed me the first time I heard it, even though the toe rag doing the yelling couldn't possibly have known my address.

Mum was always my first concern. What if some mad bastard picked on her or broke into the house when she was on her own? After looking over my shoulder every time I walked around the area or queued for a bus, I realised I had to stop worrying about the threats or leave the job. The Crime Prevention Officer came home with me one day and advised how we could install window locks, extra door locks and a burglar alarm to feel safer. I bought every gadget going until I was satisfied the house was protected.

It was a sad indictment of our profession that Jarvis could see I was barely fazed by his words. His lined face looked more weary than usual and I guessed his four-year-old twins were causing more sleepless nights.

Paulson said, 'We just thought you should know the word out on the street. The Tally twins think they're in the same league as the Krays – they even demanded to be sent to the same prison, as if you can choose one like a Spanish hotel.' He murmured a short laugh at his own joke, so I smiled. 'You drive here from home and back again?'

I nodded. 'Mum's set up an HP agreement for a new Mini. She gave it to me as a surprise after the pub bombings. The HP's in her name so I pay her every week when I get paid. She's happy. It means I can take her shopping and we don't have to rely on buses for going anywhere. It's better for working nights as well. I feel safer.'

The two men studied me. Paulson had changed from that night he'd agreed for me to go along with Jarvis to check out the paper warehouse where we suspected the Tally twins had an interest. He'd praised me afterwards and I was grateful for his attention. After a stabbing almost disabled him many years ago, he'd been confined to desk duties and took on the welfare of new officers in addition to his station inspector responsibilities. He'd gained weight from lack of exercise and too many pints in the police social club after work, but now I noticed that his uniform hung on his skinny frame and his face was gaunt, rather than florid and heavier. Jarvis noticed me staring and caught my eye. He gave a small shake of his head and I guessed there was something going on with the inspector's health.

Paulson caught the looks between us and stood up straight. 'Cambridge Diet,' he said with pride. 'The weight's dropping off me. It's bloody brilliant.'

Jarvis and the inspector seemed satisfied about my new car. 'Well, you know what to do – be extra cautious when you're out and about. A patrol car on each shift will pass by your house just to make sure everything's OK. But there's not much more we can do if there's a mad man out there wanting to earn extra cash.'

'Do the Tallys have extra cash we don't know about?' I asked. The two men exchanged looks.

'Good point,' said Jarvis. 'We confiscated all their possessions that couldn't be accounted for and the council tried to take back the house after the Tally parents lost their main source of income from the twins. Problem is the mum has children of her own, so they have to live somewhere. Her latest husband claims benefit so we'll keep an eye on him if he looks like he's got more money than he should. We'll try to find out who could have the means to pay someone to cause you trouble.'

He picked up his raincoat, which was draped over a bulging briefcase. 'I wouldn't worry too much, though. Without the drugs money they're unlikely to be in the millionaire bracket. The inspector chuckled at the pathetic joke but neither man stopped frowning.

Sitting at my desk afterwards, the angry photographs in the mug shot book flicked past me in a blur. I had to repeat the exercise three times before I could finally focus and concentrate on the job. I couldn't shake off the suspicion that something was worrying Jarvis and Paulson. We'd all agreed that I shouldn't take the threat too seriously, but my thudding heart told me I was shaken by it.

Maybe it was time Mum and I took a holiday somewhere. I could use my savings and we could book a nice hotel in Bournemouth or somewhere like it. She'd like that.

12

Evelyn

'Will you be here for Sunday lunch, Janice?'

What was that supposed to mean? I was in the bathroom preparing to shower off the grime of my day when Mum called through the closed door.

Too much steam fogged the mirror to see myself being interrogated.

'What?' I shouted back. Mum knew my shift patterns better than I did. Anything I mentioned about my days or nights or working at a different police station in the county was written in her turquoise diary and added to the calendar.

With one glance at the kitchen wall, Mum knew where I should be – night or day. She couldn't control the times I eventually arrived home, though. Generally, I could get word to her even if I couldn't call myself to let her know I would be late.

She knew perfectly well that this was my weekend off and even though I might not get up early on Sunday I always roused myself for her delicious roast dinners. When I was young and money was tight, Mum hardly cooked anything other than a tasteless stew or a thin soup with floating potatoes and carrots.

Instead of sitting at the kitchen table smoking and gossiping endlessly, Mrs Chant, our neighbour from two doors up, had taught her domestic science. After watching Mum frowning at the instructions on the back of a box of Vesta Chow Mein she'd rolled up her sleeves and insisted she learned to cook properly.

'You can't feed rubbish like to that to Janice after she's been at work for eight hours or more. If the food's better in the canteen she'll never come home.'

That was enough to frighten Mum into action. She peeled potatoes and mashed them instead of opening a packet of Smash and adding too much water to the miniature hydrated cubes. Mrs Chant died from a sudden heart attack one day when I'd been working but she'd left a legacy of recipe books and instructions that elevated Mum into a much better cook. Thank goodness.

After I stepped out of the bathroom with a towel wrapped around my wet hair and belted my Japanese-print satin dressing gown, I confronted my innocent-looking mother with great suspicion.

'Why are you asking if I'll be home on Sunday?'

She sat at the table with two steaming mugs in front of her. Wafts of hot chocolate drifted around the small kitchen. We often enjoyed cosy chats there rather than sit in the cold living room. I watched her as I sipped the boiling liquid, which was so much better than anything served at work.

Self-centred as I was, it was a shock to see how Mum had changed without me noticing. She'd always been much too thin after the war rationing and then saving precious food to give to me while she nibbled on toast. But she had plumped up enough now to have an attractive bosom and curves. Her own crimson silk dressing gown, my Christmas present to her, clung to her body and I had to accept that Mum was an attractive woman and she wasn't that old either.

With a small shock I realised that she had to be the same age as Francis Jarvis, and he was still working at a fast and vibrant pace with ambitions to progress in his career. I mentally compared our own ages.

She was eighteen when she had me which meant she was still in her late thirties. Oh yes ...

Mug in hand I leaned back in the kitchen chair and grinned. 'So, what's happening on Sunday? Do you want me out of the way?'

Mortified at the suggestion, she shrieked, 'Of course I don't. You're hardly here as it is.' I raised my eyebrows. DC Williams had mentioned after a shared interview that I looked very intimidating when I did that.

Williams must have had a point; Mum looked down at her mug. A shifty reaction. In an interview room I'd be preparing to caution her.

'No, I've invited a friend to lunch with us – his name's David and I want you to meet him. He's just a friend.' She insisted with a shy smile.

'Oh.' I wasn't sure I liked my mother having male 'friends'.

'Where did you meet him? Where does he live?'

'Sutton Coldfield. But I met him in the library in Erdington.'

'Sutton Coldfield? What were you doing in Erdington Library – and what was he doing there?' Sutton was the posh part of Birmingham and there had to be a particularly good reason for a native to cross the border over to our side.

Mum didn't look at all bothered by the unusual place for her to meet and talk to a stranger. 'He tutors in English Language and Literature and the library had a book he needed.'

'And you …?'

'To be honest I was only there because it had started to pour with rain while I was in the high street. I was looking at the noticeboard when he literally bumped into me. We started talking and then went for a cup of tea in the cafe across the road. You'll like him, Janice.'

What was I supposed to make of all that? It sounded innocent enough and I decided it was the best idea for him to come to our house for lunch. He would have to make a good impression on me, and I could ask him enough questions to check him out at work.

Mum's friend David Brown was a bit of a shock. In my mind any man who could be considered as a boyfriend for my mum would be a tall, gentlemanly person with his own car and lovely manners. Someone like Sean Connery but without the womanising nature.

David, while nothing like Sean in appearance, was still very impressive. He was tall, at least six foot, with shoulders that stooped slightly. He was much older than Mum and had bushy grey eyebrows, thick spectacles, a handsome face and clear, smooth skin.

He shook my hand with a firm grip and that redeemed him. Even if his handshake hadn't won me over slightly then I was completely lost when he smiled. Then I knew why Mum liked him and immediately I worried that she would be hurt by this good-looking man.

His even white teeth gleamed with expensive dentistry and his smile crinkled the skin around his dark brown eyes. The glasses had heavy black frames, like the ones Michael Caine wore in *The Ipcress File*. 'Blooming heck,' I thought, 'he's gorgeous'

Relieved, I noticed Mum completely relaxed around David. She didn't seem at all ruffled that he was standing in the middle of our living room, sniffing the air and sighing with genuine pleasure as he announced, 'Mmm, roast beef – smells delicious.'

We left David sitting in the lounge sipping a sweet sherry which I'd poured from a bottle I never knew we had in the sideboard. Bought for the occasion no doubt. David's long legs were crossed as he sat back leafing through *The Sunday Times* which had also appeared without my knowledge.

'I'm not even going to ask if I can help,' he called through into the kitchen hearing us banging around with pots and pans, ladling gravy over crispy potatoes. 'But I do insist on washing up afterwards.'

Mum and I looked at each other and then around at the devastation of a World War Three blitz on every available surface.

'Deal,' I shouted back and Mum swiped the singed tea towel at me.

The roast beef was delicious. During the meal we tried to outdo each other with suitable adjectives for the food. I'd taken Mum's cooking for granted, not really appreciating how much she'd improved our diet as the shops were stocked with better produce. Admittedly, though, this Sunday lunch did include far more variety than the usual meat and two veg. Who had told her you could roast parsnips and they would taste amazing?

David entertained us with little effort, delighted when we laughed at his jokes and successful attempts to show off his vocabulary.

He wiped his mouth on an embroidered napkin that I usually saw at Christmas and we both allowed Mum to clear away the plates. My heart sank a little as I realised that I would have to be the heroine and wash up – leaving them both some time to themselves. It was only fair.

'I've just retired from teaching English Literature and Language,' David said when Mum disappeared to check on the apple crumble and make custard. Being older and wiser than me he'd known I wanted to hear as much as possible about him. Retired? He was older than I thought. Sixty?

Reading my thoughts, he grinned. 'Retired early, I should say. When the government threatened to change the grammar schools into comprehensive schools, I decided to finish gracefully and change career to private tuition instead.'

'Have you missed teaching in a school?' I really wanted to ask him if he was a good teacher – and was he popular. Thinking back to my own school – a grammar school that had seen better times – I wished I'd had a teacher like him and was sure I would have worked even harder.

He nodded and sat back in the dining chair, with his arms resting on the tablecloth. I wondered if he knew I used my police training to read his body language. David relaxed and smiled with a confidence neither Mum nor I possessed. Nothing to hide, I concluded, and my heart skipped a beat with sheer pleasure for Mum.

'The thing is with English language and literature, Janice, it will never change for me. I'll always love it and apart from keeping up with the latest novels it's not like geography, with countries changing names and leaderships.' His eyes twinkled behind his magnified lenses. 'That's too much effort for me. I can teach what I love and hopefully pass it on to new students.'

Mum appeared with a rose-patterned china jug brimming with creamy custard. So, we weren't having it ladled straight out of the saucepan then. I bent my head to smile at my hands. Did David appreciate how all this effort was especially for him? Or was that unfair? We rarely had guests for any meal so how could I know how Mum might behave on occasions like this.

I'd glanced at the jug and frowned, trying to remember if I had seen it before, and almost missed David's eyes meet Mum's across the table. They both shared a smile. There was I, thinking David was here for me to assess when it was suddenly becoming obvious: my approval wasn't needed.

We gave up finding superlatives for the pudding and enjoyed savouring the taste, squabbling over the last spoonful of custard.

David was the guest; but Mum had cooked; and I deserved the last dribbles because I had a 'demanding job protecting the public'. When had Mum and I laughed so much together except at Morecambe and Wise or Benny Hill?

'Do you enjoy your job?' David asked as he scraped the last of the custard from the jug into his dish. Guests trumped a lowly police constable. It was a new rule. Mum and I insisted he obeyed.

My hand shot out to grab Mum's wrist as she reached for my empty bowl.

'I'll wash up. You can entertain our guest.' Her cheeks flushed a light pink colour, but she stayed seated while I answered David's question.

'I love it. It's hard work and there's lots of things I see that I wouldn't ever tell anyone about – but that's what makes it great. I watch people shopping or sitting in the pub with a pint and I'm glad they'll never know some of the things going on around them. I can't do anything about the newspapers but even they can't tell the actual truth sometimes.'

David nodded again and I noticed his greying hair was trimmed just above his collar. He looked respectable but not old-fashioned. There was a lot more to him than I'd first thought. I should have known better than to judge him from a first impression. But in my defence, I assessed him as my mother's boyfriend and not as a dodgy witness to the mugging of an old lady.

'I can't imagine what the job must really be like,' he agreed, 'but in my profession it's sometimes better to use discretion when talking to parents otherwise some of the pupils might not appear at all. Complete honesty isn't always the best policy. So many mothers, especially mothers, are convinced their child is a genius and a saint. And do you know,' another of his mischievous grins, 'they very rarely are either.'

David's charm had worked like magic on me and I was totally hooked, proud he was Mum's friend. I wasn't sure about the boyfriend bit.

After lunch, we all sat in the living room, drinking coffee poured from a tall ceramic pot I had never seen before. David asked me if I would be OK if he took Mum to meet his parents in Kent.

'They're frail and elderly but very independent. Dad was too old to serve in the last war but they both worked at a place called Bletchley Park in Buckinghamshire, doing whatever they could for some of the personnel stationed there. Don't ask me what,' he said with a frown. 'I'm always quoted "loose lips sink ships" when I ask. I expect it was cleaning and cooking. Neither of them would mind what they did if it made them feel useful.'

David spoke with a soft and cultured tone. He reminded me a little of the chief constable, whom I'd only met once.

He'd been incredibly polite and well-spoken. It had been hard to imagine him as an aspiring police officer.

'Do they live alone?'

'It's a big old house so my cousin lives with them to help out. Your mum will have the best room at the back, overlooking the garden and with a lovely view of the Medway. My room is the same one I had when I lived there and it's full of stuff from when I was a boy – more of a lethal booby trap than a bedroom.'

Message received – loud and clear, I thought. Mum would be treated with respect and maybe help with the cooking for his parents. She'd like that. It would be a lovely weekend away for her. Safely away from home.

'Sounds great. More sherry, David?'

13

Pat

I'd appreciated the 'nod' from Jarvis and Inspector Paulson advising me to be cautious out on the streets and at home. We suspected the Tally twins had connections all over the city and, rather like the Kray Twins, wouldn't let confinement inside four draughty brick walls stop them carrying on with business.

The drug squad hadn't reported any progress in finding the chief who organised the drug imports found in the boxes in the warehouse. The haul hadn't been huge but Detective Superintendent Thomson who led the team was convinced the surprise visit, seizing the drugs on site and subsequent arrest had at least prevented further use of the premises.

'The cannabis was packaged ready to hit the streets, courtesy of those two idiots. This is just part of the chain. What we're really after is where the operation begins. Cannabis arrives here somehow, and we need to find the source,' I'd overheard Thomson telling Jarvis, and both agreed it was like talking to the wall when they interviewed potential suspects.

'It's quiet on the street,' Jarvis said. 'Maybe we've underestimated the twins. Something's definitely spooked people out there since they were put away.'

The Tally twins had been interrogated for days but not even the dangling carrot of them serving their sentences in the same prison could persuade them to give up any names. Thomson and Jarvis finally concluded they were part of the chain but the clever plan to keep everyone on a 'need-to-know' basis had worked. The twins couldn't reveal what they never knew in the first place.

Word of their hire of a hitman to harm me or Mum soon spread around the station. It was always a mystery how police and civilian personnel knew what was going on within an hour of any information passed to one person. Long-serving officers approached me, eager to give me advice and anecdotal support. They assured me most criminals knew better than to seriously harm a police officer. Generally, the rumour was circulated to frighten the arresting officer, which in my case had worked one hundred per cent.

I encouraged Mum to spend as much time with David as possible. She didn't need reassurance that her relationship was alright with me. Most of her free time was spent either cooking small meals for him in our kitchen, out at the pictures to see the latest films (twice if there was nothing better on the following week) or on weekends away to see his parents.

Did David have some idea that Mum shouldn't be left on her own, I wondered? Whatever his intentions were, their friendship was a great relief. Mum always insisted she was home after my shifts and even though I tried to catch them out I'm sure he never stayed overnight or she with him.

After a few months of suspiciously assessing everyone I saw at railway stations or the supermarket I began to relax. I never wore my uniform openly when off duty, covering it with my own coat or leather jacket and changing the flat black shoes for high heels. Did I fool anyone? How could I know for sure?

Like many if not all officers around me, I learned to take these threats with a pinch of salt. If I didn't then I would go mad or insist on a 'desk job' which I would have hated.

Life continued in frenzied 10-hour days in CID, working on case after case with only a glimmer of respite to attend further training courses on interview techniques, welfare or advanced self-defence. There was never any refusal for training in the department. Jarvis encouraged us all to be up to date with the latest developments, especially with psychology and advancements in technology.

'You're a good team and we get results, but we don't sit back we move forward. Make sure you always know what's new before anyone else,' Jarvis would bark at us on a weekly basis in our morning meetings.

Computers were creeping into the station. There was a new VDU in CID and it stood proudly on its own desk in the middle of the office. Only authorised officers could use it. I wasn't on the list and was envious of Carter and other key detectives who would sit in front of its blinking display. Carter stayed late most nights, studying a manual the size of a house brick. He was determined to understand everything it could do for him. In spare moments I pulled a chair as close as I dared and watched over his shoulder as he played with the keyboard and green coded letters pulsated onto the screen.

Facial recognition was advancing towards more sophisticated computerisation and I beamed like a smug kid when Jarvis booked me on a two-week residential course with one of the detective sergeants. Not only was I a natural for this skill but I relied on it helping me to identify Linda, who would be twenty-one now. My problem was trying to remember any distinctive features she may have had when I played with her during school holidays.

That was difficult. All I had to look at were overdeveloped colour Kodak photos Hazel had supplied to the initial investigation. Even they had faded over the years despite good intentions to keep them in a sealed envelope in the file which Jarvis had kept in his drawer.

With his permission, I took it with me to the course and after sessions I would lay out the four photographs while I studied and prepped for tests, applying my new knowledge to build up a photo-fit of a 21-year-old Linda. It was tempting to read through the file again from the beginning to the date when CID had had to leave their investigations and move on to other crimes.

Since the nineteenth century, when French criminologist Alphonse Bertillon invented the mug shot, all law enforcement agencies relied on the facial recognition method of using eleven physical measurements. The handout with its mapped-out face showing all points was kept in my folder inside a plastic wallet, protecting it as though it was an ancient manuscript. I kept copies folded inside my police notebook and tucked into a compartment in my bag.

In class my attention was gripped by the various speakers who cagily shared some of their experiences with the development of facial recognition and experiments to compile a computerised database of portraits to match. The great 'ideal' would be a program that could extract facial features without human input. That sounded like impossible science fiction to me.

If only I'd taken more interest in computer science at school, but as it was maths based, I struggled to be interested. Instead, I'd enjoyed dabbling in art, which at least helped when it came to compiling e-fits from victims' descriptions.

Filled with fresh enthusiasm I was keen to find better photos of Linda and try to build up a picture of what she would look like if she were alive. She was a year older than me, so she should be twenty-one. Surely, she was of an age, if living, to break free from any captor and seek help? When I had a clearer photo of her face, one where her nose and eyebrows showed clearly, I should be able to draw a good picture of her.

Hazel, Linda's real mum, may have more photographs I could examine, and I resolved to one day visit her and Lonnie in their home next door. Perhaps her real grandmother, whom she'd believed was her mother, had other photographs I could use.

Jarvis was right about all the pressures of the job preventing me from seriously checking out the file and sifting through the evidence to possibly form new conclusions. Incoming work overwhelmed the department and as the most junior I could be deluged with minor tasks like checking documents or carrying out door-to-door enquiries with a uniformed constable.

It was too indulgent to seriously open the cold case when we were looking for a vicious rapist or following up leads on a potential drug empire thriving under our noses. Finding Linda would have to wait a little longer.

Another distraction was my reluctant friendship with Pat. After our first outing to the nightclub and the subsequent visits with me trying to find Rob again, we'd met up every now and then for a meal at the local Berni Inn. We both liked the faux Elizabethan décor and even though we were now twenty we felt more grown up among the celebrating couples as we drank Blue Nun or pink Mateus Rose.

Pat still chattered on about her job and the odd comings and goings of the owners. They either didn't realise they were being watched by the girls on the shop floor, desperate for any diversion from the whining sewing machines and *The Jimmy Young Show*, or they didn't care. Always mindful of my career I listened carefully to everything she said, hiding behind my menu and pretending to deliberate between the chicken cordon bleu or the half roast chicken, which was 30 pence cheaper.

'You'd be amazed what goes on during the night shift, Janice ... prawn cocktail, T-bone steak and the meringue fountain.' She snapped the menu down onto the table and looked up to catch a waiter's eye.

'You have the same every time. What goes on during the night shift?'

'No, I don't. Last time – and I mean the last time – I had the sorbet sensation because you said I'd like it. It was horrible – too watery. Never again. I like plenty of cream.'

I pushed my hair back behind my ear and lay my menu flat down next to my red paper serviette. 'Taramasalata.' Pat shuddered as though a tarantula had crawled over her and stuck her tongue out. 'Chicken and then the cheesecake.' It wasn't the best of choices: unlike Pat, who could eat anything and never lose her Farah Fawcett like figure, I had to be careful of adding a few pounds when I often spent more time than I would like sitting at a desk.

After the embarrassed waiter had left us with our order – and Pat's telephone number stuffed into his trouser pocket – I tried again. Filling her wine glass from the bottle of Blue Nun I asked, 'So go on then, what happens on the night shift? I thought you just did days and a couple of Saturdays.'

Pat's eyes followed the waiter weaving his way through the busy tables, willing him to turn around. When he didn't turn, she slumped her shoulders and drank half of the glass. 'I don't usually but I swapped a shift with one of the women who's got a kid starting nursery. You get paid more but I'd rather have my nights free for someone like him – if you know what I mean.'

I leant forward and scratched the back of my neck where there was once two inches more of my hair until that morning. 'Suits you like this,' the hairdresser had said, and I think she was right.

'At least it's a bit quieter at night.' Pat twiddled the stem of her wine glass. 'It's mostly packing what the girls have run up during the day. Sanjay, the big boss, has new orders that need to be delivered in a three-day turn around.'

'Orders? Marks and Spencer?'

Pat snorted. 'You've got to be joking. What we produce is more likely for the market stalls. But it's not cheap tat!' She stared at me with unusual concentration. I got the impression she was proud of her work and wanted to defend it. 'Some of the styles are good enough for the West End but the material's cheap – and yeah, a bit nasty sometimes. Foreign, but cheap.'

She brushed her hand dramatically down her body from shoulders to her waist and preened with her other hand behind her head. 'This is one of the designs they do. It's OK isn't it?'

It was more than OK and as the waiter deftly dropped a plate of pink mush and wilted toast in front of me, I could almost hear my brain whirring around in my head.

I'd rushed to the loo when we arrived at the restaurant and joined Pat sitting at the reserved table. It was only now that I really took notice of her outfit. My hand shook as I plastered pink stuff onto a triangle of toast.

'It's lovely. You always look good. Do they let you buy clothes at discount?'

Discount! There was no mistaking that vivid blue colour, which was exclusive to Yves St Laurent.

Pat discarded green lettuce ribbons from the glass dish and swished the prawns until they were all covered in Marie Rose sauce as pink as the goo on my plate. 'Sometimes,' she screwed her eyes and wiggled in her seat as she chewed a prawn. 'Only the rejects, mind. Not that anyone's going to see the wonky seams on the other side of the blouse – well, he might.' She winked and stabbed her fork in the direction of the waiter grinning at a sixteen-year-old sitting with her mum and scowling dad.

I told my sergeant and inspector everything Pat had said, and we pondered over a few theories about what could be going on behind the innocent-looking doors of the Sanjay and Sons garment factory. The medium-sized building was situated on an industrial estate close to the canal, a few hundred yards from the disused paper warehouse. The area had once been run down and going to ruin, but new businesses were renovating previously abandoned warehouses and dividing them into two or three buildings for rent. The estate was thriving with small manufacturing businesses and a driving school and there was always plenty of incoming and outgoing traffic during the daytime. Nights, though, were quiet apart from white vans loading up at the factory. Patrol cars visited as part of their rounds to make sure the van drivers weren't bothered by unsavoury characters and the officers were adamant there was nothing untoward with the activity. The clothing factory received deliveries of materials and sent out their own vehicles loaded with cheap fashion clothing.

'We need someone on the inside to give us more details,' DS Jones said, and I was pleased he was taking my intel seriously. The detective sergeant could be chauvinistic and uncouth, but he was well respected for his knowledge and determination to follow up leads. 'What about your friend Pat?'

Jones sat on the corner of my desk while I swivelled side to side in my chair. 'Not a good idea. I don't know her that well, but she never stops talking and I wouldn't trust her not to blurt something out to the wrong person at the wrong time.'

'You're sure she's not mixed up in this and can't stop herself from showing off her clothes?'

I shrugged and breathed deeply, not entirely certain. 'She wasn't that bright at school. But then again, she takes home £20 a week more than I do and works less hours. So maybe she's not so stupid after all.'

Jones grinned. 'Ah, come on. Does she have a canteen like ours? Lukewarm food and swimming in grease – and bacteria, I shouldn't wonder.'

DI Mercer, smart in his navy-blue suit and unstained tie, didn't appreciate the banter. He'd lingered at my desk, carrying a well-worn raincoat, listening to my conversation with Jones. He was more abrupt and to the point. 'I'll have a word with Jarvis and see whether we can get someone in there for a few weeks.' Our eyes turned to DS Stephanie Whittle, who had worked undercover on occasions.

She'd recently joined our CID at the station and stood up for herself with the men. Stephanie was a neat woman who always wore a plain dress and matching jacket with effortless style. Off duty, though, or working undercover, she transformed into a scruffy tart with cheap shoes and smudged eye shadow, fooling even those who worked closely with her. She would be ideal to work alongside Pat and find out what was going on.

I was kept out of the loop with any plans for Sanjay and Sons, which was a relief. My friendship with Pat wasn't something I particularly cared about, but I preferred not to get involved too much with a stakeout that could potentially end in her losing her job. The day after my talk with Jones and Mercer, Stephanie breezed out of the office with a wave. 'See you all. I'm off to see my aunt on the coast for a few weeks.'

Those of us left in the office grunted, 'Have a nice time' and exchanged knowing looks with each other. I was starting to recognise Steph's coded short breaks.

14

Rob

It was my day off and I could afford to spend a lazy morning in bed, sifting through the photocopied reports from Linda Bateman's file. I still needed to call next door and speak to Hazel about any photos of her daughter she might be able to lend me. Being cowardly I kept putting off the visit, afraid of the memories it would stir up.

Mum often spoke to Lonnie and Hazel and always bought Easter Eggs and a Christmas present for Rosie, their daughter. I didn't get involved and always had work as an excuse not to meet them for any social get-togethers.

With one eye on the clock, I showered and dressed ready to head out and meet Pat during her half-hour lunchtime. I'd checked it out with DS Jones and assured him we often met like this when I was off duty during the week. It gave Pat a good excuse to escape from all the noise and intense concentration in the factory.

'I don't see any reason why you shouldn't meet her – every now and then. It could look more suspicious if you suddenly stopped. Just don't make eye contact with Steph if you see her.'

'Don't worry, I won't. It's only twenty-five minutes and then she's back at work.'

After my shower I tried on a couple of things to wear.

I didn't want to look like an off-duty police officer when there was an undercover operation in progress. The flowing, patterned gypsy skirt and white blouse were as far from my usual tailored outfits as I could manage. The sun appeared through the clouds. It was still warm outside, so I plonked a wide-brimmed hat on my head to add to my attempt at a casual image.

It wasn't ever a very satisfying arrangement for me: the rushed scalding coffee and greasy burger standing next to a food van smelling of fried onions and chips. But it meant a half-hour walk to and from the factory rather than just sit in the house and dwell on my job, study for my sergeant's exam or feel frustrated with Linda's file.

Keeping to our plan I arrived ten minutes before Pat's lunch break started and ordered two burgers: one with and one without onions. Holding each, wrapped in thin napkins, I waited for Pat to appear from the mud-spattered doorway at the side of the factory. She was out of the building within a few seconds of noon and quickly ditched a tall, thin, middle-aged man wearing a brown overall that buttoned up at the front. Lighting a cigarette, he moved towards the large skips, watching Pat all the time.

'Nice skirt,' she said and bit through the soft bun, soft onions and even softer meat patty that resembled a burger. 'You look good, but ...' Another bite and I was left in suspense while she chewed her lunch as though it was a gourmet meal.

'But ... what?' I nibbled at my own burger. How could something so nasty taste so good? Bob had a secret knack with frying food and when smothered with either red or brown sauce it was better than anything you could taste within two miles of the site. Not that there was anywhere else to eat within two miles of the site.

We shuffled away from the growing queue of Pat's machinist friends and other workers from businesses nestled in nearby terrapin units.

Pat took a moment to answer and looked me up and down while she scoffed her food. She was tall and svelte and no matter how much she ate or drowned in cream she never seemed to gain a single pound. 'It's my Italian genes,' she'd once told me proudly. 'We're all the same. Mum fits in my clothes even at her age – and she's had four kids.'

My eyes followed Pat's scrutiny of my dark brown and turquoise paisley swirled skirt. The pleats swished when I deliberately swayed my hips. I nearly choked when the air filled with wolf whistles.

'Don't do that around here,' Pat advised. 'They're animals.'

She flicked an impolite two-fingered gesture towards a group of men in dark blue overalls and then laughed along with them.

'Seriously, Jan, I'd love to make something for you one day.' She wiped the corners of her mouth with the sauce-stained napkin, screwed it into a tiny ball and threw it on top of the overflowing bin at the side of Bob's caravan which doubled as his kitchen. 'You look good – don't get me wrong.'

Her hand went up, palm facing me as I started to protest. The last thing I needed was for Pat to pass a 'knock-off' dress in my direction and then expect me to wear it in public.

'I'm talking hand-made. I've been making my own clothes for years. Come over to my house one evening and I'll measure you. Then we can go to my uncle's place for material.'

'Not here then?'

Pat shook her head and smoothed her pale green tabard into a neat shape, covering her own outfit underneath. 'No, not here. They don't do retail. I mean it, Jan. I can make you look sensational. Call me when you're off duty next time.' She pushed her sleeve back from her slender wrist. 'Damn, time to head back.'

I waved her back into the factory through the grubby side door, with crossed fingers that Stephanie wouldn't appear, then looked up at the sky wondering if it would rain after all. The clouds were heavier and greyer, but I was sure I could walk home before any showers. I ruffled my hair and rearranged my hat.

The sun, when it appeared, was warm and it felt good to be outside despite the constant passing traffic on one side of the pavement and dubious-looking canal water on the other. My platform shoes were uncomfortable, so I walked slowly.

'Jan.'

I couldn't be sure the shout was for me. After all there were more than one 'Jan' in the town. Only Pat called me Jan, and this was a male voice. I couldn't think of any man who would be calling my name.

With studied nonchalance I glanced over my shoulder, just in case there was someone I knew behind me.

The only people following me were a group of teenagers sharing a tray of chips from Bob's burger van.

'Jan, over here.' The voice came from a bright red sports car parked at the kerb on the other side of the road. Leaning out of the driver's window was Rob, looking more like a sandy-haired David Cassidy than I remembered. I gasped and waved with stupid delight, almost stepping out in front of a slow-moving bus. The loud honking horn warned me to watch what I was doing.

'Don't kill yourself on my account,' Rob shouted with a concerned frown clouding his gorgeous face. I'd crossed safely after looking both ways first and joined him on his side of the road. He wound down his passenger window as I arrived so I could speak to him. 'I've been wondering if I'd see you again. It'd be a shame if I had to scrape you off the road.'

Wishing I'd reapplied lipstick and the smell of fried food wasn't drowning my patchouli perfume, I told him I was pleased to see him. My stupid grin must have given me away.

'I looked for you at Cassandra's last time I was there, but I didn't see you.' I might as well be truthful, I decided.

Rob grinned and something inside fluttered. He'd seemed genuinely concerned at my lack of road safety awareness and brush with death by the Number 57. I wasn't used to that from anyone except for Mum.

'Is that where you work?' He nodded towards the industrial site without taking his eyes off me. 'This isn't the nicest place to go for a stroll – not dressed like that anyway.'

'No, I had a bit too much to drink last night and a greasy burger was just what I needed for my hangover.' I pointed my finger at him, and the sun gleamed on the twisted steel ring. 'But if anyone asks, I have a bad migraine and I'm not fit to be handling a typewriter.'

Rob grimaced at the description of the burger but laughed anyway. He reached towards the door handle as though to invite me to sit in the passenger seat and then hesitated. His smile faded and he retreated behind the steering wheel.

'I've got to meet someone in five minutes – a business contact on the estate. No way I can get out of it.'

'That's OK.' I was disappointed and relieved at the same time. 'I'm meeting my mum when she finishes at the school. She likes to smother me when I'm not very well.' I turned down the edges of my mouth and hoped I looked like a cute chick rather than a sick clown.

Rob tapped nicely manicured fingertips on the leather steering wheel. 'I'd like to see you again – if you want to.'

This time my stomach somersaulted in a fight between the burger and excitement. A good-looking man in a red sports car said he wanted to see me again. Was I daydreaming or was this a real David Cassidy moment and there was a chance we could arrange a date?

'When are you going to the club again? This Saturday?'

Damn. My clown face was back. I was back on late shifts by then. 'Not this weekend. There's a family get-together at my aunt's house.'

My name is Janice Morton and I am rapidly becoming a professional liar.

'Saturday after, then?'

Was I fooling myself or did he seem genuinely hopeful I would be there? If I changed a shift with someone, I could do that Saturday and I was pretty sure Pat would be up for a night out. I needed to make time for her to measure me for a new and sensational outfit before seeing Rob again.

'OK then. I'll meet you in there with my friend.'

Rob looked thoughtful. 'Your friend – is she the one you were with the last time I saw you?'

I nodded and felt as though a pin had burst my bubble of happiness. Pat could easily be a model – gorgeous with long black hair and an empty-headed personality that men liked. Especially men like Rob.

He winked and switched his engine on, pressing his foot on the accelerator and letting it roar. 'Let's hope there's a new crew of bouncers to distract her then – unmarried ones this time.'

I stepped back before he closed the window and drove off into a stream of traffic to turn into the industrial estate. Surely with my police skills and over six months of CID experience I should be able to work out if he liked me. My cheeks were burning, and I knew they were pink. My heart thudded from the sheer unexpected delight of our encounter, but I couldn't help having self-conscious doubts.

Pat said I looked good in my peasant outfit, but I still couldn't fathom why someone as good-looking as Rob would want to be seen with me. If only I hadn't had that burger …

I didn't want any distractions from my career, but I knew I liked Rob – a lot. What I needed to work out now was a good and convincing story about my job and hope I didn't put him off seeing me.

The gathering clouds above darkened from slate grey to thundering black, but I ignored them. My mind rambled on as I gripped my hat in the whipping wind and wondered about a life with Rob and could it be forever.

15

Nightclub

Good for Pat. She didn't say no when I suggested a night out at Cassandra's two weeks later when it was my next weekend off from work. I didn't mention anything about Rob, even though every detail of our two conversations played through my head. How could I be sure he really would be at the club? My underlying misgivings convinced me that on one hand he would not be there and then if he were, he would ignore me in favour of a more attractive woman.

'What is it with you and the bouncers?' I asked Pat as we combed our hair through in the ladies' toilet. The booming beat from the other side of the door was muffled but we both swayed and nodded our heads to the Fat Back Band's 'Bus Stop', preparing ourselves for the hours of dancing. 'Every time we come here you spend most of the night leaning against the wall waiting for one of them to speak to you.'

Pat had stopped disappearing without a word and usually let me know when she was leaving me to find out when Shay, Mo or Dave were due to have a break. I could understand the superficial attraction of the bow-tied men wielding power over who they would and would not let into the club. There was always bucketloads of charm for the attractive ladies and Pat certainly fell into that category.

She puckered her lips into a Marilyn Monroe-like kiss and undid another button on her halter-neck scarlet satin blouse. 'They're just so sexy, dahling,' she squealed, 'and they like me. Anyway, why not?'

'Pat, you could have any of the men in here. You just ignore them most of the time.'

'D'you think so?'

My mouth, looking sultry from its newly applied Max Factor wet-look deep red lipstick, fell open. How was it possible that Pat had no idea of her looks and, ahem, charms?

'Seriously, Pat ...?'

Pat stopped preening and studied her reflection. 'My nose is too big and so's my mouth. My brothers have always called me the ugly duckling and warned me about men pretending they like me.' She leaned closer to the mirror and I had a bird's-eye (or should that be bouncer's-eye) view of her chest and breasts down to her navel.

Brothers warning their little sister about men! I began to understand Pat's naive uncertainty about her good looks. It was understandable her three brothers would be protective, but would they ever realise how much damage they were doing? Pat's beauty could scare off genuinely nice guys, but the bad ones would always try their luck and she'd fall for their rubbish just to have a man take notice.

'You're crazy. Look, stay with me tonight and I'll nudge you when I spot a guy you should dance with. Don't bother with the losers on the door. They'll just use you and move on to someone else next time they're working here.'

Pat's eyes watered and I felt hurt for her as well as ashamed at my own attitude towards someone I should have seen was vulnerable. She liked me and trusted me whereas I couldn't care less if we stayed friends or not –

and I had used her to arrange a night out at the club so that I could meet Rob. At least if he didn't appear, or ignored me, I wouldn't feel such a fool.

'Trust me,' I found myself saying and I meant it. She'd designed a short black dress that fitted me perfectly without looking trashy. It was a joy to wear and the cut accentuated my curves. She hadn't even let me pay her, insisting the material was from an old dress of her mum's.

'What if Mr Gorgeous is out there?' Pat dabbed at her eyes and stiffened her long lashes with even more black mascara.

'Who?' I blustered. This woman was truly surprising me.

She winked at me in the mirror. 'Did you think I didn't notice him that first time we came here? I was watching the pair of you before I had to butt in so we could get a taxi. I've felt bad about that ever since.'

My wide-open eyes stared into hers through the mirror and then we both smiled at each other in a way we hadn't done before – like friends.

'You ready?' She snapped the clasp on her wide patent clutch bag and slipped a bare arm through mine. 'You never know, he might be here tonight. He likes you, I can tell.'

I grunted.

'Yes, he does. Trust me.'

I was on my second Cherry B and feeling a little queasy if I was honest. Pat was shouting 'What did you say?' every couple of minutes while a stolidly built young man yelled into her ear, trying to be heard over the music. Eventually he pointed at her empty glass and my near full one and then at the bar.

She nodded but I couldn't face another sickly red drink and shook my head. With an almost imperceptible request for my permission 'Danny' kept his arm around Pat's shoulders which he'd placed there to get closer to her ear.

I made a quick assessment – he was a little taller than Pat in her 5-inch heels and despite the heat wasn't too sweaty even though his curly black hair looked thick and heavy sitting on his collar. Despite his overpowering Aramis aftershave, I decided he was a safe escort for Pat. In fact, when he thought no one was looking, he seemed pleased and proud to be with her.

As Pat's guardian for the night, I grinned quickly to show it was OK for him to take her away from me. They walked through the crowds towards the heaving bar area and I knew it would be a while before they'd be served. I was in for a long wait for their return – if they came back.

'Is she behaving herself?'

My hands trembled and my fingers gripped the Cherry B glass to stop the bright red liquid from overflowing and spattering my Patricia-designed dress.

Rob, taller than I remembered, towered over me, his brown eyes kind and amused. Trying not to fall flat on my face, I shuffled my bare feet back into my high-heeled sandals to elevate me almost to his height. Inside my head a silly voice was screaming, 'He's here!!!'

The glass was taken from my hand and Rob grimaced with mock disgust. 'Is that the best you can do? Follow me and I'll buy you a proper drink. Gin and tonic?'

He held my hand to lead me away from the crowded, smoky room, but I held back, searching for Pat and Danny at the bar.

'She'll be alright,' Rob said, reading my mind and

hesitating at my reluctance to leave Pat. 'I know Danny – he's a nice guy.'

'You know him?' I asked in a normal voice when we reached the quieter room where couples lounged on mock-leather sofas and red velvet chairs.

He handed the barman a £5 note in exchange for two tumblers of clear liquid with ice and lemon bobbing in them. I was impressed. Who knew the bars in the club, with its sticky floors, had supplies of lemon slices? Rob fluttered his fingers and walked away without his change. This was a new world for me.

We searched the room for two empty chairs and spotted a couple leaving, arms around each other, lips locked together. With two steps, Rob's long legs reached the studded brown leather sofa before anyone even noticed it was vacant. Still holding the glasses, he gestured for me to sit before he slumped down next to me. The aging leather whispered with our weight and moulded around us.

He passed me a glass and when I grasped it, he bent his head to stare into my eyes, 'Nice to see you again, Jan.'

We clinked glasses. 'Nice to see you again, Rob. You don't come here very often, do you?'

A creased frown marred the clear, tanned skin around his eyes. 'What do you mean?'

'I thought I might see you again after we met but whenever I came, I never spotted you – it was only twice afterwards.' I rushed to add, not wanting him to think I'd been hunting him down.

He sipped his drink and lifted his chin with smug triumph. 'So, you missed me then.'

'Sort of. Pat's had a thing about bouncers so it would have been nice to have someone to pass the time with.' I sipped my drink, unsure if I liked the bitter taste. My eyes roamed around the room, pretending I wasn't as bothered as he implied.

The sofa, though small, was generous with space and there was room for Rob to sit with legs slightly apart rather than squashed up against me. I breathed in Paco Rabanne aftershave and thought he was the loveliest man I'd ever sat with. There were good-looking men in the force and one or two in CID, but they all had a cynical air about them that was off-putting and unattractive.

'I've been abroad for six weeks – Spain. My family's got a small restaurant out there so I go and help when it gets busy.' He leaned in closer to me as though to share a secret. 'I cook a brilliant paella, Jan.'

16

Spain

Thank goodness for Vesta and their packet versions of paella: bright yellow rice with tiny shrimps and peas. I'd tried it once, but I really preferred the Vesta Chow Mein, especially the crispy noodles, which always amused me and Mum when they curled up in the frying pan.

'I'll make it for you one day. But you'll have to come to Spain for it – that's the only way the octopus will be fresh.' His eyes twinkled over the rim of his glass, which was nearly empty.

I nodded wisely. I could play this game. I knew you could eat octopus even if it wasn't one of the Vesta ingredients. 'I can't wait. Just let me know the time and the name of the restaurant and I'll even watch you cook.'

It was all bluff. It wasn't likely I'd ever get to Spain, now that Mum had her new friend, David. I had expected she and I would go on holiday together at some point but now I wasn't so certain.

What's your full name? Address? Date of birth? Occupation?

My mind ran through all the questions I would usually read out from a prepared form at work. But off-duty Jan had to block out the on-duty Janice's instincts and learn to smile and dredge up every bit of witty banter I barely possessed. I allowed just one thought to dominate my slightly alcohol-sodden brain: *please, please like me.*

I forced myself to sip the next G&T, already feeling my head swim and not wanting my words to slur or my face to droop with too much off-guard relaxation. While we talked, supremely attractive women passed us by, each with sensational body curves emphasised in short, tight dresses. Rob barely looked at them and his attention seemed to be genuinely focused on me.

When I arrived at the club, I'd felt sexy in my new dress with chunky red beads around my neck. But sitting with Rob, seeing my knobbly knees beneath the short hem, I felt frumpy in comparison with these women who could easily compete with any of the Three Degrees.

While we talked, he draped an arm across the back of the sofa and his hand brushed my hair and shoulder. The nearness of him was a stronger intoxicant than any gin and tonic. He wore a light jacket, like a lot of men in the club, but he didn't sweat or look uncomfortable. The whites of his eyes emphasised his tanned skin which had faded since we met two weeks ago, but still suited him. My stomach flipped each time I felt his hand touch the skin on the back of my neck.

Rob talked a little about himself and asked banal questions which were easy to answer. I confessed I'd never been to Spain but yes, I would like to visit there one day. He confirmed it was hot, sunny and a great place to dance to good music until dawn sometimes and then have breakfast on the beachfront.

He wasn't too impressed when I described my week in a caravan with Mum in Wales, where it rained for three days and drizzled for four days. His laugh was infectious and showed his even white teeth. I covered my mouth when I laughed, unsure how my own teeth appeared against this perfect dental competition.

'Jan, you look fantastic – as usual.' He kissed the knuckles of my hand and I stopped worrying about my knees. His lips were dry and warm.

'What do you do when you're not in Spain?' The question felt natural and I had plenty more to ask.

Rob didn't flinch so I didn't feel I was overstepping the mark. He'd finished his drink and swirled the melting ice cubes around the glass. 'I'll be honest with you, Jan; my dad's done well in Spain. The restaurant is busy from breakfast time to late at night. He and his girlfriend work hard in the spring and summer when the tourists are in Palma. Locals usually dine in the evenings in the autumn and winter. When customers start to disappear, Heather insists Dad takes her to Bermuda for January.'

'Bermuda,' I mouthed. 'That sounds nice.'

He shrugged. 'I've been once – full of loud Americans. Dad and Heather like it. Mind you, they're pretty loud themselves.' He thought that was funny, but I wasn't sure whether I should laugh at people I'd never met so I smiled and patted the skin below my eyes, checking my mascara hadn't smudged.

'They pay me well for working for them, but I prefer being in England which is why I'm looking around for a place where they can open a new restaurant over here.'

'In Birmingham?' I almost choked at the thought of it.

'Maybe. I'm working out how fresh the fish can be if it was here. Much better to have one on the coast of course but it's more commercially viable to open a Spanish restaurant in a city like this. More people are going abroad for holidays and hotels in Spain are being built all the time – so they could still enjoy the food when they are back at home.'

I thought of Mum and me, squashed in our shabby caravan on a crowded park in Rhyl. Rob could be right about the attraction of holidays in the sun rather than shivering in wet and windy English summers. Wales was nice but Spain was a better option with its sunny blue skies every day.

Before we could delve further into his ambitions for a business in Birmingham, Pat appeared with Danny still clinging onto her waist, looking a little soppy. She hesitated slightly before interrupting us.

'It's nearly one, Jan.' Where had the time gone?

'When Will I See You Again?' filtered through from the main part of the club and I pictured the last dance shuffle. Part of me wanted to feel Rob's body close to mine but I didn't have the courage to suggest we dance. For the past hour he'd held my hand as we talked. As though we were a couple. I didn't want him to let go if we moved.

I looked up at Pat and Danny, a little dazed. Pat's face shone and Danny's fringe was stuck to his forehead like a row of crazy Roman numerals. Their cheeks were flushed, and their eyes shone with something I didn't recognise. Perhaps it was happiness. Pat was holding her shoes and suddenly looked petite and fragile next to Danny's chunky body.

'Oh!' I leaned forward and immediately slid back on the slippery leather. 'Yes, we'd better find a taxi before the queue starts.' I glanced at Rob who was tapping at an LED watch peeking from his shirt cuff.

'Can't you stay longer? The club won't close for another hour ...'

I wanted to stay with him for a lifetime – not just an hour.

'Danny's got a car. He's gonna drive us home,' Pat said with pride. Not too many men would drive their own car to a nightclub, I thought.

Danny's eyes met Rob's and then looked away. 'Well, it's a van really. I use it for work – but three can sit in the front easily.'

'Does it "Clunk, Click with Every Trip"?' I tried to sound light and flippant while my stomach muscles tightened, and nausea jumped into my throat. My first morgue experience had been an autopsy on two dead bodies after they'd been flung through the windscreen of an uninsured white van. The mangled remains weren't easy to forget.

Danny muttered towards his feet. 'Yeah, it's got seat belts. I'm a plumber and the van's my livelihood. It's sound.' He added quickly when I opened my mouth again. 'And I don't drink – never have. I can't afford to turn work down if I'm hungover from a night out. It's not worth it. I'm saving for a house.' He looked at Pat shyly, but she was fussing with the bra strap slipping down her shoulder.

I heard Rob breathe out heavily. Had he been as concerned as I was? Accepting the lift was the right thing to do so I said goodnight to Rob. At least this way he didn't have to offer to see me home and then find out where I lived. That part of my life could be kept under wraps for a while longer.

As I placed both hands on the sofa to help lift myself up, Rob leaned over and kissed my lips, not caring about the two people watching us. His hand on my shoulder drew me closer to him and his skin felt cool next to mine. My limbs and my insides melted into each other in a way I'd never experienced before. Drawing away, he crinkled his eyes and kissed my nose.

Danny and Pat had moved closer to the door, leaving us to say goodbye. Rob stood and gently pulled each of my hands so that I could join him as elegantly as it was possible. I didn't want to let go but he broke the spell, leaning over again and touched my lips with his mouth.

'Give me your number and I'll call you.'

Riding home in the van I stared out of the window at darkened streets, shrouded homes and dimmed lights, trying not to let Pat see the tears sliding down my face. It had been a night I would replay in my head for days and weeks to come. But even as I'd watched Rob write my phone number into a small black notebook, I just knew he'd never call, and we'd never share a paella in Spain.

Feeling numb and upset, I leaned forward in the van to peer around Pat who sat between Danny and myself.

'Danny, how long have you known Rob?'

He concentrated on the lack of traffic and slowed right down towards the green light waiting for it to turn red. This was going to be a long drive home.

'I don't know him. First time I saw him was tonight with you.'

Strange. 'He told me he knew you.'

Danny shook his head. 'No, I've fixed the boilers at the club a couple of times. He must have seen me working there.'

Very strange.

17

Overtime

I tried my best to sleep after I finally crawled into bed but lay with eyes wide open until I heard birds singing and daylight framed my heavy curtains. There was no reason to get up and I dozed for as long as I could, knowing Mum wouldn't disturb me. I held a faint hope Rob would call and suggest we meet up for a picnic in the country and I didn't want to look pale and tired.

In my mind I saw his face, tanned skin with brown eyes that lit up when he talked about the plans for a future business in town. He understood numbers, balance sheets, profit-and-loss accounts and I wished I could have been more open about my own job. My brain retained the facial features of men, women and children and I was proud of my skills. But the last thing I wanted was to tell Rob what I did for a living.

It wasn't that I was ashamed of being a policewoman, but I preferred to at least have the title of detective or be able to say I'd been in the force for more than two years, relating serious crimes I'd helped to solve. Apart from the Tally twins episode, I spent my days sifting through mug shots, making tea and coffee for everyone in the department or being hauled off to accompany a senior officer with bad news for a family who wouldn't see a loved one again.

None of that was as entertaining as Rob's larger-than-life dad and hilarious tales of clueless tourists who only ever wanted sausage, egg and chips when they were on a Spanish holiday. I smiled at the ceiling, remembering how he'd stroked my hand when he spoke of his father, unsure whether he'd known what he was doing.

I turned over and buried my head in my pillow. Rob's glamourous life was a million miles away from my own. There was no way I could fit into his world – sports car, expensive clothes and a watch that probably cost more than my annual pay. It didn't stop me imagining life with him, though. I was going to drive myself crazy expecting him to call me and wondering if I'd ever see him again.

Even before the first ring of the phone faded, I shot out of bed. Leaving my dressing gown hanging on the door my heart pounded in rhythm with each step as I ran downstairs, screaming, 'I'll get it.'

By the second ring Mum had grabbed the receiver and was saying our number before I reached the bottom of the stairs.

'Yes, she's here.'

Obediently Mum handed me the phone and I tried to breathe normally, holding it next to my thumping chest before I could speak. I lifted it to my ear with a grin widening across my face.

'Janice. I know it's Sunday, but we need you here today. ASAP. It's 8.30 now. I'll send a car round to you in half an hour – twenty minutes preferably. I expect you were out on the town last night so best you don't drive. Get your mum to make you a strong cup of coffee. I need you alert and firing on all systems by the time you get here.'

I held the phone to my ear and listened to the dialling tone. Jarvis was never one for chatting and when there was a serious crime, he was even sharper and to the point. Mixed with disappointment that he'd been the caller and not the lovely, handsome Rob who talked about paella, I wondered what had happened that needed my so-called expertise.

Dressing quickly after a hasty shower and gulping hot black coffee I cursed the two gin and tonics and disgusting Cherry B I'd drunk the previous night. There was a nasty throbbing behind my eyes, which I guessed was due more to lack of sleep than a hangover. From habit I swallowed two Anadin with the last slurp of coffee and brushed my hair, straightening the waves I'd carefully emphasised the night before with the curling tongs.

Jarvis hadn't mentioned anything about wearing casual clothes, so I was in full uniform when the panda car arrived. PC Nick Watson was driving, and Mum trailed after me to the vehicle, pushing a paper bag into my hands before I could shut the passenger door.

'There's toast in there,' she said and looked across me at Nick. 'Enough for two.'

Nick was talkative at the best of times but as we pulled away, he bit into a warm, limp slice of buttered toast and, with his mouth full said, 'Your mum's a nice lady. Are you adopted?'

I tried to bite into the bendy toast and snorted. It was funny.

'Ha, ha, Nick the comedian. Don't call us, we'll call you,' I managed to splutter with a mouthful of rubbery toast wrapped around my tongue.

I knew the lads at the station, not just in CID, saw me as a serious, sometimes stuffy studious woman. I rarely joined them in drinks at the pub after a shift.

What was the point? I couldn't have alcohol when I was driving, and I knew how quickly the loose tongues delivered their gossip on the after hours' behaviour. Most of the policewomen I knew had slept with at least one of the male officers, regardless of rank. None of them ended up in serious relationships, but they did end up being labelled as 'mattresses' or worse by their colleagues. Strange how the men weren't maligned in the same way.

I thought of Rob for a second or two. I was so glad my instinct told me I could trust him at least. This call into work from Jarvis meant I wouldn't spend the day at home waiting for the phone to ring, resigned to the certainty that I was far from Rob's thoughts.

I turned sideways to watch Nick drive with all the confidence of his latest Grade 3 Pass from Driving School. He hardly touched the steering wheel, but the usually sluggish panda car flew along the almost-deserted, early-morning streets and across roundabouts. It was a joy to be chauffeured rather than sat next to one of the more jaded sergeants on a never-ending night shift. Screwing my eyes tight, I felt the ache in my head fade.

My eyes fluttered from side to side while I chewed the last mouthful of toast, exaggerating the movement as I studied Nick's features. His profile highlighted his long Roman nose and high cheekbones. His jet-black hair was straight and hung around his face, not quite long enough to break the regulation length but still with some movement to make him noticeable. And yes, I had noticed him before that day.

Startled when he suddenly faced me full-on as we drew up to a red traffic light, I jumped slightly and stared ahead out of the windscreen. Please don't let me blush, I begged to no one in particular. Nick was a very good-looking guy and we were sitting close to one another.

'So which slimeball do I look like then?'

'Uh?'

'I can feel you weighing me up to add to your file of suspects.' Back in gear and almost at the station Nick patted a spot beneath his left eye. 'Identifying feature: small brown mole below left eye.'

Deliberately I bent around him to examine the 'mole'. 'I never noticed that before,' I said truthfully, not wanting to pander to his obvious ego. 'In fact, I was going to say …'

'… that I look like Brian Ferry. Loads of people tell me that. Although my mum says I remind her of Dirk Bogarde.' When he grinned, he showed white teeth reminding me of Rob. His top lip curled over them and I realised Nick was shy as well as arrogant.

I pointed across the station car park. 'Actually, I was going to say there's a space over there next to Jarvis's Toyota.'

Due to the shift patterns the small car park was never quiet and today was no exception and even though Nick was already driving towards the empty space I could at least salvage some of my dignity after our slightly flirty exchange. Slightly flirty? Yeah, there was definitely something going on there.

My brief Sunday morning freedom and chauffeur driven ride to work soon crashed into a reality of near nightmare for the next six hours.

Jarvis had requested me for overtime after the night shift were called out to deal with a serious assault against a teenage girl raped by three men on her way home from a party. Through an endless flood of snotty tears and mascara-blackened eyes she managed to describe her ordeal to a room of not-very-sympathetic CID officers.

The senior detective, also called out on his day off, spoke to Tanya as politely as he could, advising her that I would take down all the details she could remember about the men who attacked her, dragged her into the nearby park and raped her. Then he left me with Detective Sergeants McIlroy and Shepherd, who rocked back on their chairs and pretended to be bored while watching Tanya's every emotion.

At first Tanya was too upset to make much sense. All she could say repeatedly between sobs was, 'Please don't tell my dad.'

From what I understood, the PCs had been unable to find anyone at Tanya's house when they arrived to report what had happened to someone's precious daughter. Apparently, the neighbour next door, roused from her bed by the officers banging on the door of the flat, let them know Mr and Mrs Addison were probably still at the wake from a funeral on Friday.

I felt sorry for Tanya as she relapsed into an exhausted sniffle after a lukewarm cup of coffee and a delicious fried egg sandwich from the twenty-four-hour cafe at the end of the road. Big Al knew where he could pick up his best business when the station canteen was closed at the weekend. Sometimes he even got paid.

Pencil ready to take notes with my folder of face shape outlines, eyes, noses and ears, hair colours and styles in front of me, I settled myself down to work with Tanya. My own egg sandwich had dripped onto my tie and I tried to ignore the stubborn stain while I asked all the usual questions to help me sketch pictures of the men we needed to find. I placed the box of cardboard eyebrows, noses, eyes etc on the chair beside me as another visual aid.

We worked together for three hours with McIlroy or Shepherd chipping in every now and then with their own questions. They took it in turns to leave the room when there was little they could do except write down their own notes.

The jigsaw-like pictures in front of me began to take shape and I was pleased with the results. I even felt strongly that I recognised all three of them and searched through the files in my head to remember where I knew them. I even heard their voices. Had we interviewed them for something during my time in the job?

This wasn't my first rape case, but it was the first time I hadn't sat quietly with two male officers, handing out tissues and sympathy to the victim. Stifling a yawn that could have swallowed the desk in front of me, my numbed brain switched to another channel.

I was almost finished but I paused to scribble a note and passed it to McIlroy.

He glanced at it and snapped his head towards me in a double take. With a deep sigh and more than a hint of weariness loaded into it, he shuffled to the door and left me asking Tanya again about the colour of each man's hair.

'You're sure this one is blond and his nose is snub, making his face look round and podgy?'

Almost asleep with her head on her arms on the table, Tanya mumbled, 'Yeah.'

There was hardly any oxygen left in the room after the hours we'd spent inside it. McIlroy, Shepherd and Tanya had smoked continuously, and the overflowing ashtrays littered the middle of the table. I felt grubby and knew I must stink from the cigarettes and lack of air. The only window in the room was thickly painted over the edges and never opened.

Shepherd replaced McIlroy and handed me an envelope with a nod. His red-rimmed eyes opened wide with an undisguised query which Tanya missed. A moment later Detective Sergeant McIlroy entered the room and I saw he was wearing his suit jacket and had straightened his tie. He also nodded to me, indicating I could take over the questioning.

18

Monkeying Around

'Tanya, wake up.' My voice was kind even though I had just wasted hours of a precious free Sunday and the possibility of a seductive picnic with Rob. But when I shook the girl I wasn't as gentle as I could have been. 'Tanya, I want you to look at this.'

Bleary-eyed and with smudged mascara almost wiped away, Tanya looked even younger than the sixteen she claimed to be. She lifted her head and sat up in the seat she'd occupied for almost twelve hours. I pushed a garish colour photograph towards her, forcing her to look at it.

Instantly she recoiled and stared at me. 'Who's that? What are you showing me that for?' Her tearful voice confirmed my suspicions.

'Tanya, that woman there was raped – like you say you were – but she was also kicked and beaten with a rolling pin. She survived with broken bones but it's a wonder she wasn't killed.'

'Did you catch the bloke? Was she able to tell you what he looked like?' Tanya whispered and reluctantly she held the photograph gently as though she could smooth away the woman's dreadful injuries revealed in their bloody and purple vividness.

'We caught him, Tanya, but not because of any description she gave us. In fact, she didn't report the attack or the rape. We arrested the man for another attack on a woman and found that photograph on his camera. He was so proud of his work he took photos of her and developed them at home.'

Tanya gagged, holding her hands over her mouth. Tears spilled down her cheeks, merging with the dirt on her face.

I continued. 'The police officers managed to get this man to give us more details about the woman, so we tracked her down and when we visited her, she confirmed what had happened. But Tanya, she hadn't reported the rape.'

'Why not?' The waif in front of us leaned forward and finally here was the justification for all the wasted hours we'd spent in that room.

'Because she'd met the man in a bar and had a drink with him. She didn't think the police would believe her. She was scared to come into the police station or even go to hospital. She just wanted to lock herself in her home, leave her job so she didn't have to show her boss her broken nose and bruises – hoping she could forget about it.'

Tanya and I locked eyes. McIlroy gave me a weak salute in farewell and left the room. Shepherd continued with his notes.

'You know why she was scared to come to the police for help don't you, Tanya?'

The girl wilted in her seat, still sobbing softly.

'You weren't raped, were you? You've made this story up haven't you?' She nodded, head down, letting her tangled hair screen her face from us. 'Tanya, do you understand that what you've done is the reason why so many police officers don't believe women claiming they've been raped. Their first thought is that the woman was "asking for it" – messing around with men they know or men they don't know. The men think they're on to a good thing and when the woman changes her mind it's too late to stop anything from happening.'

I reached out my arm and squeezed Tanya's small thin trembling hand. Even at such a young age her fingers were nicotine-stained and I'd noticed her yellow, rotting teeth when she talked.

'Tanya, were you attacked and raped in the early hours of this morning?'

She shook her head and mumbled 'No.'

'Tell us what really happened.'

'I went to a party with some mates. On the way home they started messing around with me.' Her tone was flat, unemotional. 'When I told them to leave me alone, they ran off and left me in the park. I was running home when I bumped into the copper and I told him they'd raped me to get back at them.'

Shepherd sighed and stabbed his pencil on the last full stop, mumbling obscenities under his breath.

I separated the three mock-ups across the table in front of her. 'These are not possible IDs of any men who attacked you, are they?' Tanya shrugged. 'Have you seen them before?'

Tanya looked away and I sensed her leg beating a rhythm under the table. 'Me mum knows them.'

DS Shepherd lifted his head with fresh interest, but I flashed him a slight shake of my head.

'I'd be surprised if she knows them personally,' I said, wanting to end all this nonsense and freshen up in the ladies' locker room shower. Pointing to each 'picture' in turn I named the men. 'David Jones. Micky Dolenz and Peter Tork. They were in a group called The Monkees a few years ago. Your mum was a fan, wasn't she?'

Another embarrassed shrug. I refused to look at Shepherd. McIlroy saved the day by entering the room again.

'So, was there a rape?' he almost snarled the question.

I shook my head and the three of us gazed at the forlorn and pitiful sight of Tanya weeping into her arms spread out on the desk, fingers brushing the discarded cigarette ends. We'd seen other 'Tanyas' many times. Left alone at home. Uncaring parents who couldn't be bothered if she ate, washed or wandered the streets.

McIlroy, as the senior of the sergeants, said, 'Tanya,' forcing her to look at him. 'I've spoken to my governor, Detective Superintendent Jarvis, and he's agreed you won't be charged for wasting police time – a lot of police time.' Tanya sniffled and I wished I had a clean handkerchief to pass to her. The box of tissues was empty, and no one had bothered to fetch a replacement. Without one, she wiped her nose on her clammy arm.

'Your mum and dad still haven't returned home so one of the officers will drive you back to where you live and drop you off at the end of the street. You can get back into your flat and they'll never know what's happened.'

Tanya covered her face with her hands and brushed them through her thick corn-coloured hair. Relief lined her young face, which already showed the beginning of wrinkles around her lips. My heart ached for her and I wondered what kind of a future she would have with no one to love her and always seeking love from anyone who would give it to her.

A report would be sent to Social Services with a request to check out Tanya's home life but none of us had any expectation of her circumstances changing.

I could have gone straight home once I'd straightened up my composite box and written up my own report for the CID tray. Instead, I decided to shower the filth from my skin and hair before asking someone to drive me. It was wonderful to feel hot soapy water on my skin and wash smoke from my hair, leaving it smelling of Pantene shampoo.

The cheap table in the interview room had snagged holes in my black tights. I dabbed at them with the pink nail varnish in my locker, to stop ladders running down my leg. The strong smell of pear drops was overpowering, and I massaged drops of Aqua Manda on my wrists to drown it out.

Feeling better, and with my shirt collar open, I left the women's locker room breathing cleaner air and pleased with my own handling of Tanya's case. She'd wasted our time but if I hadn't spotted the weakness of her descriptions, every officer on patrol and the whole of CID would be out looking for three members of The Monkees for days or weeks.

As I walked along the corridor towards the front desk, I heard a chorus from 'Daydream Believer' sung very badly from behind me. Looking around I saw Nick Watson, off duty and without his tie and jacket. Like me, he'd slung on a bomber jacket to tone down his appearance with an attempt at a casual look. Neither of us would have fooled anyone.

'It's all around the station, Janice. Bloody Monkees, eh? Before my time but I've seen some of their daft shows on the telly.' How could that be when he was older than me?

It was disloyal I know but when Nick smiled, it wasn't easy to conjure up an image of Rob. He attempted another line of his song, so I stopped him with my hand up as though directing traffic.

Ignoring my attempted hint, he grabbed my hand and whirled me around, singing loudly, 'Cheer up sleepy Janice' and mumbled made-up words from the song. I stumbled away from him before I started to enjoy the attention.

'McIlroy and Shepherd are going for a curry down the Bristol Road. They're the only places open on a Sunday night. You coming?'

How could I resist? If I'd stayed home, I would have studied for my sergeant's exam. I had to be back on my shift at 2pm the next day and I really should have said 'No' to Nick. But I couldn't. It would be fun to spend some off-duty time with the lads after the day we'd had.

'OK then. What's a real curry like? I've only had a Vesta beef curry.'

'Bloody hell, Janice, you've got to stop living life to the full and relax a bit. Vesta? Are you joking?' He flung an arm around my shoulders, keeping a small distance between us. 'I can see I'm going to have to educate you on the finer dishes of Indian cuisine – don't look like that – I'll make sure it isn't too spicy. If you don't like it, you can order an omelette and I'll eat yours.'

As I followed him out of the station and joined the others, squashing into the back of Nick's Hillman Imp I decided that no matter what happened I would learn to love curry as much as Nick, even though an omelette sounded wonderful to my hungry stomach.

19

Nick

At the Indian restaurant Nick sat next to me. The chairs were narrow, and our legs touched beneath the small table. We ignored the contact, but he was very attentive during the meal and I liked the friendly and easy conversation. As uniformed officers we were intimidated by the two detective sergeants who mumbled to each other while they shovelled chicken vindaloo and poppadoms into their mouths. Nick entertained me and helped me choose a mild korma, patting my shoulder every now and then, as he ate and laughed at my comments.

The evening ended early after the meal finished and we all threw in an equal payment towards the total charged. The men insisted on paying for me and I struggled to accept the offer.

'It's one-time only, Janice. First time you've been out with us – and well done for today.' DS McIlroy raised his glass with a mouthful of lager swilling in the bottom of it. The others beat the table with their hands, and I was duly embarrassed.

I stood up to pull on my jacket and Nick grabbed my arm. 'Where are you going?'

'To ask one of the waiters to order me a taxi.'

'No need, I'll drop you home.'

DS McIlroy appeared at my shoulder. 'Janice, you can share our cab. Where do you live?'

'It's no problem. I picked her up this morning. She's not far from me.' Nick stood his ground and all I could do was wait helplessly for them to decide my best choice of transport.

The detective sergeant took control and faced Nick. 'If I don't make sure she gets home, I'll have Frank Jarvis on my back.' He was serious and for the first time I thought about the contract on my life. DS Shepherd tottered over to us.

'Mate, they're young. Let him take her home.'

McIlroy wasn't giving up and prepared a lecture for Nick. 'Straight home. Make sure you see her in the door – you'll have the third degree from Jarvis, take it from me.'

It was a relief when their cab turned up and the guys left Nick and me to walk alone to where he'd parked his car. We made small talk about my first curry and ignored any reference to Jarvis and a contract out on my life. Shepherd was right. We were two young people and just wanted to enjoy an evening. I was very tired, but the meal and laughs had perked me up.

Nick unlocked the passenger door and opened it for me, standing close. 'What do you want to do, Janice? I can take you home – or for a coffee back at my flat. You can trust me – and I'll get you back to your mum's.'

'Aren't you tired, Nick?'

'Not really. Today's my last shift and I'm off for four days. What about you?'

'Two 'til ten tomorrow, so I can stay up really late.'

He drove like a madman again, confident and sure of his abilities and parked outside a sixties-designed block of flats built over two floors. His two-bedroom apartment was on the upper floor, but it was too dark for me to see the surroundings. We were in Edgbaston, I knew that – and I was a long way from home.

He opened his front door, which was opposite another flat in a dimly lit, carpeted corridor. With the door partly open, I grabbed his arm and blurted out, 'You can take me home if you've changed your mind.'

He laughed at my sudden apprehension. 'Bloody hell, Janice. You're coming in for a coffee – I'm not selling you into white slavery.' With a small push, he propelled me into his warm, welcoming home.

It was my innate curiosity of course that had encouraged me to accept the offer of going to his place. I wanted to see where the gorgeous Nick Watson lived and entertained his harem of fabulous women and girlfriends. I didn't kid myself I was one of them.

At the curry house, we'd laughed out loud with each other, especially when I'd tasted each of the dishes and tried not to choke from the sharp, biting spices. I'd entertained him with descriptions of each of the singers from The Monkees and he agreed with me that his childhood was the poorer from never knowing much about them. I promised him a poster for his wall ... and then he'd suggested I choose the right space for one.

'Close your mouth, Janice. It may not be much – but this is my home.'

The spacious flat was nothing like I had expected. He turned on small table lamps rather than the overhead light, which would have fiercely lit up the old-fashioned heavy furniture and paintings of country scenes on the wall. The three-piece suite was framed in heavy dark wood. Clothes and books were strewn over the worn velvet cushions, which looked as though they would be comfortable to sit on. A matching mahogany sideboard was set against the window with framed photographs and books piled high. Two guitars sat together on an armchair like lovers in a Dali print.

I followed him into the large kitchen with its generous array of cupboards and watched him spoon Nescafe into two pottery mugs. 'Have you got any hot chocolate?' It was almost 9pm and I thought caffeine wasn't such a good idea.

Nick frowned and paused halfway through pouring milk into the second mug. He opened a cupboard and shuffled through various packets, jars and tins. 'No. No hot chocolate. You should have said earlier.'

I shrugged. 'We have hot chocolate. Perhaps we should have gone to mine.'

He held up the two mugs. 'Stop being difficult and follow me.'

We walked through the unattractive lounge and along a thickly carpeted passageway into his bedroom, where he set the mugs down on a bedside table. Once again, I was staggered at the layout of the room. I walked around, picking up old Beano annuals.

He watched me with his hands on his hips.

'*To Nick, Happy Christmas, Love forever, Ruth, kiss, kiss, kiss.*'

'Sister Number One.'

I chose another annual.

'*To Nicky, Lots of Love at Christmas … Hannah …*'

He interrupted me, 'Sister Number Two.'

'… *only one kiss* ... I guess she doesn't love you as much as Ruth.'

He took the book from my hands and opened it to read the message. He checked the year of the annual – 1964 –

and screwed up his face to think back to that point in his history.

'That could be the year I started trying on her shoes. She didn't like that.'

I twanged the string of another guitar, leaning against a chest of drawers.

'Nick, is this really your place? Have you just picked on this flat because you knew it was empty?' He exaggerated a glance around the walls of bookcases filled with books, magazines, old comics and dusty trophies from sports days. It was like a teenager's bedroom not that of a professional man.

'What?' He pretended to be hurt while he tossed his bomber jacket into the wardrobe and then guided me to sit on the end of the bed next to him. 'Of course it's my place. At least it has been for the past month. I like it. Don't you?'

He removed my jacket and placed it carefully on the back of an old wooden dining chair, stacked high with thick law books. The room was also lit by side lamps and its dimness relaxed me. It felt good to be close to Nick, but I wondered why he'd moved so quickly when I'd never given him the impression I was there for anything but coffee.

Was I being naive? Just agreeing to the invitation from someone like Nick must indicate I was prepared to sleep with him – except there wouldn't be much sleeping. I felt a tingle of excited anticipation, but I knew this was a bad idea. McIlroy had guessed what he had in mind and tried to warn both of us not to do it. This was my own stupid fault and now I was going to mess everything up.

Well, he'd find out he'd made a big mistake soon enough, and I'd be back in his Hillman Imp on my way home.

Unsure where to look, or what I was expected to do or say, I studied every inch of Nick's possessions on display around the room, looking everywhere except at him. Apart from the experience of my job, I'd never been in a man's bedroom before and wondered if they all looked like this. It was nothing like what I saw on TV in programmes like *The Saint* or *The Avengers*.

My sudden cry of 'Oh!' was smothered by Nick's mouth on mine. He'd encouraged me to lie back on the bed and kissed me, gently at first and then with more urgency, forcing his tongue inside my mouth. It wasn't unpleasant and I tasted chicken madras and lager. I lay quietly and wondered what the bloody hell I was supposed to do.

His strong arms lifted me slightly from the bed and positioned me higher. I didn't object and the touch of his hands was thrilling. I couldn't deny it. Still kissing me, he ran his hand over my uniform skirt and gave a small groan, before ruffling it higher and feeling my suspender belt and top of my stocking. He lifted his head and looked down at me. I half smiled, unsure what I should do next.

Somehow, I couldn't bring myself to touch any part of him and wondered if I was supposed to undo his shirt buttons. I was still pondering the next move, when he sat back and said, 'Janice, have you done this before?'

'No, have you?'

He gasped a laugh. 'What? You've never done this before?'

'No. Should I have?'

He grinned with surprise. 'No. Of course not. So, you don't expect me to …?'

I sat up to face him. 'No. Should I?'

'I knew I liked you, Janice.' He fetched our coffee mugs and we sipped the hot liquid sitting side by side. 'You're the first woman I've brought here – and I just thought as we hit it off tonight, I'd be expected to leap on you and do all sorts to make you happy.'

'Actually, Nick, you make me happy with or without that.' I dropped my head and peered up at his face through my hanging hair. 'Do you mind?'

'I like you better for it, Janice. But how is it ...? I mean, never?'

I shrugged. 'When would I? I went to a girls' grammar school, then joined the police. I live with my mum and I don't go out much. I'd always vowed I'd never date anyone from work – so what the hell I'm doing here, sitting in fifteen-year-old Nick Watson's bedroom ... I do not know.'

'You like me.'

'I do like you. But I'm not your type, Nick, so this would never be something with a future. Not that I want that. I need to pass my sergeant's exam ... that's all I'm bothered about.' He nodded, seeming to understand.

'Why aren't you my type? What is my type? Silly, giggly girls? Serious, frowny ones?'

I hazarded a guess. 'Beautiful models with long legs and perfect bone structure. You are "Gorgeous Nick Watson", after all. You shouldn't settle for less.'

He too gazed around his teenage boy's state of a bedroom. 'Do you think this would impress a beautiful model with long legs and what was perfect ...?'

'Bone structure. Do you usually take your women to hotels then?'

He looked at me as though I had two heads. 'You have a very strange impression of me, Janice. I want a career in this job – just like you. I don't have time for messing about with women I know I don't want to see again.'

'I would never have guessed. Seriously, I wouldn't.'

'Do you know who started that stupid expression "Gorgeous Nick Watson"?'

With my head on one side, facing away from him, I bit

my lip and shrugged my shoulders. 'It could have been me. It sounds like something I'd say.'

He was thoughtful and took the mug from me, laying both on the floor. 'If I hadn't stopped … what were you going to do?'

I laughed without any embarrassment. 'I was waiting for you to tell me what to do. I thought that if I had to do it with someone, you were the best person to do it with. You know, get the whole "first time" thing out of the way. Over and done with.'

His horrified expression made me laugh out loud, and after a moment he joined me, pushing me back on the bed. We laughed together like a pair of silly teenagers.

'Janice.' He lay beside me and held my hand as we gazed up at the ceiling. 'Shall we just be very good friends – for as long as we both shall live?'

I loved the idea and agreed. My heart had thumped so loudly while he kissed me, and it was a relief to feel it settle into a more relaxed rhythm.

'One thing, Nick.' We faced each other and he leant his head on his hand, straightening my ruffled skirt with the other. 'Will you teach me how to kiss a man? I'm useless, aren't I? And I want to be better.'

He squinted his dark blue eyes and I noticed his long eyelashes. He really was a very good-looking man. 'You've met someone you like.'

'Yes – No. I mean, I like him – but he's not interested in me.'

'How do you know?' He stroked the outline of my face with his finger and I loved his tender expression. This was going to be a very good friendship if I could talk to him so freely.

'Not calling me – that's a hint, isn't it?' I felt disappointed at the reminder of Rob not telephoning even though he'd asked for my number. I'd checked with Mum when I rang to tell her I would be late home and she confirmed there were no messages for me.

'What's his name?'

'Rob.'

'Rob, who?'

'Don't know.' Nick opened his mouth wide in pretend shock. 'I never told him my real name – just Jan. I don't know what he does for a living – and he knows nothing about me.'

Nick drew me closer to him and I felt the warmth of his body through his shirt.

'I see. So, it's still new then.'

'Sort of. I met him at the end of last year. I only see him at Cassandra's nightclub and I can't manage to get there very often – with shifts and everything.'

'Mmm.' He stroked my hair as he pondered what I'd said. 'When did you give him your phone number?'

'Last night,' I said miserably. 'He hasn't …'

Nick released me and pushed himself away. 'Last night! Well of course he hasn't rung you … I'd give him a week at least. A bloke would never ring the next day.'

'Are you sure?' There was a note of hope in my question.

'Janice, Janice, Janice – am I sure?'

He kissed me and again his tongue explored my mouth. I let him and enjoyed the sensation of his closeness. He paused and whispered, 'You can kiss me back, you know.'

The mistake I made, was closing my eyes.

20

Grandad

The loud bang of the door opposite to Nick's flat woke us. Startled, we both sat up abruptly.

'What time is it?'

He checked his watch. 'Just after 3. My charming neighbour is a hospital porter and gets home all sorts of hours.' He yawned and stretched. 'Are you OK to stay? I could drive you home if you want …'

I blinked my tiredness. 'When did I fall asleep?'

'In the middle of me teaching you how to kiss. I don't think it was an overly exciting lesson. When I realised you were out for the count, I fell asleep next to you.'

'I hardly slept last night – Saturday night – morning. Whatever. It's comfortable here. Do you mind?'

Nick grinned. 'Hardly. I like your company, Janice – even if sleeping when I try to make love to you – to get it over and done with – is a bloody insult. Will your mum worry?'

I wasn't sure. I'd told her I was going for coffee with another officer I really liked – and trusted. She hadn't asked when I'd be home – but it wasn't like me to stay out all night. Maybe it should be.

'Hopefully not. I am twenty – not twelve.'

'Let's hope she doesn't ring Superintendent Jarvis – or I can say a sweet goodbye to valuable parts of my anatomy.'

'More valuable than my virtue.'

He studied me. 'Why is he so interested in you? I don't believe there's something going on between the two of you. I'm not that crass.'

I studied the bookcase, but he wouldn't let it drop. 'There is something isn't there?' He stroked the skin beneath my lashes. 'Is it why your eyes always have a touch of sadness in them?'

'It's not what you think. I first met him when I was nine years old. He was a detective inspector. My friend disappeared – he never found her. She's still missing.'

'Oh.' He frowned. 'He feels sorry for you?'

I screwed up my face. 'I'll tell you about it another time. I lied to him – thought he was a bit stupid.'

He grinned. 'So many detective inspectors are stupid – not Jarvis though.'

I sat straighter and crossed my legs like I used to in school assembly. 'He'd never heard of Francis Drake – he thought he was a boy in my class at school.'

Nick dropped his head to the side. 'Ah, so the man whose name had been Francis since birth had never ... heard ... of a ... British hero ... with the same first name ...' He held my face in both of his hands. 'Seriously, Janice, you fell for that?'

The penny dropped and he laughed annoyingly at my slumped shoulders, admitting I had indeed fallen for the charade. It was no use, I had to thump him until he stopped snorting at my stupidity.

'I'm awake,' he said after sobering a little. 'Coffee?' It sounded like a good idea. 'Stay here and we'll try that kissing thing again.'

The next time I woke it was a more decent time of 6am. The bedroom curtains were open and I watched the trees swaying in the spring breeze outside the windows. It was birdsong that had woken me and I lay listening to the chattering calls, enchanted by the sound. Next to me, I heard Nick's soft breathing.

We lay on top of the bed. I was still dressed but he'd loosened the fastening on my skirt. The duvet was folded over half my body. His left arm held me protectively and his head nestled against mine.

Nick too was dressed but he'd pulled his shirt loose from his uniform trousers and undone the top two buttons for comfort. He snored gently each time he breathed in and I lay as still as I could. On the bedside table I saw a mug full of coffee, and guessed I'd fallen asleep when he went to make it.

My eyes, even after several hours' sleep, were still tired and sore, but I was sure I wouldn't fall asleep again. Nick stirred and I regretted the end of our time together. It really was the cold light of dawn and time for me to go.

The last thing I expected was for him to pull me closer and kiss me with a new passion. This time I responded without any instruction. My body felt the heat from his and I wanted to draw closer. I copied how he'd kissed me earlier and hoped I was doing the right thing. The small groan he gave reassured me.

His right hand drew me into him and then he moved my whole body until he was fully on top. Was he awake? I opened my eyes and saw him looking directly at me, trying to read my drowsy expression. All I could do was smile tentatively. After all, we had agreed to be friends.

Although he pulled his body away from mine, with his arms extended keeping his hands on the bed, he kept his mouth on my lips. My hands cupped his face, not wanting him to release just yet. But common sense prevailed and with panting breaths we lay side by side, holding hands tightly. Friends again.

Somehow, I knew we'd never be so close and I couldn't resist it. I leant over and kissed his lips, holding his head in my hands. He was a truly lovely man. I wasn't his type, but I would always be his friend. The serious, frowny girl.

He stroked my hand when I stopped kissing him.

'Would you like breakfast in bed?'

'Oh, yes please. I would like ...' I counted on my fingers, '... bacon, sausage, egg, mushrooms, tomatoes, hash browns, buttered toast, jam and peanut butter in separate little dishes. You know, the cute ones. A pot of tea – no sugar.'

He grinned. 'I'll make that two. Anything else.'

'Yes. A blob of red sauce next to the egg – which must be runny. And a blob of brown sauce next to the sausage.'

He sat up and checked his flies. All was decent. 'Coming right up.'

'Excellent. Don't take all day, I'm very hungry.'

Ten minutes later he appeared in the doorway with a wide tray, bordered with woven plastic.

'Where did you want the blob of red sauce?'

'Next to the fried egg.'

'Damn.' He set the tray between us on the bed. On it sat a large brown earthenware teapot, two mugs and half a packet of Rich Tea biscuits with the wrapper twisted to keep in the freshness.

I poured the tea and he poured the milk from a cow-shaped jug. Nick opened the biscuits and took one out to offer me.

'I would have thought that with you being posh, there would be a plate for the biscuits.' I crunched mine noisily.

He broke his biscuit in half and popped it in his mouth, speaking with crumbs flying everywhere. 'I decided that as you are not posh, it wasn't worth it. Oh, don't dunk it in the tea – you'll only make a mess – see, I knew you would.'

I put my mug on the tray, yawned and stretched. With my legs crossed schoolgirl style again I re-examined the bedroom, staring at the bookcases and old-fashioned wardrobe. My mind tried to work out the back story to Nick's living style. I blinked when he waved the palm of his hand in front of my face.

'Don't do that. It's very irritating.'

'It's like you're in a trance. What are you thinking?'

'I'm thinking,' I said and dipped another biscuit in my tea, avoiding the soggy piece floating in the mug, 'that this was your ... grandad's flat. He's either letting you live here – or you're storing your stuff here.'

Nick didn't contradict me and seemed impressed. 'Alright, Madame Arcati, why grandad and not grandmother?'

'I think you are very like your grandfather ... and your grandmother gave up trying to make him stop going out with beautiful models with long legs ...'

'... and perfect cheekbones ...'

'... and perfect cheekbones. Sadly, she passed away before him.'

'Not bad. My grandfather died two months ago and left me this flat in his will. My sisters are married now with their own homes. I moved all my stuff here from Suffolk where it was in my bedroom at my parents' house. Granny died last year from a broken heart, having been jilted for a beautiful, perfectly proportioned, model.'

'I knew it. Will you stay here? Or sell and buy something more fitting for a future police sergeant/inspector etc etc, with an excellent choice in friends?'

'Janice, stop making a mess of that tea. That's the second biscuit that's ended up in it. You're worse than a child.' I tried to scoop out the soggy biscuits with a teaspoon and lay them on the tray, worsening his disgust. 'I shall sell, of course. Move somewhere in the country that isn't too far from work. And never, *ever* tell you my address.'

I rubbed my nose and giggled. 'I'll find out. I intend to join CID properly and have Jarvis's permission to snoop into all your affairs.'

I reached for another biscuit, but he moved them behind his back.

'Do you want to give it another go?'

'You make me sound like a car engine that needs a jump start. Why don't you chase me round the living room three times? Get me in the mood.'

He found that very amusing. 'Three times around the living room! I'd catch you before the first lap.'

'Very likely. It's like an obstacle course in there.'

We grinned at each other, both of us knowing I had to leave.

'Janice, we've been together since six o'clock last night. I've had more fun in this short time than I have in weeks.'

'Thank you for breakfast, PC Nick.'

We kissed the kiss of friendship. It was time to go home.

21

Hazel

'Hello, Janice.'

It was Linda's voice.

It came from over the garden hedge just like when we played together in 1964. I whirled around, dropping the misshapen plastic bowl with its trail of potato peelings next to the bin, scared she would disappear before I could see her.

There she stood, plaited blonde hair scraped against her pink skull and her pleasant round face smiling at me with friendly eagerness.

It was Linda – except it couldn't be. This Linda looked ten years old and it was 1976, twelve years after she disappeared.

My whole body shook and each question in my head pounded with the increasing beats of my heart thudding against my chest.

What is she doing here?

Where has she been?

Why hasn't she aged?

Who is this?

Mechanically my head turned towards the fence at the bottom of the garden. The ivy had been cleared away and the roots killed after Linda disappeared. I'd insisted on it to help me see immediately if the door ever reappeared. It still hadn't. Only the old, dried-out wooden fence panels existed.

From the corner of my eye I saw this Linda still watching me over the fence. She'd even started to chew her fingertips in the same way, uncertain whether I would agree to playing with her. Only her head and shoulders were visible above the high hedge, which had grown untrimmed; she had to be standing on the old box Lonnie had made for her.

I shook myself physically and flattened my hands on the top of my head, smoothing down my hair. No, no, no, no. I had to be seeing things.

'Rosie, what are you doing? You'll fall off. Stay where you are and I'll ...'

The spell broke. My breath gasped in short bursts, banishing the waves of nausea and growing blackness behind my eyes. Hazel's head appeared next to the girl and she nodded unsmiling at me. Rosie refused to move now that she had my attention.

'I want to talk to Janice. I want to see her uniform.'

'Janice doesn't play with little girls. Now come down before you fall. Janice has got an important job and doesn't need you bothering her.'

I forced my legs to move the couple of yards across the lawn to speak to mother and daughter.

'It's alright, Mrs Donnegan.' I struggled to speak above a whisper and decided honesty was the best policy. 'Just for a moment I thought ... It sounds silly now – but ... she's ...'

Hazel must still have been quite young, but her features were pinched and hardened. Without smiling she nodded and held tightly on to Rosie's waist.

She sighed when she spoke, looking at her daughter rather than at me. 'I know what you thought. I think it every day – especially when she was the same age as ... when Linda went missing.' My head jerked and I noticed Rosie was still biting her fingertips while she watched me from curious blue eyes. 'She's twelve now but she's small for her age.'

Fully recovered from my scare, I pulled myself together. I had another three hours before I was on duty and now could be a good opportunity to speak to Hazel about the subject I'd avoided discussing with her. With a friendly smile at Rosie I said, 'Would you like me to pop round in my uniform before I go to work later?'

The wet fingers grabbed Hazel's arm with excitement. 'Can Janice come to tea, Mummy?'

It was a simple question, but I detected a faint undertone suggesting Rosie expected her mother to say 'No'. This wasn't a child who always had her own way – unlike spoilt Linda.

Before Hazel replied I needed to find a way to persuade her to see me. I needed a distraction from my studies and preparing a meal for Mum. 'Actually, Hazel I've been trying to find the right time to ask you about Linda.' I lowered my head, hoping I looked embarrassed and slightly shy. 'Would it be alright if I came to see you in an hour's time? I won't stay too long.'

I'd promised Mum I'd cook sausage and mash and peas for her before I left for work. Instead, I quickly chipped the potatoes and left them soaking in cold water with a brief note propped up next to the bowl. I rushed to have a quick bath and change into my uniform, checking I looked as smart as if I had a meeting with the chief constable.

It was a while since I'd last looked at Jarvis's file, always kept in the bottom drawer of my office desk. Fortunately, most of the meagre details were committed to memory.

Rapping on the Donnegans' front door I nervously patted the hair peeking beneath my hat and stood up straight. I needed to make a good impression. Hazel hadn't looked at all pleased to see me talking to Rosie.

The young girl didn't so much lead me inside the house as dragged me into the kitchen where a plate of sandwiches lay in the middle of the table. Next to it was a Lyons cream and jam cake with sugar sprinkled over the top. I sat on a red plastic banquette next to Rosie, who bounced into her seat.

'So, you like my uniform, do you?' I'd rehearsed my questions, keen to appear kind and interested in her, winning her friendship. Hazel only glanced at me when I entered and then turned away. She hadn't moved from the kitchen sink and fussed with the teapot.

I gave Rosie my hat to wear while we ate salmon paste sandwiches on thin white bread. She only nibbled hers and chattered on about wanting to be a policewoman like me when she was old enough to join. Unlike Linda, who had been plump, Rosie was slim, and I must have imagined the round face: hers was more angular, with a pointed chin.

Hazel finally joined us. She refused to eat and sat sideways in her chair smoking and looking out of the kitchen window as though expecting to see someone in the garden. Linda perhaps?

'Hazel,' I spoke softly, slightly intimidated by her hostility, 'I'm sorry I haven't been to see you. I didn't know what to say.'

She held the cigarette in her left hand and tapped ash into the glass ashtray she held in her other hand, waving the smoke away from the food. Rosie stopped speaking and nibbled even more slowly. Sitting so close to Hazel I saw she also was thin, with stick-like arms uncovered by

157

a sleeveless dress. Another long drag and a loud exhale, Hazel stubbed the cigarette out in the ashtray and threw the contents into a bin under the sink. She washed the glass clean, dried it and placed it on the window ledge.

When she joined us at the table, she reached for the knife lying next to the cake and cut it into eight small slices.

'I should have come and seen you,' she said, lifting the top half of her cake slice and copying Rosie's delicate nibbling action around the edges of the sponge. Like mother, like daughter. Had Linda eaten her cake in the same way? I only remembered us both stuffing our cakes greedily into our mouths and spluttering crumbs as we laughed in each other's faces.

'I've been asked to look at Linda's file to see if there's anything I remember from those last days.' Thank goodness I found it so easy to lie. 'Would you mind if I asked you some questions … doesn't have to be today …'

'Ask what you like but anything I knew back then should all be in the file. Nothing's changed. We never heard anything from her if that's what you're wondering.' She placed the nibbled cake back on her plate and then patted the crumbs with her ring finger, only to flick them back afterwards.

Rosie stared at her mother and gently placed her nibbled quarter sandwich on her own plate. No wonder they were both so thin if this was how they ate. I'd already polished off 3 small quarters and I didn't even like salmon paste.

'I wasn't wondering about that,' I admitted, waiting politely to be offered a slice of cake. 'Do you have any photographs of Linda that I could look at? I'm sorry but I was very young when she disappeared, and Mum and I didn't take many photographs. The photo in the file is a school one.'

Without a word, Hazel got up and walked into the lounge. I heard her strike a match and smelt a lighted cigarette. When she re-joined us, she passed me a small pack of colour photos and fetched the ashtray before sitting down. She watched as I scrutinised each one of them, five in total. They were still in the Kodak envelope with the negatives and I wondered what had happened to the others from the roll of film.

Used to searching for facial recognition motifs and used to studying drawings, mug shots and photos – black and white and colour – I examined each one in turn. Rosie's curious eyes bore into the side of my head. I felt the hairs on the back of my neck prickle against my cold skin. How could I meet Hazel's eyes? I knew what reaction she expected from me – and I hadn't disappointed.

Puffing smoke from her cigarette into my face, she leaned on the table and I smelt the tobacco on her breath.

'She idolised you, Janice. Worshipped you. She thought you were the most wonderful friend in the world. You didn't know that did you?'

This time it wasn't just the hairs on my neck that prickled. My eyelids scratched when I blinked, and my eyes filled with unshed tears. Avoiding the question, I shuffled the photos, quickly at first and then slower, using my preferred working method. This was work – looking for information on a cold case of a missing ten-year-old girl.

Except this was also my friend Linda. The five photographs showed Linda and me playing in our gardens. Lonnie had taken them, and we posed like silly kids, sticking out our tongues and giggling. Nothing unusual – no suspicious angles when we were in bathing costumes jumping in and out of the paddling pool. Just ordinary photos of two friends playing in the school holidays.

What had shaken me so much, though, were Linda's expressions. While we were goofing around, her eyes were always fixed on me with an endearing expression of love and affection. Where I posed with my arms flung in the air, she did the same. In fact, we had the exact same pose – Linda copying me. I didn't remember anything about the occasions.

Seeing the unshed tears in my eyes, Hazel stubbed out the quarter-smoked cigarette and patted my shaking hand. 'Children can be very cruel.'

It wasn't said with any accusing malice – just stated as a fact. She glanced at Rosie, who had silently finished her sandwich. 'I make sure no one calls Rosie names. We gave Linda too much – it wasn't her fault she was ...' Hazel lowered her voice, '... fat.'

I wanted to protest but instead I continued looking through the photographs, mesmerised by the images of myself at nine years old. Posing and being silly was one thing but anyone could see I deliberately ignored my older friend. Even holding hands, she gazed at me and I looked straight at the camera pretending she wasn't there.

'You can keep them if you want,' Hazel said, washing up the ashtray as before. 'You'd better make a move if you've got to get to work.' She looked up at the clock and I tried to recall the kitchen from when I'd known Linda. The banquette was new. In 1964 we'd sat at a spindly card table with low chairs.

A thud in my chest reminded me I'd sat in this kitchen with Linda eating fish paste sandwiches and Victoria sponge cake, pretending we were friends. The kitchen had changed but the clock on the wall was the same one, round and pale green with solid black hands.

I stood up and smoothed out my creased skirt, playfully taking my hat from Rosie's head, pretending it was stuck and having to pull hard. She shrieked with laughter and I vowed I wouldn't ever treat her how I had treated Linda.

'Would you like to come to the station with me one day when I'm not working? I can show you around – we can even go into the cells where the prisoners are taken. At least you can see what it's like to be a policewoman. I warn you; the ladies' toilets are freezing. It might put you off.'

It was agreed with mother and daughter that I'd set up a date for me and Rosie.

Before I left, I grabbed a mean slice of cake and opening my mouth as wide as I could, took the biggest bite, finishing it in two mouthfuls. I gestured to Rosie to copy me and with a reluctant nod from Hazel she did. Even Hazel laughed and I wondered how often she did that. After all, she'd lost her first child and must wonder every day what had happened to her.

'Thank you for the tea, Mrs Donnegan,' I said, with all the politeness my mother had instilled in me. I settled the hat on my head and joined her at the sink to wash the sugar and jam from my fingers. We stood shoulder to shoulder and I whispered without looking at her. 'I'm going to find out what happened. I'm going to spend as much time as I can finding Linda.'

22

Cameron

Bruce the Bruiser was aptly named by friends and enemies. He was a tall, thin man who lived permanently within the four walls of Cassandra's nightclub. The slightest pressure on his pale skin lifted ugly purple welts that lingered for weeks.

He counted the cash on the desk with lightning rapidity, crooked fingers bundling £20, £10, £5 and £1 notes into curled cylinders which he then tightened with fresh elastic bands, snapping them into place. Licking thumb and forefinger he rubbed each note as he counted to eliminate any possibility of two being stuck together. There were never any accounting mistakes when he was in the office – which was every waking hour, all eighteen of them.

Each breath he took puffed the roll-up cigarette dangling from his lips. He'd given up smoking after his fifteenth birthday but still liked to taste the tobacco on his lips. He never inhaled but left the growing ash to fall on his old brown knitted tank top, enjoying the smoke stinging his squinting eyes. A vividly specific film on cancer and its effects on the body had scared the life out of him but not enough to stop him sending the youngsters out to buy him Rizla papers and a tin of Drum tobacco.

While he heaped the 50-pence coins into £10 stacks, he looked across the small office towards the floor-to-ceiling darkened window. From his position he couldn't see beyond the glass, only the back of the boss's favourite: a tall blond-haired young man. He was leaning forward with his forehead on the glass and one arm flung above his head, suggesting to Bruiser that his companion was less than happy.

'Penny for 'em, Cam,' he said and scooped around fifty quid's worth of pennies into the charity bucket. The boss hated the new pennies, even though Bruiser argued regularly for the total value he 'threw away' just because he couldn't be bothered to carry the extra weight to the bank.

The young man didn't move or reply. Feeling the need to stretch his legs, Bruiser stubbed out the finished cigarette, brushing ash from his chest and knees. He left his desk to join Cam, wondering what was absorbing so much of his attention. Below them the nightclub dancefloor gradually filled with lovely young women dancing within a few inches of their carefully placed handbags.

'How they can move in those platform shoes I'll never know,' Bruiser muttered to himself. The whole layout of the club was visible from the tinted window, deliberately put in place so that no one below, including the kids working behind the bar, knew they were being watched.

It was early in the evening and the club was only a quarter full of the early punters. They were the really young ones – almost certainly under the eighteen years age limit. Even from their elevated position Bruiser could tell the girls were pretty and having fun.

He thought it was wonderful to stand there pretending to be God Almighty looking down on the little people. They thought they were having the time of their lives while their hard-earned money poured into the tills. Bruiser shrugged his thin shoulders into his neck – it was 'win-win' as the boss always boasted when he greedily looked over each night's takings. At weekends he could take in one night what everyone in the club put together barely earned in a year.

Bruiser, captivated by the sights below, knew he should move and finish the hourly banking, bag it up and store it in the safe for the boss's visit. Hardly able to move his eyes away from two women dressed like the hot girls in Abba he sneaked a glance at his friend.

'Hey.' No response. 'Hey,' he shouted and lifted a strand of Cam's long hair to reveal his ear, trying to break into the guy's catatonic concentration. Sometimes when he was in the office, he could be good company, joking about his life in Spain and the lewd and crude tourists out there. Bruiser couldn't remember ever seeing him so morose.

Recalling a conversation from a week ago he turned back to the glass and scanned the crowd below with increased interest, trying to recall Cam's description of the woman.

'Is she there?' It was hardly worth bothering to ask with Cam's uncommunicative mood so apparent.

'No, she's not. She's working tonight.' He scowled. 'Nights.'

Having broken the spell Bruiser returned to his desk, groaning loudly at thousands of scattered small silver coins. He looked at the clock. This was going to take forever to count. But boy, would it be worth it.

The young man turned to face him, his back arched, with his shoulders resting on the reinforced, bulletproof glass, and his arms folded; his tired eyes were glazed from staring through the window.

The twenty-pence pieces chinked as Bruiser slid them two by two off the desk into his hand until he had £5 to stack in front of him.

'When you gonna do it, Cam? Boss is wondering what's taking so long – said so only yesterday. He'll be here in half an hour and he'll ask you himself – if you're still here.'

His words impacted on the young man like a bucket of cold water. Roused from his thoughts, Cam reached for the soft tan-coloured leather jacket and shuffled into it. He patted his trouser pocket and took out a bunch of keys with a slim fob showing two interlinked gold Cs.

With three strides he reached the heavy steel door, punching in the security code to open it. 'There's no rush. No one said anything about a date in the diary. I'll do it when I'm ready – and not before. See you later, Bruise.'

Bruiser's pallid eyes waited for the door to slide back into place with the expected soft thud. With one finger poised above a line of stacked coins he shook his head and tutted.

'Five, ten, fifteen, twenty …'

23

Ray Bolton

Jarvis was bent over his desk, writing notes with a fountain pen on a typewritten report, pausing to think before he scribbled more words. DC Mick Carter and I hovered in the office doorway waiting for him to look up. When he carried on writing, seeming oblivious to our presence, Carter cleared his ex-smoker's throat.

Looking down and reading through the report, Jarvis said, 'No need to remind me you're standing there. I'm hoping if I ignore you both, you'll take the hint and bugger off.'

That was enough for me. I turned away but Carter stayed firm, whistled through his teeth and tapped an S-O-S on the door frame. Hesitating, I waited to see if Jarvis would show some curiosity about our presence. He tossed the report into his out-tray and picked up a green file from his in-tray. Before he opened the cover, he acknowledged Carter's persistence and nodded for us to enter.

'You two should have your own police series. I saw you both with your heads together last night when I left.' He exaggerated a frown and screwed his lips to work out what we could want from him. I looked at Carter and he in turn stared at our boss, who blew out air and sighed, 'Go on, sit down and tell me.'

Mick is a gentleman as well as a ruthless, hardworking detective. He waved a hand at one of the plastic chairs and waited a fraction of a second for me to sit before he took a seat.

'Ray Bolton's out of the Scrubs.'

Jarvis sat back, opening his arms, and loosening his hands in a defeated gesture. 'What? Any other old news you've got for me? He's been out for six months – and unless you're about to surprise me, he's kept himself clean.' His eyes narrowed. 'Have you got something to tell me?

Seeing experienced detectives doing what they did brilliantly always sent a thrill through my body. My skin tingled when I saw Jarvis's expression – keen, interested. His eyes met Carter's and they did that invisible signal thing between them. It was just a tiny nod of the head sideways or a raised eyebrow. Somehow the gestures conveyed more than half an hour of conversation.

'Ray Bolton shared a cell for three years with that creep Len Ward after he appealed against his solitary ... He was the one who found him slumped over the slop bucket when he had his stroke.'

Jarvis sifted imaginary files in his head. 'He did. Ward died from natural causes – a stroke – two months later? I thought it was a heart attack.' No one in the room expressed any sympathy.

Carter turned to me and waited for me to speak. It was up to me to explain what we needed, or Jarvis would lose patience and throw us both out of his office, roaring at us to stop wasting his time.

'Sir, I'd like to meet Ray Bolton and ask him if Len Ward ever said anything about abducting Linda ... you told me you had your suspicions of Ward, but he said he couldn't remember her.' My voice sounded small in the quiet room.

That wouldn't do at all if I were to get permission for the interview. I leant forward in the chair and spoke louder. 'It's the only lead we have, and we all know how cell mates boast to each other.'

Jarvis answered me, but stared at Carter when he spoke, 'Well done, Morton, for finding out that information. Did you have any help?'

Carter wasn't embarrassed. 'I thought it was worth mentioning. Bolton's living with his daughter in Sheldon. Local nick says he's keeping his head down – he's more scared of her than he was of her mother. A chat with him might give Janice the lead she needs.'

'It's worth a try,' I insisted.

Ever since Mick had told me how some crimes were solved with the luck of a remark from a suspect's cell mate, I was determined to speak to anyone who had shared a cell with the man Jarvis had interviewed five years ago. He'd been kept in solitary confinement for his own safety for years, but then moved to a cell with Bolton.

'I'll go with her,' Carter offered. 'I'll soon spot if he tries to play silly beggars and mess her around.'

'Too right you'll go with her. You know what he was in for, don't you?'

'Attempted kidnapping of a minor,' I confirmed, trying not to show off my knowledge. 'He claimed he was trying to take his five-year-old nephew away from his brother – he was certain the brother was abusing the child. It was for his nephew's own good.'

Jarvis agreed. 'Kid was too young and too traumatised to back up the story. But it gave us a chance to put him in with Len Ward. Anyone else would have killed the bastard. But we got nothing from him. You'll be wasting your time.'

I lifted my chin, determined not to pass up the opportunity of this only chance of finding out some information that could lead to finding Linda – even if it was her body.

My voice wobbled when I spoke and I was thankful only Carter and Jarvis were in the room. Ever since our encounter with the Tallys on the night of their arrest I always felt safe with them. Jarvis had ranted on at me many times when I hadn't completed tasks he'd set me – or brought him the wrong bacon sandwich or undrinkable coffee – but he'd always pass on advice or find time to help with any questions I had.

'Sir, I really want to see this man. There could be a chance he says something that may help me to remember another detail from that night – or the day before ... it could ...' My words tailed off into a miserable nothing. Jarvis was probably right, and I would be wasting my time – but surely no real detective ignored even the faintest and improbable lead?

Again, Jarvis met Carter's eyes, and again I saw that imperceptible nod. 'I'll do the talking, Frank. Keep her out of things as much as I can.' He turned to me. 'No uniform. Ex-cons never like that.'

I straightened up in the chair, my head swivelling between each man in dignified outrage, and opened my mouth to protest. Jarvis held his hand up to stop me.

'He's right. Stay in the background as much as you can. I don't want Bolton blabbing about you asking questions about Linda. Mick will soon know if he's telling the truth – and if he doesn't know anything that will be that. Janice, I've told you before, villains will manipulate you and you'll never see it coming until the chief constable asks to see you ...'

He knew exactly what he had to say to scare me to death and make sure I did what I was advised. I sighed under my breath but agreed to take notes while Carter did the talking. At least we could go and see Bolton – that was something.

Ray Bolton surprised me. He was expecting our visit and waited in the annexe at the side of his daughter's detached house. Marianne was a petite, no-nonsense woman in her early forties. She was in the middle of cleaning windows when she opened the door.

'Can't you lot ever leave him alone?' she said with a weary smile. She wasn't hostile and seemed resigned to her father having regular visits from the police while he was on parole. 'He's through here …'

We followed her into the one-bedroom, self-contained apartment which had once been a double garage. It was light and airy with comfortable furniture. I sat in a chintz armchair leaving Mick to sit closer to Bolton on the sofa. His bulky frame sank into the soft cushions and Marianne barely hid an amused smile.

'I'll leave you to it.' Bolton's eyes watched her leave with a fond expression and small wave that said, "Don't worry, I'm fine."

I'd dressed demurely in a mid-calf, flowery print Laura Ashley dress with a frilled collar under my chin. I couldn't have looked less threatening and hoped the man would relax and help us.

Bolton sat upright in the Ercol armchair with his hands loosely balanced on each of the polished teak arms. A close glance, though, and it was possible to see his fingertips gripping the wood. He was plumper than I expected. Ex-cons could be lean and thin from smoking too much, with gaunt faces puckered from years of bitter hatred at being locked up. This guy seemed pleasant with his round Mr Pickwick like face, small dark eyes and fluffy white hair.

I reminded myself he'd been convicted of abducting a small boy and thought how deceptive those kindly looks could be to children.

'This is nice,' I said, looking around the room at the paintings of horses on the walls and bookcase of Dick Francis hardbacks. Mick shot me a stony look. I forgot I wasn't meant to speak.

Ray was pleased with the compliment. 'All down to Marianne. She and Jon fixed this place up and made it ready for me to move in as soon as I came out.' He dropped his eyes to the floor at the reminder of prison. 'They call it a 'granny flat'. He chuckled and looked out of the window where a tall hedge obscured any view of passers-by.

'You like it here then?' Mick asked with some scepticism and I understood his meaning. The room was furnished by a woman and apart from the books and paintings it didn't feel very masculine.

'Are you kidding? I was inside for nearly eight years. This is a palace compared to where I've been living – I'm thankful for every day I wake up here.' He gestured towards a closed door. 'Through there I've got my own bedroom, kitchen and bathroom. She does all my shopping and I do my own cooking.'

Mick didn't turn his head but watched Ray who was watching me. 'Good for you, Ray. Part of the problem for ex-cons is finding a decent place to live when they get out.'

'Tell me about it. I'm not likely to give this up in a hurry. Nancy died while I was inside, but Marianne stuck with me.'

'Why was that?'

'They both knew I was doing my best for the kid. Social Services – and your lot – wouldn't believe me.' He ran his fingers through his hair, leaving it sticking out at the sides. 'My twin isn't identical, but he's still got these kind grandpa looks. He can charm anyone.'

I'd read Bolton's file and wondered myself why he'd received such a harsh sentence. Doctors had confirmed his nephew's abuse and his brother had received a harsher sentence than Ray. But he'd enticed the boy into his car and driven him to a cottage in Wales where his addled, well-meaning brain thought he could keep him safe.

Mick shrugged. 'It couldn't have been easy doing time when you didn't harm him.'

Bolton's face lost its honeyed innocence, clouding into a dark scowl. 'They kept us away from the regular prisoners, but you still hear the shouts at night – every night, making sure you spend the daylight hours petrified someone will get at you.'

Neither Mick nor I looked sympathetic. 'Let me tell you why we're here, Ray. Then you can watch the racing ...'

Bolton brightened at the thought but was puzzled. 'Superintendent Brian Young knows everything that Len said. I don't have anything more to say – and my memory's like a piece of fudge these days. Soft and dense.' He pointed at the books. 'I've read all of those about five times and I never remember a thing about them.' He sighed and stared into space.

Was this going to be harder work than we anticipated? Who, I wondered was Brian Young?

'So you reported everything to Young?'

Bolton nodded as though it was a well-known fact. 'Every month. You must know that. Talk to him. One of his WPCs would visit. Right from the start. We made out she was my cousin's daughter. I'd tell her everything Len had said since the last visit.'

Mick rubbed his straggly moustache. 'Did he talk much?'

'Too bloody much. You know what those people are like ... never shut up about what they've done and how they've been cleverer than the coppers. Trouble is they think everyone wants to hear about it. Made me sick. I was inside for trying to save a kid from someone like Len.'

'What did you get then?' Mick asked while I wrote notes. 'Shorter sentence for sticking with it?'

Ray nodded. 'Earlier parole. It was worth it once that door opened, and I was shoved out into the freezing cold with Marianne waiting in her car for me.'

My heartbeat quickened and I wondered if this visit was a waste of time. Did Jarvis know that this Superintendent Young already had reports of what Len Ward may have confessed to Bolton? And if there had been any mention of Linda, then surely Jarvis would have been informed. I chewed the plastic pen top, nibbling the end of it.

Mick leaned closer to Bolton. 'Let me tell you why we're here. In 1964 a little girl went missing one night from her home. Me and my guv'nor were on the case but we never found her. Ward said he couldn't remember if he'd taken her. We just want to know if he ever mentioned a lass called Linda.'

'Linda? Yeah, there was a Linda.'

Saliva flooded my mouth and I underlined 'Linda' on my notepad. I sensed Mick giving me a sharp warning look at the mention of her name. I kept my eyes on the pad, not trusting myself to look at Bolton even though I wanted to spring over to his chair and demand he tell me everything.

'What did he say about …' Mick began.

'There was more than one Linda …' Bolton cut in. He needed to speak, and we let him. His fudgy brain had melted into something much sharper. 'There were two Lindas – the one brought up at his trial and then one he talked about in the cell. Linda Rogers was the first one – from Cannock.'

We knew about her from the file and press cuttings. She was younger than Linda Bateman and had short dark hair cut into an uneven bob.

'The second one …'

'He never said her last name – just that there was another Linda, but the police would never find her.'

My hand flew to my mouth. The saliva was turning into something more bitter and sinister and I choked it back.

'Any chance of a cup of tea, Ray?'

Bolton blinked as though emerging from a trance. 'Oh. Yes.' He walked over to the connecting door leading to the house and called to Marianne for drinks and a plate of biscuits. Carter and I knew then that he'd decided to trust us. The police were rarely offered hospitality until the homeowner decided we were decent coppers.

'You reported the second Linda to Young?'

Bolton nodded. 'Of course. But I didn't trust him on that one. Some other copper had asked him about a missing girl called Linda and he pretended he couldn't remember if he'd known her or not. Complete bollocks. He remembered every disgusting detail.'

'Did he say where he'd snatched the second Linda?'

Marianne joined us with a tray of clattering teacups and set it down on the coffee table, cleared of any magazines which were stowed in a rack next to the faux fireplace. I offered to pour, and she left us alone. My hands shook and tea slopped into the saucers, but I couldn't help myself. This was what we'd come for.

'Yep. Lickey Hills. Saw her looking out of her bedroom window and beckoned her down to join him. Then buried her somewhere on the Hills. You alright, love?'

Milk overflowed the shallow cup, but I mopped it up and passed the pale drink to Mick. 'I'm fine,' I said faintly with undisguised disappointment.

Bolton helped himself to a biscuit and left the insipid cup of tea on the tray. 'You sure she's a copper? Looks like she's gonna faint any minute.'

Nightmare #2

Like an unofficial sentinel I watched over the moonlit garden below. In my usual place I sat on a padded stool at the bedroom window, curtains apart, waiting for a sign – any sign – of Linda. The inanimate Sindy had never moved from the spot where she'd been placed in 1964, a symbol of my hope that if Linda returned she would be welcomed by her favourite doll.

At last, she was there.

Standing in the middle of the lawn, she still wore the plaid dressing gown and suede fur-lined ankle boots. Our eyes met when she looked up, searching for me inside the house. Neither of us waved but I shouted to her to wait for me. My words were lost against the glass barrier of the window and before I could be sure she'd heard me, thick clouds settled around the moon. The garden, and Linda, were plunged into blackness.

Turning from the window I tried to run downstairs and join my friend, knowing that I could help her over the privet fence into her own garden.

Something was wrong. I couldn't move across the room to my bedroom door, which was firmly closed. My single bed had changed into a king-sized monstrosity that filled the room. It was covered in huge, satin, padded cushions and when I tried to climb over it, I slipped on the shiny material. Falling onto the carpet I looked out of the window, shouting to Linda to wait for me.

It was too dark to see her.

I tried to scramble around the end of the bed, struggling to push it aside and make room for me to pass. The wooden frame was too heavy for my weak, feeble hands. It wouldn't move an inch, so I crawled across the cushioned obstacles, scattering them aside. The distance across the bed was too great and I floundered on the thick, quilted eiderdown.

Finally, I was at the door and wrenched it open, but I overestimated my strength and the doorknob fell into my hands and rolled onto the floor under the bed. I was trapped and couldn't leave the room to join Linda.

But there was an alternative. This door – this 'dream' door – opened both ways and when I pushed it with all my strength, it slowly inched open. I ran down the staircase which increased in length as I attempted to descend. 'Wait for me, Linda,' I pleaded with every step.

Then I was in the garden, lit up by the bright shining moon. All was silent in the black and white stillness of the night.

Linda had gone.

Slowly, slowly, I turned in a circle on the spot, searching for her.

She wouldn't have been able to climb over the privet fence into her own garden without help. Spying the back gate, I guessed she'd gone out to walk around to her own house.

If only the bolts weren't fastened so tightly. If only my small hands could force them to move across and the gate open to let me through. Every second counted if I were to catch up with Linda. I had to tell her something important. I had to tell her I was sorry.

Like the bedroom door, the gate eventually gave way and I dragged myself along the path to the street. It was too dark to see where I placed my feet. Slowly, my hands felt the wall at the side of the house, moving forward into the blackness towards the front.

My legs refused to carry me, and I crawled with my hands outstretched to reach the pavement. I was exhausted and desperate to catch up with Linda before she knocked on her front door, waking Hazel and Lonnie. I had to speak to her. I had to tell her something important.

Weeping, I knelt and called to Linda. She stood with her back to me, her dressing gown belt trailing each side of her waist. My voice was so small and quiet, it would be impossible for her to hear me.

'No,' I screamed inside my head. But it was no use. The driver of the waiting car, engine throbbing loudly, with its passenger door opened wide, gestured with a brown-gloved hand to the seat.

Linda climbed in and closed the door.

'No,' I screamed again. My knees were glued to the pavement. Linda hadn't seen me or heard me. With its door closed, the car drove away.

Registration. Registration. Get the Number. Get the Number.

The night was dark again and I peered into the gloom. A streetlamp briefly shone on the number plate as the car passed it.

W8 4ME.

24

Tanya

I couldn't help notice PC Watson appear in the doorway of the CID office and hesitate before walking into the room. He wore his helmet and it made him look even taller than his six-foot height. It was unusual for a bobby to keep his helmet on indoors. They were designed to make officers taller, but all the men hated wearing them.

In uniform, with helmet off, they were figures of authority to be trusted or feared.

In uniform, with helmet on, they were figures of fun to be ridiculed and taunted.

He must be in a hurry, I thought, and didn't blame him for being reluctant to enter the office. As usual it stank of cigarettes. All the detectives smoked except for me and three others. Ashtrays were rarely emptied and even if they were, the contents missed the bin more times than not.

Cleaners were discouraged due to the nature of CID's work and their natural distrust of everyone. We were supposed to do our own clearing up. Jarvis had seen a documentary on the way the Japanese worked and had barked one day that none of us were to go home until we'd cleared everything off our desks and locked files away.

Nothing should be left out for prying eyes to look at or nose into.

We'd all agreed but the practice lasted about two days. Carter was so good at locking everything away that while he was out interviewing one morning, Jarvis couldn't find some vital paperwork he needed. Undeterred by a padlock on Mick's desk drawer, he angrily smashed it open and after that no one bothered again.

I was supposed to wipe down the kitchen area where we kept a kettle and a toaster with a small cupboard and sink. Dirty cups, plates and cutlery were strewn everywhere and, for once, I took a stand and refused to clean anything except what I'd used myself. Even Jarvis backed down when he saw I was furious at spending my time cleaning like a housewife.

Watson stepped into the unwholesome fug and gave me a weak smile that barely creased the lines around his eyes. He tapped on Jarvis's door and mumbled something to him before making his way to my desk. I'd been looking through Linda's file and had followed his progress with some curiosity.

'Janice,' he said in a low voice, 'I need you to come with me. Jarvis says it's OK.'

Puzzled, I tried to reason, inside my head, that this wasn't anything sinister. It was always in the back of my mind that one day I would be asked to leave the job for something stupid I had done. Surely though if that were the case, it would be Jarvis, not a PC, who would notify me of such a dreadful decision.

Nick lowered his tall, athletic frame towards me. 'Tanya Addison's in the General – been beaten senseless. I need to try and take a statement from her – and visit her family.'

In seconds I was on my feet, shrugging into my own uniform jacket which was on the back of my chair. I followed Nick's long strides to his police car and slipped in beside him.

My whole being seemed to be racked with guilt these days. I was consumed with guilt over my part in Linda's disappearance. That never left me. And now, I was filled with guilt over Tanya Addison. After she'd been driven home after her false claim of rape, I'd never followed up what happened to her when she arrived – nor had I checked that Social Services had been involved with her home life.

'That's not your job,' Nick muttered grimly as we sped past vehicles that slowed down for our blue flashing lights and siren and moved aside to make room on the congested roads.

'I could have made time,' I protested. 'She was a vulnerable minor and all the signs were there she was being neglected.'

Sitting in Ray Bolton's comfortably furnished 'granny flat' drinking tea and eating biscuits hadn't achieved very much. The time could have been better spent with a visit to Tanya. I said so to Nick, but he countered it smoothly.

'We were keeping a low profile if you remember, Janice.' He spoke with more authority than a police constable. Mick Carter was right when he said that Watson was destined to become a very senior officer at some point in his career. 'If you had turned up at her home, you could have caused a lot of questions …'

It was impossible not to agree. But I made a mental note to contact Social Services and find out the results of their visits.

At the hospital, we spoke to PS Fay Wilson and PC Ken Knowles, who had been alerted to Tanya's bruised body lying half dead on a park bench.

'A couple walking their dog found her,' Knowles said, consulting the recently made notes in his pocketbook. 'At first they thought she was dead or out of it on drink or drugs. The bloke's an ex-magistrate and a bit judgemental if you ask me.'

'No one's asking you,' Wilson coughed her warning. 'We called an ambulance straight away. To be honest, her injuries are so bad it was hard to tell if she was alive until we checked her breathing.'

I turned away to watch a white-coated doctor and two nurses talking to each other over a bed where a drip had been set up. They obscured the occupant, whom I guessed to be Tanya. Leaving Nick with the other two officers to check the details I walked slowly into the ward and joined the doctor.

No one had yet dressed Tanya's injuries, but they had quickly drugged her against the pain. Something I didn't recognise tugged at my heart and flipped my stomach. The little girl, barely a teenager, looked tiny lying in the bed. Her straggly unwashed hair was matted with blood and had been spread across the pillow, away from her face.

Both eyes were swollen and the cut on her cheekbone had exposed a bloody mess. Whatever had hit her had not been a light object or blow from a puny hand. This was meant to do damage.

'WPC Janice Morton,' I held up my warrant card to prove my identity and convince the young doctor he had to tell me everything about this sad case. 'We need a statement from her as soon as possible. Whoever did this is walking around out there.'

The doctor nodded to the two nurses and one of them gently folded back the crisp, fresh sheet to expose Tanya's frail naked body. The recent bruises were already turning blue and purple, standing out against faded black ones.

Dr Raj, as his badge confirmed, explained that they were waiting for a theatre to become free so they could prep Tanya for emergency surgery and try to patch up her insides.

Raj spoke with an Eton-accented tone that thinly disguised his horror at what lay in front of us.

'You would only need to flick a heavy duster at this girl to cause her some inconvenient pain – kicking her with leather boots and punching her with fists … you get this.'

'The damage …?' I tried to speak calmly and not to picture an unknown thug battering this waif, relishing the result of his actions. She must have screamed in agony.

'It won't be good, Constable.' He pointed delicate fingers to Tanya's blue-tinged lips. 'We're doing all we can … but those bruises indicate her organs could stop functioning at some point.'

Tears sprang into my eyes. I didn't want to cry but this was too much for me. Needing to hide my expression from the other officers, I bent over Tanya and stroked her hair.

The nurses efficiently covered her body with a hospital gown, ready for the bed to be moved by two porters into surgery. They were kind but their actions were brusque. One of them grabbed the stand with its saline and morphine drip and I stood up to help her.

'Let me take this,' I offered as she moved it to keep pace with the bed. She shook her head and smiled.

'You're alright, love. I'll need to scrub up when I'm down in theatre, so I have to go anyway.'

I waited for her to mumble something about Tanya being 'alright' and 'not to worry' but we were both too professional to pretend. The doctor had a duty to help the patient, but I felt sure the little girl would never wake up.

Nick Watson had let the other two officers leave, so we replaced them on duty. He filled me in on the sketchy story they had obtained from the former magistrate and his wife.

'It was the dog that alerted them,' he explained. 'It ran up to Tanya lying on the bench and then sat down whining. It's a German Shepherd – possibly once in training for the canine branch.'

'Which bench? Which park?' I asked as we walked over to a vending machine selling packets of crisps, sweets and even fruit. Nick shoved in some coins, bought me a Mars bar and an apple for himself.

'Hamilton – just around the corner from where she lives. Knowles and Watkins are off to make enquiries and find out if anyone saw anything. They might get lucky, but whoever did this probably scares the life out of everyone out there.'

'There has to be a motive,' I suggested. We sat side-by-side in two visitors' chairs placed around the space where Tanya's bed had stood. Nick crunched his Granny Smith, sucking up the juice while I nibbled the chocolate around the caramel and soft mousse. He frowned at my childish effort and tutted. 'Eat it properly, Morton – you're not six years old.'

I ignored him and we sat in silence, pondering our own theories of what could justify a small girl being beaten by a stronger male. Neither of us could contemplate the thought of a woman hitting Tanya in such a manner.

'Some of the bruises were old,' I told him. 'She'd been hit with something hard before today.'

Nick's handsome face lost its mild expression and became hard. 'Parents. One of them at least. Either them or a brother … someone who wanted to make certain she did as she was told.' He glanced at me, still nibbling the Mars bar. I ignored the silent reproof.

We'd both experienced incidents of domestic violence and in some cases a brother or father beating a child into submitting to rape either by themselves or someone paying for the depravity. I steeled myself to accept that this could be a probable cause for Tanya's injuries.

My fingers were a chocolate mess after ten minutes of nibbling the Mars bar. I was being childish, just as Nick had accused me. I told myself that the longer the Mars bar lasted, then the better Tanya's chances were of surviving surgery. Dr Raj spoke like a man to be trusted and I hoped and hoped there was something he could do for her.

I disappeared into the ladies' toilet to wash my hands and give in to my emotions about the poor state of Tanya and the miserable life she must have led. Dabbing at my eyes with a wet tissue I had to hide all trace of tears before I re-joined Nick. If Carter was right, then one day I might be sitting in front of him at a promotion board and couldn't risk him thinking me a weak officer.

While we waited, Nick disappeared into the corridor to check on updates on his radio. Knowles and Watkins had visited her home looking for her parents, but no one was there, except an unhelpful man who said he was the lodger. The next-door neighbour suggested they try one of the pubs in the area and when asked 'which one?' by Knowles, she'd answered, 'all of them'.

When he returned, he asked me what time I was due to finish my shift. I checked the clock on the wall. 'Two hours ago. What about you?'

'I was just starting my 2 o'clock when I heard this come in. Sheer coincidence I was standing next to the new radio operator. My sergeant suggested I attend the hospital and I thought of you.'

New radio operator! He meant the red-headed

WPC who'd transferred from Solihull. Trust him to be coincidentally standing next to her.

'You can go if you need to be somewhere,' Nick continued and I felt bad for my accusatory thoughts. 'You'll need to clear it with Jarvis if you want to stay ...'

I didn't have permission to do overtime for this job, so I called CID from the hospital phone. Jarvis had been informed of Tanya's beating and the pessimistic prognosis. He and some of the other detectives were on standby, waiting for this to turn into a murder inquiry.

'Sooner we catch this thug the better,' he said. 'You stay there and tell me everything she can remember. She knows you, doesn't she?'

'Yes. And PC Watson drove her home that day after the rape claim. When she wakes up ...' I deliberately trailed off to impress on Jarvis the unlikelihood of that happening. '... we'll both be familiar faces.'

'Any description at all will be helpful. We're keeping an eye on the lodger and uniform are still searching for the parents.'

It was doubtful there would be much chance of Tanya telling us anything, but Jarvis was more encouraging.

'You'd be surprised, Morton, how resilient the body can be – especially when it's in good hands. I've seen a few miracles in my time.' He murmured something and I guessed he had a visitor. 'There's always a shred of hope.'

No goodbye as usual.

Two different porters pushed Tanya's bed back into the ward. She looked worse than ever. Her hair was covered in a plastic cap and her pale face was deathly white. Dr Raj joined us after a few minutes.

He explained that all her ribs were broken or fractured and her spleen damaged. 'Her heart is still strong and I'm arranging for her to be put on dialysis.' He shrugged his shoulders and patted my arm. 'The body is a wonderful thing – we have to wait to see how she responds.'

I watched a young woman in a matron's uniform check the equipment at the bedside. She monitored Tanya's heartbeat with her own watch against the bleeping machine. 'You want to talk to her, I suppose.' She snorted breath into her nostrils and smiled. 'We'll all be thankful if whoever did this is behind bars before the day ends.' She glanced fondly at the girl and stroked her small fingers, still stained with dried blood. 'The anaesthetic will wear off shortly and she should wake up …'

My chair was closest to Tanya's head and rather than hold her hand and risk squeezing it too tightly, I copied the matron and stroked it instead. Without a word, Nick dampened some paper towels and gave them to me. As gently as I could, I wiped the blood from Tanya's hands and face. Nothing improved the vile bruises, but the open gash on her right cheek had been sewn together.

The restless Nick Watson was in the corridor again for the latest update on the enquiries for Tanya's parents, when her eyes fluttered open. Hurriedly, I pressed the button for the nurse, who took the wet flannel from its dish and dabbed it on her lips which were cracked and dry.

'Hey, Tanya,' I smiled, 'do you remember me? It's Janice. I'm here with Nick.'

She'd been given a lot of morphine for her pain so I was confident she wouldn't be too uncomfortable. Nick joined me and greeted Tanya with relief when he saw her eyes were open. We waited for the nurses to re-check the machines and her drip and talk soothing words to her. They nodded to us and Nick asked if one of them could stay a little longer. Nurse Marie Andrews stood on the opposite side to us with her arms folded.

In a soft voice I barely recognised I said, 'Tanya, I need to ask you some questions.' Nick opened his notebook and hunched closer to my side. 'Can you lift one of your fingers?'

Nick flinched. That wasn't a question he expected me to ask. Tanya slowly lifted her middle finger a fraction from the bed. 'That's brilliant. Now if you want to say 'yes' to a question lift your finger. If the answer is 'No' then leave it on the bed. Do you understand?'

With her limpid eyes fixed on my face, Tanya lifted her finger. I could feel Nick and the nurse watching me and Nick held his pen against the paper in his notebook.

'Do you know who attacked you?'

Finger raised. It was a 'Yes' but instead of lowering it, Tanya switched her gaze from me and looked fully at Nick, turning her finger to point at him.

Ignoring his intake of breath, I asked her, 'Did Nick attack you?'

The finger dropped.

'She's on very strong medication,' the nurse said and was rewarded with one of Nick's most charming smiles.

'Did the person who attacked you look like Nick?

Finger raised.

I think we all breathed freely when we saw that.

Without looking at him, I nudged Nick. 'Stand up.'

'Was he as tall as Nick?'

The finger dropped.

Nick lowered himself to around 5 foot 10. The finger didn't move. He dropped another two inches.

Finger raised.

'You little darling,' the nurse said in an accent that reminded me of Lonnie.

'Did he have black hair?'

Finger raised.

'Brown eyes?'

Finger raised.

I could feel Nick's elbow bumping my arm as he wrote everything down.

'Does he live in your flat?'

Finger raised.

'Was it your dad?'

Finger did not move.

'Was it the lodger?'

Finger raised and a snuffling cry.

Nick was on his feet and away, switching on his radio as he walked towards the corridor.

'You're safe in here, Tanya. The nurses and the doctor will look after you. You just need to get better. We'll make sure nothing happens to you again.'

Tears fell from her eyes and I brushed them away with a tissue, concerned the saltiness would mingle with the raw, new scar.

'Your mum and dad will be here soon,' I promised, hoping they would be sober when they arrived. Tanya's fingers scrabbled the sheet in agitation, and I caught them with my own.

'Do you want to see them?'

No fingers were raised.

'I'll let Matron know and tell the front desk,' Nurse Andrews said and rushed out of the ward, passing Nick as he entered.

I quickly told him of Tanya's reaction when I mentioned her parents and he swivelled around and switched on his radio again.

25

The Halter-Neck Dress

Tanya pulled through from her injuries but would need to be hooked to a dialysis machine for most of her life. Dr Raj was sure that advancements in dialysis were looking good. She never went back home but lived with foster parents for the duration of her treatment.

The information I'd obtained from Tanya with Nurse Anderson as a witness was swiftly relayed to CID detectives via Nick and Jarvis. The lodger living with Tanya and her parents was so convinced he hadn't done anything wrong he was still at the address where Watkins and Knowles had found him. Confident he was in the clear after the officers left without taking much notice of him, he was sprawled on his bed eating chips and leering over *Playboy* magazines, when Sergeants McIlroy and Shepherd kicked the door in. They flashed their warrant cards at him and as he was stoned off his head, he gave little resistance. He was handcuffed and hustled into the back of a police car. The detectives confiscated the bag of weed he'd carelessly left on his bedside table.

Tanya's parents, Joe and Elaine Addison, were an enigma of complete and utter cluelessness. They seemed not to have a brain cell between them and after intense questioning we discovered that they were brother and sister who had lived in the flat after their parents died in

1972. Tanya was their niece, left behind by an older sister who escaped to London after her daughter was born.

Neither of the adults could look after themselves properly, let alone a child, and spent all their benefit money at the pub and on fish and chips. Social Services had visited the home on several occasions but when no one answered the door the caller had to move onto her next case. The system had failed the little girl and I couldn't see the situation improving.

The lodger was Ivan Lebedev, a Russian seaman who'd jumped ship in Liverpool and travelled on a canal boat down to Birmingham. When he saw, all too clearly, the vulnerability of the Addisons he talked his way into moving into their flat and sleeping in Tanya's bedroom, so that she had to use the sofa.

The beating he gave her was because of her reluctance to buy cannabis on his behalf, from a local supplier. Edgington CID had been busy with comings and goings from the drug squad officers. They might have been dressed for undercover work outside, with shabby clothes and long hair, but inside the police station they stood out like the proverbial sore thumbs. I wondered if the bag of cannabis found with Ivan had sparked all the activity.

I guessed correctly when I heard that Detective Superintendent Thomson and a couple of officers had interrogated him rigorously. He refused to give up the supplier's name, claiming he never knew it, but did confirm suspicions they had about drugs transported along the canal.

Fingerprints taken from Lebedev were circulated to Russia and Interpol, which revealed that he was wanted in Moscow for the murder of his teenage girlfriend. An order was made to deport him back to Russia, avoiding an appearance in court and saving Tanya from being cross examined. After she came round from the heavy medication, she could remember little of what she had told us and a good defence lawyer could have destroyed her in court. McIlroy and Shepherd escorted Ivan on his flight to Moscow and handed him over to four grim-faced uniformed *militsiya*. 'I almost felt sorry for him,' Shepherd said on his return.

I was relieved to have had a significant part in resolving an attempted murder, with the attacker caught without any difficulty. Nick Watson and Frank Jarvis agreed that my swift and sympathetic questioning technique had resulted in a quick response from Tanya that hadn't caused her any further distress.

I felt justified in the commendation I received for my part in the incident – and the overtime pay. But part of me wondered whether Tanya's co-operation, before the drugs in her system knocked her out for twelve hours, had more to do with having Nick at my side. Few females could fail to be charmed by that man.

A few days later, I sat at my desk with my head lifting higher every few minutes like a cute wild animal I'd seen on TV in a nature programme. Every time I checked, Jarvis was still absorbed in his phone call.

'You waiting to see Jarvis, Janice?'

It was Steph, dressed down in Chelsea Girl jeans and a C&A blouse. I nodded, 'Yeah, but he's been on that call for nearly an hour.'

'I know. I can't wait any longer. I'm due at the factory – they think I'm at the dentist and Sanjay hates it when you take time off. He'd be happy if you just bled quietly at the sewing machine so long as you didn't make a mess of a frock.'

She held up a thin, blue plastic bag and pulled out a gaudy piece of fabric with streaks of scarlet slashed through the pattern. 'When he's finished can you give this to him?'

'What? Who's he bought this for?' I shook out the material and it transformed into a halter neck dress which could only fit a slim frame like Steph's.'

'Sanjay offered a rack of clothes to all the staff yesterday. £1 an item. It would have looked strange if I'd said 'No'. This was the only one that fitted me, thank goodness. I can't keep it, obviously, so Jarvis can book it in against the job.' She winked and swung out of the office in her Littlewoods white patent sling-backs, with scuffed black marks around the heels.

She had only just disappeared down the corridor when I saw Jarvis drop the receiver back into the cradle. I sprang to my feet before he could start another call. At least I had a good excuse to disturb him with Steph's dress. I draped it over my arm and then laid it on his desk.

'Steph said it's from Sanjay's factory. She paid £1 for it.'

Jarvis was as startled as if I'd thrown a dead dog before him. 'What is it?'

I picked it up and again shook it into the shape of a dress.

'It won't suit you, Frank.' It was Detective Superintendent Thomson. He stood in the doorway with another man, tall, slim built and wearing a smart navy-blue suit.

They both entered the office with a swaggering sense of entitlement and neither gave me more than a glance. I was meant to disappear – and probably make them tea.

I felt foolish holding up the dress and my arms drooped with it in my hands. Thomson, with his arrogant manner, snatched it from me and frowned. 'How are you supposed to wear it?'

Hadn't he seen a halter-neck before?

'How'd you usually wear women's clothes, Doug?' His friend smirked.

Thomson slipped the material through his hands and used it to gesture towards the other man. 'Frank, this is Senior Investigating Officer Adam Byrne, Customs ...' He trailed off when he realised he'd spoken in front of me. 'Milk and two sugars, darling – Adam will have the same, but you'd better find him a clean mug.'

'Doug.' Jarvis spoke sharply and stood up to shake Adam Byrne's hand across his desk. In the office he always kept his jacket on the coat stand, preferring to work without it. His wide tie hung from his loosened collar. He didn't compare too favourably with the smartly dressed Byrne.

'This is WPC Janice Morton – she picked up the intel on the Tally twins and encouraged the information on Lebedev from Tanya Addison.' I tried not to flash a smug glance at Thomson, but he was busy playing with the cheap dress. Byrne, though, nodded to me with an impressed look on his young face. 'And she tipped us off that something could be fishy with the Sanjay factory ...'

'I see,' Byrne said in a more cultured voice than I was used to hearing in CID. 'Fancy switching to Her Majesty's Customs and Excise ...?'

'Don't even think about it,' Jarvis tried to smile but he wasn't happy with the remark.

Thomson was more interested in the dress that had baffled him. He held the material to his face and sniffed it – and then inhaled more deeply. He passed it to Byrne, who almost backed away, but was intrigued enough to take it from him.

Locking eyes with Thomson, Jarvis and I watched him crumple the material into a silky ball and then take a further sniff of the fabric.

'It's faint …' he pronounced. 'But there's definitely something …'

There was silence in the office, and I was irritated at the two men making fun of the dress Steph had tried on at the factory.

'Er … Janice,' Jarvis said, 'make us all a cuppa, will you? Don't worry about clean mugs.' He shot a look at Thomson who closed the office door behind me when I left.

On my return with a tray of mugs I kicked at the door to ask for it to be opened. The lively hum of chat I'd heard on my approach ceased as soon as Thomson opened it enough to meet me on the threshold and take the tray from me.

'Thanks, darling,' he said and shut the door in my face.

What else did I expect? A medal for my part in solving the crime of Tanya's attacker. A little sit-down in Jarvis's office with soothing words about my ingenious method of interviewing a near-unconscious victim? A pat on the back?

My commendation was enough, and it was all in a day's work. I shouldn't be disappointed that life in crime and detection moved on. It was back to work as usual.

I slumped into my seat and shuffled a pile of filing. The phone ringing was a welcome interruption. An interruption that turned out to be near-fatal.

26

A Night at the Opera

It wasn't pleasant being jostled by the increasing and feverish crowd of people coming towards me from all directions. I checked my gold Timex watch and jiggled it on my wrist as though that would help my situation. Only one minute had passed since the last time I'd looked, and ten minutes after the 7.30pm time Nick Watson had warned me to meet him outside the Birmingham Hippodrome Theatre. 'No later, Janice. Performance starts at 8 o'clock.'

The welcome interruption had been Nick.

'Are you busy tonight?'

'Do you need me? Jarvis is here. I can ask him to spare me …'

He smiled a laugh. 'No. Nothing to do with work. I've got two tickets for the theatre. My mum just cancelled. I thought you might like to go with me.'

The way I'd been feeling after the encounter with Thomson and his vile way of treating Steph's dress, I'd have been happy to sit in a greasy spoon cafe with Nick, eating egg and chips.

'Theatre? A play?'

'Erm … it's … well, do you like musicals?'

'Like *The Sound of Music*? Yes, course I do.'

'Great. Then you'll like this. Seven thirty at the Hippodrome. Plenty of time after you finish your shift, yes?'

I quickly calculated that if I left the office right then, I could drive into town and buy something new to wear – and stock up on sweets.

'Yes, that'll be great. I haven't been to the theatre since …'

'What was the last thing you saw?'

I breathed through my teeth as I tried to remember. 'I think it was *Aladdin*.'

'Bloody hell, Janice, it's like you live in a cupboard. You'll like this then. Very similar to a panto. See you later – and don't bring sweets. They make too much noise.'

I stared at the phone. I didn't live in a cupboard, but I did live in a world where I re-lived Linda's disappearance and tried to make sense of a secret door that had closed and never been seen again. My life was so different to other people's lives, but here was an opportunity to enjoy an evening that Nick took for granted.

With my light summer jacket half pulled around my shoulders I bobbed outside Jarvis's office, hoping he'd spot me. When he did, our eyes met and I did my own version of a pantomime to let him know I was leaving. He never minded our comings and goings, and he knew I rarely left early. I flashed him my best smile and waved a goodnight. The other two men realised something was going on and looked over their shoulders at me.

The halter dress was laid out on Jarvis's desk in a spooky replica of a dead body. My boss didn't smile but he did nod and held up one finger to indicate I had his permission to leave. Within a second, the men continued their discussion in low, urgent voices.

I knew the theatre trip wasn't a date with Nick, but nevertheless I didn't want to let him down and look out of place. He would know the right thing to wear for every occasion, but I didn't have a clue. With my shiny plastic credit card in hand, I walked into Rackhams and asked the assistant for her recommendation for my evening.

Waiting for Nick I wasn't sure I'd made the right decision and kept taking my black velvet jacket off and then putting it back on, depending on the outfit I'd seen another woman wearing. My final choice was a demure knee-length burgundy and navy patterned silk dress with a square neckline and long sleeves that finished in a frilled cuff at my wrists. It was a loose fit and when I walked in my kitten heels it swished around my hips. Daphne, the ladieswear assistant had declared it 'just perfect'.

At almost a quarter to eight, I was deflated, certain Nick had either played a horrible joke on me or, even worse, taken one look at how I was dressed and hidden in the crowd for a quick get-away. There was an urgent bustle towards the entrance as a loud voice announced, 'Curtain Up in Fifteen Minutes. Fifteen Minutes.' This caused a wave of murmurs and smokers hurriedly took final drags of nicotine into their lungs before throwing away smouldering cigarettes.

I wasn't the only person waiting alone and had already been approached by a nervous-looking man holding a single red rose, asking, 'Are you Sandra?' A tall, red-haired lady also wove her way around the crowds and more than once our eyes met. Her cascade of curls wafted around a tight, dark green leather jacket, which I thought wasn't as appropriate as my dress for the theatre. But she looked about fifty and, guessing she was probably more used to this than me, I began to have doubts again.

The jacket was back on and then I saw him running across the small road outside the theatre, dodging taxis offloading other latecomers. The red-haired woman roamed closer to me and I smelt her perfume. It wasn't one I'd ever liked.

I stepped forward to attract Nick's attention and felt a sting in my side. Surely, I hadn't trapped a wasp inside my jacket. It was too late to check as I was hustled firmly by Nick, towards the open doors.

I stood my ground in disbelief. 'We're not going in here are we?' I pointed to the two giant posters either side of the entrance. 'I thought we were going to see *The King and I*.'

'What? What are you on about? King who?'

He was distracted, fumbling in his inside pocket. He held his arm protectively around me as we bumped along beside other patrons, clutching their own tickets. He pushed towards the STALLS sign and muttered something about needing to pee, but it would have to wait.

'Nick,' I spluttered, 'I've never heard of this. What's it about'

We waited while everyone sitting in our row stood to let us pass and reach our seats in the middle. '*Madame Butterfly*. You'll like it. Set in Japan.'

The orchestra began playing a fast-paced musical piece that almost had me open-mouthed and quite excited. I turned to Nick with bright eyes and mouthed, 'Thank you.' He could be right, and I was going to enjoy this more than I expected.

How wrong I was.

My side began to throb from the wasp sting – or maybe someone's umbrella had prodded me. As I rubbed it, I felt something wet on my dress. I held Nick's arm and he inclined his head. 'I think someone's spilt a drink on me. My dress is wet.'

He didn't reply and kept his eyes firmly ahead, fixed on the stage. But he did fumble in his pocket and passed me a clean handkerchief. I laid it across the side of my waist and felt better, though puzzled. How could anyone spill a drink while we rushed from the street to our seats?

The throbbing didn't ease and each time I felt intense pain, I breathed in sharply.

'Stop fidgeting,' Nick hissed and I felt the man next to me pointedly stare in my direction. I pointedly stared ahead and tried to concentrate on two men standing and singing in what I presumed was Italian.

Slowly, slowly, I inched my fingertips to feel the handkerchief. It was sodden and when I stroked the material, I stiffened. If there was one thing I knew the feel of, it was blood. I pulled Nick's handkerchief onto my lap. Could I be wrong?

I nudged Nick's elbow, which he'd leant on the arm of the seat, dreading his irritation. Sure enough, he gave me a tolerant glare that said, stop messing about. I gripped the material of his jacket to stop him from looking away and passed him the wet handkerchief. Our eyes met in silent horror – and then the nightmare began.

Nick jumped to his feet. 'Bloody hell, Janice. You've been stabbed.' He called to an usher who appeared the moment Nick raised his voice, holding up his warrant card. 'Call 999 – police and ambulance. This is an off-duty police officer and she's been stabbed.'

He lifted me in his arms and the shocked people in our row stood to let us pass. But first he insisted my neighbour walk in front. 'You're coming with us – and you're under arrest on suspicion of grievous bodily harm to one of Her Majesty's police officers.'

The poor man couldn't be more shocked and protested his innocence all the way to the foyer, where Nick laid me down on the crimson carpet. 'Stay right there,' he ordered the theatregoer, who must have wished he'd stayed home and watched *Coronation Street*. 'Someone fetch me something to stop the blood.' He peeled off his smart jacket.

Theatre staff were rushing around, assuring him an ambulance was on its way. To my dismay he bent over me and with both hands parted my silk dress at the side seams. It ripped like a cheap envelope, exposing my side, now oozing rather than seeping blood.

'Nick … it's new,' I whispered.

His cold fingers felt for what we both knew he'd find.

Our eyes met and he nodded. He bundled his jacket and held it firmly against the wound. 'Talk to me, Janice. You've usually got plenty to say.' A young constable ran up to him. 'PC Ray James, Nick. What can I do?'

Nick swore as though reciting the alphabet and looked up at the ceiling. 'Check all the bins in the area. A knife – small blade. Don't ruin any fingerprints. And don't stop looking.' Then he shouted. 'Janice, talk to me.'

He bent his head when he saw my lips move. 'Red hair … curly … green … leath … jack … Charlie … Greek …' I tried to point my finger.

The last thing I heard was the muffled sound of sirens and Nick screaming my name.

Nick Watson's blue eyes were the last thing I saw before I passed out and the first thing I saw when I regained consciousness. His white shirt, which had been pristine when he arrived at the theatre, was soaked with my blood. It was smeared on his face where he'd wiped his hands across his eyes and cheeks.

He sat on a plastic chair like the one he'd used when we'd sat with Tanya. 'Why didn't you just say you didn't like opera?'

'I was enjoying it.' My voice was faint and croaky, and he lifted a glass of water to my lips. When I tried to sip it, cold liquid leaked down my chin and onto my gown. 'Thanks a lot, Nick. I'm soaked.'

He bit his lip, trying not to smile. 'How are you feeling? They patched you up before you lost too much blood. How could you not have known what happened?'

'I thought it was a wasp.' As I lay my head back on the pillow, I heard a man's voice repeat 'wasp' with disbelief. Then I saw Nick and I weren't alone in the room. He scraped his chair back so that I could see Superintendent Thomson standing in the doorway.

It was instinctive to try and sit up. 'Sir.' The man always managed to intimidate me.

He'd changed out of the scruffy clothes from when I'd seen him with Jarvis and wore a clean pair of jeans and a grey sweatshirt. His eyes weren't as malevolent or as arrogant as usual and in his right hand he held a slim buff folder.

'How are you feeling?' He didn't say my name or my inferior rank of constable. 'If it helps, nearly every officer in the county is searching bins, car parks and drains looking for the weapon used to stab you. And we will find who did this.'

He approached the bed and Nick stood to give him his seat. Thomson picked up the glass of water and holding his folded handkerchief under my chin, encouraged me to take another sip. It was more successful this time. 'Nick … PC Watson … told Control what you said before you passed out at the theatre.' He checked from his notebook. 'Red hair … curly … green leather jacket … Greek – possibly called Charlie. Can you make sense of it?'

I stared at the blank wall ahead of me and thought of the half hour wait for Nick to turn up.

'Morton. Janice. Are you listening to me?'

Thomson spoke sharply, but I needed to concentrate. Nick stood behind him, trying to look relaxed with his arms folded.

'Wait a moment, sir. I've seen her do this before. She's thinking.'

The superintendent grunted.

'Outside the theatre, while I waited for Nick. A tall … my height …' I turned to Thomson. 'Five foot six. Female. Red curly hair.' I stroked my finger across my chest just above my heart. 'Down to here. Slim. Around 45 to 50. Smoker. Green leather jacket. Wears that awful perfume – Charlie.' I licked my bottom lip and bit down on it, picturing the moment I'd seen Nick and moved away from the spot where I'd waited with apprehension. 'Nick arrived. She walked across the road … there's a Greek takeaway …'

Thomson wrote in his notebook and nodded. 'I know the one you mean. This is particularly good observation, Morton. You've got a photographic memory. Big help.'

He held up the buff folder. 'I'm fairly sure I know who this woman could be – based on the threat against your life. In here …'

Frank Jarvis appeared in the doorway and Thomson stopped. 'Anything?'

Jarvis looked grave and tired as always. He too was dressed in jeans but still wore his shirt from earlier and a sports jacket. Nick stood aside to let our senior officer approach me. 'How are you feeling?' He was the third person to ask me the question but the first person to wait for my reply.

'OK. Confused.' I gingerly felt the dressing on my waist. It was thick and the sticky plaster pulled at my skin. I realised for the first time I was completely naked beneath the hospital gown and slowly shifted my body further beneath the sheet and blanket. 'Sore.'

'I'd add lucky to that list.' He spoke more to the superintendent and Nick than to me. 'I've just seen the X-rays.'

He held up a large envelope and extracted a black and white X-ray. 'This is our copy,' he said to Thomson and held it high up to the light above my bed. All three men examined it. I sat forwards trying to understand the image, pushing Jarvis slightly so that I could see better. It looked faintly obscene and I wasn't at all pleased to see my inner self displayed for them all to examine.

Jarvis pointed to a shape in my pelvis and a small incision mark. 'You can clearly see the wound is centimetres from her left kidney. I think the knife was aimed at the kidney area. This was attempted murder without a doubt.'

'Nick, you saved my life.' Thomson, Jarvis and I stared at him and he joined me again and sat on the bed, carefully avoiding the area which was bandaged. 'She was standing next to me. I saw you and I stepped forwards. That's when I felt something like a sting in my side.' I breathed in and then exhaled slowly through O-shaped lips.

'Has she ID'd her yet?' Jarvis asked Thomson, who opened the folder and scattered six colour photographs on the blanket in front of me. 'Recognise any of these women, Janice?'

I heard the urgency in his voice. If they had their suspicions, then Thomson probably had officers waiting close by with a warrant to search premises where the red-headed woman lived or worked. My eyes swiftly studied the photographs and I gathered up three of them – wrong age and wrong shape of head. I passed them back to Thomson who took them from me without a word.

My fingers tapped another two photos. It was obvious their hair colour was fake. My charming friend was a natural redhead.

'This one's wearing a wig.' I looked closer at the young woman's features and smiled at Jarvis. 'That's Steph.' His one-sided grin confirmed my statement.

I discarded the two photographs and Thomson returned them to the folder. He and Jarvis exchanged glances but didn't speak. I held up the remaining photograph of a mug shot of the woman I recognised. Her distinctive features were worth a re-examination. Why had she been so obvious in the crowd, with no attempt to hide herself? Because she hadn't expected me to live?

Thomson opened the folder and from the back removed two more photographs which he added to the bed. Same woman but this time they were surveillance shots of her and in each one she wore the green leather jacket. I locked eyes with Jarvis and nodded slowly.

'It's her. These were taken recently,' I added, and he grinned again, checking with Thomson.

'Two days ago.'

'Well done, love.' Inside, I cringed at Jarvis's slip-up. He never usually said words like 'love'. Would he have said that to a male officer? Of course not.

I expected Thomson to rush off, but even though he was on his feet, he hesitated. 'Have a closer look at her face. Can you see who she's related to?'

Jarvis leaned forward and placed a hand on my bed. Nick was sure he was too close to my wound and politely pointed the fact to him. He swiftly removed it. 'Janice?'

I blinked and focused on the woman's eyes and nose. The nose was sprinkled with freckles and almost confirmed what I'd thought earlier. But it was ridiculous. Thousands of women had red hair and freckles. But not all of them were involved in drug smuggling and attempted murder. This woman must have some connection with drugs if Thomson was leading the investigation.

'Tally twins – mother?' She was too old to be a sister.

Jarvis actually showed his teeth.

Nick wondered what was going on. 'Are you saying this woman is the Tally twins' mother and just happened to turn up tonight with the intention of killing Janice? She didn't know she was going to the theatre until late this afternoon.'

Thomson spoke quickly. 'After you told us what Morton said, we decided there was a chance it was related to the contract out on her life. From what she just told us, I reckon … her name's Red by the way … she must have spotted Janice and then did her best to be sure it was her. We've checked the nearest phone box and taken prints. There's a good possibility Red rang the person we think has the contract and checked if she could do it instead. We'll have confirmation of numbers rung from that box in due course. It was sheer coincidence and opportunism.'

'Who do you think she phoned?'

Jarvis shook his head when Thomson checked with him. 'We'll keep that confidential for now. But there's a good chance the contract may be cancelled after we've spoken to Red.'

I stared at the detective with fresh eyes. While I'd been unconscious, he and probably half the Force had been working on finding the culprit … working with the sketchiest of information. I was impressed. Something else occurred to me. I opened my mouth to speak but closed it. Everything seemed too far-fetched.

'What?' Jarvis spoke sharply. 'Something else?'

I shrugged and shook my head. 'No. It's silly.'

Thomson drew closer to the bed again. He held his police radio and hesitated. 'Doesn't matter. Say it.'

I blew air and groaned when the effort seemed to strain the dressing. 'When Nick called – I knew I didn't have anything decent to wear …'

Nick was startled. 'Bloody hell, Janice. What did that matter …'

Thomson and Jarvis told him to shut up and waited for me to continue.

'I went into town – to Rackhams – and asked the assistant what women wear to the theatre and she helped me find a dress – and the velvet jacket.' I saw Nick raise his eyes and shake his head with sincere despair. 'I paid with my credit card – it has my name on it – Miss Janice Morton. She knew where I was going – the time I'd be there – and what I was wearing.'

Jarvis checked with Thomson for his reaction. 'I'll get Mick Carter over there tomorrow before they open – what was the assistant's name?' I told him. 'OK, Doug?'

Thomson spoke into the personal radio in his hand, relaying my identification of Red and confirming the need for a warrant to enter her home. 'When you have it – tear the place apart. I want that weapon.'

A static voice replied, and we all listened carefully. 'It's just been found. A PC Ray James headed into the city centre and checked all the bins at the bus stops. It was in the one closest to the Number 7 terminus. That bus is on Red's home route. He should have gone off duty two hours ago. But he wouldn't give up.'

Nick grinned and raised his eyebrows at me. I held up my thumb in triumph.

Thomson disappeared, mumbling into his radio. I lay my

head on the pillow. If I'd been given painkillers they were starting to wear off. My side felt sore and uncomfortable.

'Why were you late?' Jarvis demanded an answer from Nick, who unfolded his crossed arms and stood up straight.

'Working, sir. A late arrest – Dennis Parker.' He shifted a little when Jarvis failed to be impressed with the reason. 'If I'd known this one was going to get herself stabbed, I'd have let the bastard go.'

I sensed tension when Jarvis still didn't respond. Nick's excuse sounded valid to me. Jarvis must have let people down for the same reason during his long career.

'Oh, my car.' I suddenly remembered it was parked in the multi-storey near the theatre.

Jarvis looked at Nick. 'You'll need a patrol car to take you – or you can walk there.' He picked up my small handbag soaked with blood, which lay on the hospital chair. 'Janice, give him your keys and Nick'll take it to your house. Maybe pick up some things for you.'

'Mine's in the same multi-storey. I'll move it and then pick up Janice's car. You'll need clothes for tomorrow.'

'What will happen to mine? I know the dress and jacket are ruined …'

'Evidence.' Nick confirmed in a tone that reminded me of the significance of the bloody clothes.

'Yes, they're evidence. Of course, they are. Shame, I liked the dress. It was silk.'

'So did I. I never said, but you looked nice – until you bled all over us both. They'll need my clothes for evidence as well. They've got the jacket.'

Jarvis told me that Mum knew I was in hospital after an incident at the theatre and it was best if she stayed home until I arrived. I appreciated him not encouraging her to join me. The two men would soon leave and even though I hated feeling so vulnerable, I just wanted to sleep.

Jarvis confirmed that a uniformed PC would be outside my room until I left the hospital.

'As soon as you're able to, get your first name taken off the credit card. *J Morton* will do. Any problems getting it changed, let me know.'

He gazed from me to Nick and pursed his lips. 'How long have you two ...?'

Nick's eyes widened. 'We're not ... sir. I asked Janice if she wanted to come to the theatre tonight – my mum cancelled. *Madame Butterfly* is her favourite opera.' He shrugged and flashed me one of his most brilliant smiles and winked. 'WPC Morton is an admirable police officer and we agreed to be friends a long while ago.' I nodded in agreement. 'That's all.'

Jarvis twisted his mouth but seemed satisfied. 'It's none of my business, but that's a good decision.'

'Sorry your evening was ruined, Nick. You'll have to tell me how it ended. I'll never sleep not knowing.'

It was Jarvis who answered. 'It was an opera, yes? She died then. The women always die in operas.'

'Not this woman.' Nick stared straight at me, still covered in my blood, and for the second time in our short careers, gave me a mock salute.

27

Light Bulb

My recovery from the stabbing went easier than I expected. The wound wasn't deep as the knife had had to penetrate the velvet jacket before hitting my flesh. Jarvis agreed I could return to the office and go on light duties. He was the one who gave me the bad news about Red. I'd guessed he was calling me into his office with an update, but I wasn't prepared for the information.

'Sorry, Janice. Superintendent Thomson just confirmed – forensics can't find any fingerprints on the knife – nothing to connect Red with it. She was on that Number 7 bus – we know that – but no one saw her dispose of the knife in the bin. It was wiped clean, but traces confirm it's your blood on the blade.'

'So there's no proof she was the person who stabbed me?' He shook his head and the corners of his mouth turned down with regretful frustration. How many times had we all encountered disappointments like this?

'It doesn't matter how close she stood next to you – unless someone saw her push that knife into your side, then we have nothing. We put out appeals for information from anyone standing outside the theatre between 7.15pm and 8 o'clock, but we barely had confirmation Red was even there. Only two people commented about a tall red-headed woman. The owner of the Greek takeaway confirmed she was in there just before 8 o'clock and bought a kebab.'

'Shame.' It was all I could think of to say. 'At least I know who to look out for in future.'

Jarvis couldn't agree. 'I doubt we'll see her anywhere near you. Thomson's men arrested her for receiving stolen goods – including bottles of perfume. But she's got out of things before. He's happy though.'

That was difficult to believe. Not unless he was kicking puppies or something.

'It was time for her place to be visited and they couldn't justify a search until you provided the perfect opportunity from your description. The team always felt they'd missed something after the boys were arrested – they were right. Twenty grand in notes was concealed behind the wallpaper. Plenty of fingerprints on those.'

'That's good.' At least something positive had come out of the night at the opera. 'What about the Rackhams' assistant, Daphne.'

'She lives two doors away from Red. She didn't deny it. Phone records from the ladieswear department confirmed she'd called Red's number around 3.55pm on that day, just after you paid and left. Still nothing to incriminate either of them. Nothing to put in front of the DPP. All circumstantial.'

'But we know they're up to something,' I offered, feeling disappointed and miserable. Thanks to those two women, I'd missed out on my theatre night with Nick, I no longer had a set of expensive clothes and there was no prosecution in sight. The bra had cost £10, but I didn't have the courage to ask for it back.

When I'd returned to the office after a week's sick leave there was a small package wrapped in newspaper on my desk. It was a cassette recording of *Madame Butterfly* and a little note: *Another time, another place. One fine day, Morton.*

Jarvis fiddled with his fountain pen, twirling it around in his fingers.

'Why did you think you had to buy new clothes to meet up with Nick Watson?'

I wasn't prepared for the question and met his eyes in surprise. 'I didn't know what you wore to the theatre – and Steph wasn't around, so I couldn't ask her. I decided someone at Rackhams could tell me.' I shrugged. 'That's why Nick and I will only ever be friends. I'm not his type, sir. Women he goes out with would know straight away what to wear – go home, choose from two or three possibles and be out of the house in half an hour.' I was glum at the thought of my own shortcomings.

Jarvis lay the pen on the desk and shrugged. 'Women. No man on earth will ever understand you lot. Any man in this station would be proud to be seen out with you. Remember that. Nick wouldn't have cared what you wore, Janice. Honestly, you could have turned up wearing nothing at all and he'd have been happy.'

I coughed and spluttered and when he realised what he'd said, Jarvis's face reddened. 'Oh, you know what I mean. Get out of here, WPC Morton. And if there is a next time with that Casanova, make sure you're the one who's twenty minutes late.'

It was a shame no one could be charged with my attempted murder, but every police officer was outraged at the unfairness of the outcome. When I thought about Jarvis's last words, I smiled often. It helped – just a little.

I was due time off before going onto six days of afternoon shifts. Things were never quiet in the CID room but there wasn't anything I could help with, so Inspector Paulson called me for an eight-hour shift on the front desk, sorting out problems with the general public.

For my attachment to CID I still had to wear uniform and if other bobbies phoned in sick or were away on training courses, I was often pulled out of the office to cover more normal duties. I'd never minded doing that before life in the CID office, but it was difficult dealing with members of the public turning up at the front desk with lost property. Everything was recorded in the book, from one cigarette in an otherwise empty packet to a dirty plastic comb.

'Never let anyone see you don't care, Morton,' Paulson advised when I held the comb with two fingers hovering over the bin. 'It'll be on the front page of the local paper and it'll be the one time they even spell your name right.'

I clocked off my shift at 10pm the moment the night shift stomped through the door in heavy-duty boots. Dead tired, I was ready to sleep for two days but I needed to tidy my desk in CID before I left the station. One overhead strip light lit up part of the deserted office and perversely I was wide awake. With the desk cleared I decided there were two days to catch up on sleep and looked through Linda's file while it was quiet.

I'd updated the paperwork after my visit with Carter to speak to Ray Bolton. There was no chance that Len Ward had been in the Edgington area on the night Linda disappeared. Lickey Hills was miles away and it was obvious to me he'd made the story up after Jarvis had interviewed him about a 'Linda'. The one-page report had been hastily typed after a day's work so I hadn't had a chance to re-read other notes.

With the main lights muted I read by the desk lamp, hoping the ambience would lull me into tiredness. Linda's file, what there was of it, was hardly a Robert Harris thriller.

My statement, written up by WPC Alison Harper, filled almost a page. It was a faithful report of everything I'd said – leaving out the cheeky bits aimed at Jarvis. Lonnie's was just repetitions of 'No, I did not' or 'No, that never happened' to every question asked of him. It was uncomfortable to read how Jarvis tried twisting Lonnie's responses when asked, 'Do you like your wife's sister?' and 'Do you think she's pretty?'

Shaking my head as usual when I read through Lonnie's statement, I was appalled by CID's determination to obtain his confession to killing Linda and hiding her body. I wanted to know the truth about her disappearance, but I could never believe Lonnie would harm her. Tiredness started to kick in and I rubbed my eyes and yawned, willing something to leap out of the page and hit me afresh.

Other statements from neighbours who barely knew Linda were short and unhelpful. It was time to leave for home, so I quickly photocopied the fresh report on Ray Bolton before I left.

The drive home was quick and easy with so little traffic on the dark, empty streets. I crept upstairs with hot tea in a clean mug and a decent amount of milk rather than the dribble left in the bottle by selfish work colleagues. I was reaching the point on shift where I would start drinking black coffee rather than search around for milk which always ran out before I reached the office.

I tried crunching a slice of toast quietly and slipped off my black leather shoes as I sat on the edge of my bed, ready to fall back on the duvet and descend into another world. Still awake, I lay the photocopied sheets next to me and pinged my clip-on tie to free up my top button. It was a wonderful relief to change into clean, freshly ironed pyjamas.

Sipping the tea and covered by the duvet I sat up with the pillow propped at the back of my head. Wide awake again now, I wasn't going to sleep until mid-morning. The shift patterns were a nightmare. I mused over my memories of Linda's last day and night, trying to piece together a vague puzzle with a missing picture.

Lonnie loved Linda like she was his own sister or even a daughter. He'd said so in the interview with Jarvis and I believed him. His own family lived in Ireland and he had no relatives in England. He was adamant he'd never do anything to destroy what he had with Hazel and Rosie – and no, he never minded Linda coming to stay. She was no trouble.

For the millionth time I wished I had never seen the door in the fence and swapped secrets with Linda. In my mind I replayed the summer's day when we'd played with her Sindy dolls in my garden. In the orchard I'd regretted telling her about the door in exchange for what I'd considered to be a poor swap. What did it matter if Linda was Hazel's sister – or Hazel's daughter? Did it matter …?

I knew there was something wrong with the statements. I knew them all by heart, and I was certain something important was missing in each of them. Reading them again I felt my heart burst out of my chest and my brain switch on like an Edison light bulb.

I sifted through the photocopied photographs and the Kodak ones Hazel had let me keep. There was Linda's school photo – at least a year out of date; Linda in her garden next door holding up a Sindy doll to the camera with a serious expression on her pink face; Hazel and Lonnie sitting on the grass in front of the white-painted fence, laughing at whoever was taking the photo. And then there were official photos of our gardens, especially

Lonnie's freshly dug vegetable patch and the orchard, including the discarded peach with the bite taken out of it.

It was too dark behind the drawn curtains to see brunette Sindy where I'd placed her against the window frame, looking out over the orchard. The once-shiny black mac was now a dull, sun-faded matt grey at the front. A few years ago, I'd straightened her arm so that she didn't wave any more. It didn't seem fair to leave her in a painful pose. The synthetic hair was flattened at the front where her forehead pressed against the glass.

There was nothing in Jarvis's notes, comments after the interviews or summing-up reports to suggest that Hazel was Linda's mother. It was like being hit by a lightning bolt. The stupid secret had stayed a secret. I hadn't said anything. Why would I? I was nine years old; but none of the adults had said anything either!

There was a newspaper cutting in the file with a photo of Mr and Mrs Bateman and Hazel next to an article saying how much they all missed Linda and begged her to come home or for someone to come forward with information. Yet none of them could have mentioned to Jarvis that Linda was Hazel's daughter – not her sister.

Chills ran down my spine like a shower of ice cubes in tiny boots. Why hadn't Jarvis known the truth about Linda? In missing persons' investigations, we always checked the birth certificate to verify that the parents really were the right people to deal with. There was no report of any such check back in 1964.

Had Jarvis been so convinced of Lonnie's guilt he expected to do the routine checks after his arrest? Then the expensive lawyer had shown up with all his questions to Jarvis and the charges against Lonnie were quickly dropped due to the lack – total lack – of any evidence.

Wide awake, I scrambled out of bed, knocking the empty mug on the floor, and found a pen. I scribbled over the crumpled pages writing down my thoughts. Who was the solicitor?

It was a Mr Arthur Thornton-Lea from Thornton-Lea & Paige, The Strand, London. Tomorrow I would check him out in the Yellow Pages and head down to The Strand to speak to him. Why on earth would someone like him turn up at a small police station in Edgington, Birmingham? There was a chance he'd known about the case from the newspapers and there were TV appeals at the time, but why defend Lonnie? At the time, he was a butcher's apprentice earning just enough money to pay the bills.

What had interested Thornton-Lea so much he'd travelled from London to intervene for Lonnie? Solicitors never worked for free. Who had paid his fee? Hazel's mum and dad hadn't been poor, but I couldn't see them having contacts like Thornton-Lea.

My head nodded, despite the excitement of a possible new lead. Hopefully, it wouldn't end by crashing into a brick wall like it had with Ray Bolton. Somehow, I was sure the solicitor held the key to opening another door leading to Linda.

The spark was lit and settling back against the pillow I weighed things up in my head. Before I saw Thornton-Lea I needed to speak to Hazel. She probably had no idea I knew she was Linda's mother – Linda had told me in confidence. It was our secret because I'd had no idea what she was talking about. I was too young to understand how Hazel could be Linda's sister and her mother at the same time. The enlightenment was enough to send me sound asleep, clutching the photo of Linda and me playing in her garden.

By 9.30am I had tracked down Thornton-Lea & Paige through Directory Enquiries and learned that Arthur was away on holiday. I arranged an appointment with him two days after his return – Tuesday 19th May.

Hazel was an easier target to pin down. I waited until Rosie left for school, knowing Lonnie started early at the butcher's shop. He managed it now the owner had retired and hoped one day to buy it from him.

I didn't want to look too officious with Hazel by writing notes while she talked, so I hoped she'd let me use my cassette recorder to record everything she said to me. I found a pack of blank cassettes I could use. My days of recording the Sunday afternoon pop chart, waiting for the final countdown to the week's Number One, were over.

I had a strong feeling I was getting closer to finding out the answer to a question that had never been asked in the investigation. It wasn't asked because no one realised there was a question to ask.

Who was Linda's father?

It was a chilly spring day, so I ran upstairs for my lilac cardigan to wear. Mum met me on the landing. She carried her plastic washing basket and I could see my blue shirt from yesterday sitting on the top.

'Janice,' she beamed at me as though we hadn't met for months. It was partially true as we both had our own lives now. She saw David at weekends and still worked in the school kitchen during term time.

'Hi, Mum.' I kissed her in excited haste. 'I'm just popping next door to see Hazel. I want to ask her about Linda … I'll cook us something nice for lunch when you get home …'

Mum stubbornly refused to step aside to allow my whirlwind to pass. 'No need, love. I made a shepherd's pie yesterday, so we'll have that with some gravy and carrots.' She spoke in a rush, anticipating me running away from her. I guessed she hadn't finished. 'What do you want to do for your birthday? You can have a little party here or we can have a meal out with your friends. I'll pay for us all. It's up to you.'

My body slumped as though she'd punched me in the stomach, and I breathed out heavily. My birthday – my 21st birthday. I hadn't forgotten completely. We'd talked about it a while ago and I decided I just wanted a meal out with Mum, maybe David, maybe Pat as well. If Rob ever phoned me, I wanted to ask him to join us and warn the others not to mention my job. Fat chance of Pat keeping her mouth shut …

'A meal out.' Simple decision and now I could escape. 'The Berni Inn – I like it there and so does Pat. Ask David if he wants to join a table full of women. Oh, can you book a table for us – and a taxi so we can have wine?'

'Great. I'll do that. I thought you'd given up trying to find Linda.'

Mum tried to kiss me across the loaded washing basket, and I saw her smile with relief. Was I such a difficult person? Had she dreaded bringing up the subject? She'd seemed anxious so hopefully my suggestions helped her relax. I could be such a selfish bitch sometimes – most of the time if I was honest. I quickly decided to make sure we both had something nice to wear and make the evening special – a bottle of Asti Spumante even.

It was only when I knocked on Hazel's front door that I realised my 21st birthday was 19th May – the day I planned to be in London to meet Thornton-Lea. Maybe Mum wouldn't mind if we ate late.

'Hazel, I was wondering if we could have a chat.' Before she could answer I was over her threshold clutching the compact cassette recorder.

28

Hazel's Story

I let Hazel talk without interruption. She still wore her rose-patterned Brentford Nylons dressing gown when I swept into her living room and plugged in the recorder. Looking dazed but resigned she nodded when I explained what I wanted to do – what I wanted to hear – and sat down on the plumped-up sofa.

Holding the mug of tea I'd made for her in one hand, she felt under the sofa with the other until she dragged out a family photograph album. It lay unopened beside her while she talked, and I left it there as I held the microphone in position. It was old and likely to topple over and crash onto the coffee table if I let it go.

'I should have known Linda would tell you I wasn't really her sister. She adored you and would have told you every secret she knew if it meant getting closer to you.'

'I don't know why. We didn't see each other very often – just a few weeks a year in the school holidays.'

'Don't forget she lived with my mum and dad for the rest of the time – old people. They were kind and gave her everything they thought she would like. But they were old-fashioned and when she wasn't at school she didn't know what to say to them. Stayed in her bedroom reading or playing with her dolls.'

'She must have had friends from school.' That wasn't true. According to Jarvis's file Linda's headmistress said the girl was a loner – unable to fit in with the other children. Classes were busy and the teachers didn't have time to spend on a quiet, withdrawn child.

Hazel sighed and moved her mouth into a droopy line, like sadness drawn by an infant. 'She only wanted *you* as a friend. The plan was for you to join her at senior school – but then Mum and Dad decided it would be too expensive for her to go to grammar school.'

'Oh.'

What else could I say? Images of Linda at my grammar school flashed through my head: seeing her in the corridor between lessons or, worse, at lunchtimes; seeing me reject her and hiding from her.

'Will you tell me about her father, Hazel? I think it could be important in trying to find … trying to find out what happened. The police didn't suspect her real father could have taken her away because they never knew about him.'

That shook Hazel out of her miserable thoughts. The idea couldn't have occurred to her. That was strange.

'There's no way that happened.'

'Why are you so certain?'

I'd lost her again. With languid fingers she stroked the glossy album cover; the opaque plastic was cracked and peeling away from the pink fabric and absentmindedly she tried to smooth out the creases.

'I was really pretty when I was 16. I had long blonde hair right down to my waist. It was a real golden colour, thick and wavy. But then Mum and I went to see *Roman Holiday* at the Odeon and that was it. Audrey Hepburn was the prettiest woman I'd ever seen.

My friend Gina's mum was a hairdresser and I asked her to make me look like Audrey – I even told people my name was Audrey. Mum went mad when she saw my short hair – but it was nothing to how mad she was when I dyed it black.'

Hazel laughed at the memory as she peeled off the cracked plastic, secreting the sharp pieces in the palm of her hand.

'I'll show you the photos in a minute. Dad took a few – he didn't seem as mad as Mum. I didn't look like a silly doll anymore – much more grown-up. He soon changed his mind though when he saw the lads looking at me.

'He tried keeping me at home – curfew he called it. I had to go home straight after school and not mess about with the other kids – especially boys. Trouble was I could twist him around my little finger – a few tears and some pouting and he was on my side.'

'Was it one of the boys from school?'

Hazel snorted. 'Not likely. We were fifteen. You won't remember the Teddy Boys, Janice. They were so good-looking – well, some of them.'

'One in particular?'

'After the haircut, I got noticed by the older lads who hung around the coffee bar before it closed for good. They'd buy me coffee and I felt more grown-up with them – I even smoked cigarettes if they were offered. Dad could smell them on my clothes, but I didn't care. I was an only child and hated living at home. So boring.

'They gave up with the curfew and in the end were just pleased I went home at all; I was never that late – where could I go anyway? Apart from one place and that was no good once it got dark and cold.'

An unwelcome chill fingered its way up my spine and into my scalp.

'The orchard.'

Hazel emerged from her self-imposed misery, becoming alert and smiling at some of her memories. I was trained to wait during interviews when a confession was about to be made: 'Let them talk.' So I let Hazel talk.

'You must be a good policewoman, Janice.' She tilted her head in respect and placed the mug on the carpet, ignoring the impression it made in the thick paisley-patterned wool.

'It was the perfect place to have some privacy. Mr Taylor always had his dinner between 7 and 8 o'clock and hardly ever went back out to look at the orchard again. Me and Keith would creep in through a gap in the fence. He'd made it himself when he was a kid.

'I was a push-over. I realised that when I was older and I met Lonnie. But when I was fifteen, I was madly in love with Keith – and he was in love with me. In the caff we'd started sitting on our own more and more. He didn't care if his mates laughed when we held hands.'

For a moment I lost concentration and thought of Rob – was he my first love?

Hazel continued in a dreamy voice. 'At first we just kissed – as you do at that age. Keith was older but he was only 17. Handsome. Tall with sandy hair – like Tommy Steele.

'It never bothered me when we finally did it.' She glanced over at me but, really, did she think I didn't know what she meant? 'It just seemed right. I was sure we'd get married. We were meant to be together – I was certain of it. I didn't even care when I discovered I was pregnant.'

'What did your mum and dad say?'

'Janice, they went ballistic. Dad kept shouting, "I'll kill him," so I wouldn't tell them about Keith until he promised to calm down and let us get married. You had to have your parents' permission back then.'

She paused, shaking a little, and then walked over to the low sideboard where she lit a cigarette; she sat down with a china ashtray on her lap. This was a different Hazel from the other day. The mug with its nearly spilt dregs still lay on the carpet and she puffed at the cigarette, enjoying it while she continued with her story.

'Then the dream turned into a nightmare. Dad and Mum forced me to go with them around to Keith's parents and tell them what had happened. They were furious. Keith was supposed to go to university, study engineering and have a different life to theirs – not get married before he was even out of his teens.

'I was shocked from all the shouting. My dad and Keith's dad started threatening each other but the two mums calmed things down. In the end there was an agreement. They gave me £500 not to say anything about Keith and never to let anyone know about the baby.

'Dad insisted I have Linda adopted as soon as she was born but Mum was brought up a Catholic and she stood up to him. That was how we agreed to keep the baby and tell everyone it was hers. I was heartbroken about Keith – he disappeared before I had the baby and I never saw him again. I finished school and stayed at home, not caring about anything. When Linda was born, I was glad to see her every day. You'll know what I mean when you have a child.'

I forced myself to concentrate and not daydream about playing Happy Families with Rob.

'Did you tell Lonnie when you met him?'

Hazel looked around her living room's new and modern furniture with glowing pride on her face.

'No. I didn't need to. Linda was five when Lonnie and I met. We fell for each other straight away – but he was nothing like Keith. He's got a good head on his shoulders and he's so kind. This is his house. He rented it when he moved here from Dublin. His parents gave him the money to live for six months until he found a job on a building site. He met Stan Tarrant on his first day wandering around the shops and decided to take the butchering job.

'We decided not to get married – he was a bit of a hippy and didn't believe in marriage. But I never doubted he'd look after me. He started apprenticing for the butcher and I worked in the chemist next door – learning the pharmacy side when there was time. We were happy – we still are.'

Yet Hazel hadn't looked happy when I ate sandwiches and cake with her and Rosie.

'You all agreed to keep the secret about Linda and Keith from Lonnie?'

'There didn't seem to be any need. I heard Keith went away to Spain before he finished university. I never saw him again. He'd never wanted to see Linda – or me. Mum and Dad told me to wait until I married Lonnie and then tell him the truth. While we weren't married it was safer no one knew.'

'It seems strange no one knew the truth.'

'Nearly everyone in this street has their own secrets, Janice. We all know when to keep them locked away – if someone tells my secret then I might just tell about theirs.' Her blue eyes shone with a peculiar malice. 'There was more than one kid living around here whose dad wasn't the man living in the house.'

'Oh.'

'When Linda went missing, Keith's parents were the first people I tried to contact. But they weren't around. It was the summer holidays and they were away. That's why I didn't say anything to the police. After the police moved on to other things and she was never found I finally told Lonnie the truth. I loved Rosie and so did he, but I knew I could move back in with Mum and Dad if he threw me out.'

'He understood?'

She threw the burned-out cigarette end in the ashtray and lay that on the floor next to the mug.

'His family have their own secrets. He's the eldest of eight and two of his sisters ended up in a convent for unmarried mothers. The only thing he asked was for me to say *Yes* to marrying him. It was the best day of my life – even without Linda. Registry Office in town. I finally felt safe. But lately, I see so much of her in Rosie.' I nodded in agreement. 'Life seems to be slipping away … and I can't sleep wondering where she could be.'

I wasn't surprised. Hazel must have suppressed so much after her so-called sister disappeared. It would surface eventually. With her story told, I saw a small difference in her – less strained and fidgety.

'Do you think you can find her? Or find out what happened?'

'I think I'm getting closer. I still need to speak to one more person. Do you know who engaged the solicitor for Lonnie when he was taken in for questioning?'

Hazel shook her head, gathered up the mug and ashtray and in the kitchen I heard her refill the kettle.

'No idea,' she called. 'I'll make us another cup of tea. Have a look through the photos.'

I reached to turn off the tape recorder and paused. I still needed one more thing.

'Hazel,' I called back, 'you didn't tell me Keith's surname.'

'Didn't I?' She appeared in the doorway, swirling water around in the tea pot. 'Taylor. Keith Taylor. He's the son of the orchard's owners. They were all in Spain when Linda went missing.'

I stabbed at the OFF button on the recorder. I had as much as I needed to fill in most of the gaps and wasn't as convinced as Hazel that the Taylor family had nothing to do with the disappearance. I'd think about that later.

If Keith hadn't finished his university degree but had moved abroad, it didn't seem likely he could afford a top-class solicitor's fees. It was another blow to my attempts to solve this mystery.

While Hazel rattled teacups and spoons I flicked through the album, looking at photographs of myself with Linda. There were quite a few of them over a two-year period. Clasping a hand over my mouth I struggled to force back the vomit threatening to spill out onto the pages.

There we were, Linda and me. In every photograph, I saw again what I had never noticed when we played together. While I pranced around for the camera, Linda was always looking at me with a fond expression of pure love. She had really loved me as her friend. And I could barely stand her.

Not only that, but I had also betrayed her trust when I abandoned her in the orchard. I'd perverted the course of the investigation by not telling Jarvis that Linda was Hazel's daughter so he could question her real father. And even though I had been determined to find her when I joined the police force, I'd let myself be distracted by thinking about Rob and barely looked at the file.

If she had been held against her will for all these years, it was all my fault.

I prayed my silent prayer: please let me find her and make it up to her.

29

Lonnie's Story

Absorbed with the photo album I was only partially aware of the front door opening and closing. I'd assumed the faint clunk came from the letterbox, so it was a big surprise to see Lonnie walking into the living room with a paper-wrapped parcel in his hand. He was heading for the kitchen and stopped halfway when he realised I was there.

'Oh my God, it's you, Janice. I didn't expect to see you here at this time of the morning.'

I'd heard his lilting voice occasionally, floating over the hedge when he was in his garden. We'd spoken a few times in passing but I'd never stopped to chat with him for long. My reasons were the same as with my avoidance of Hazel. What was there for me to say to either of them?

After the pub bombings and the backlash against the Irish, I'd told mum to let me know if anything happened to Lonnie – or the family. I wasn't sure what I could do, but apparently it had made them feel better. When his shop window was smashed, I told him to report it to the police, but he never did. Everyone liked Lonnie and a collection was made by the locals to help pay for its replacement.

Hazel appeared, wiping her hands on a fresh tea towel, and took the package from him. 'Those the chops?' She pecked him on the cheek. Her eyes were bright with tears, but she looked very pretty.

Lonnie was startled, as though she'd asked him if was carrying a dead sheep, surprised he was holding anything at all.

'Yes,' he smiled with relief, before turning back to me. I was on my feet by this time – desperate to leave. 'I thought I'd better bring them home to you. There's been a ferocious run on lamb this morning. Anyone would think it was spring or something.'

I was mumbling words like 'Nice to see you ...' and 'I'd better be going ...' but I lingered where I stood, realising I had questions for Lonnie if he had time to answer them. He spotted the open photo album, filled with garish colour photos of me and Linda grinning at his camera.

'I've a half hour if you've still time to stop for a bit, Janice. I heard you were stabbed. How are you now? Did they catch the person who did it?'

'Not yet. They found the knife with my blood on it – but no fingerprints. I need to put it behind me – but I'm on light duties for the next month.'

He joined me and we both sat on the sofa. Hazel stayed in the kitchen, but all was quiet, so I knew she was listening. The smell of cigarette smoke wafted from the doorway and with a glance over his shoulder, Lonnie wrinkled his nose with irritation.

'After Linda disappeared, I couldn't enjoy smoking any more. It didn't seem right when we were so miserable. That's when she ...' He nodded towards the kitchen. '... took it up. But now I can't stand the smell of it. But at least I know where she is when I'm looking for her.'

If he was trying to joke, he didn't smile.

I replaced the album on my knees but left it lying there, untouched. 'D'ye remember those times, Janice?' He spoke softly and kindly, his southern Irish accent still strong. Of course, from Lonnie's point of view I was also an injured party – losing my best friend and never knowing what had happened to her.

Nodding, I closed the album, not wanting to see myself strutting around the garden with Linda following me like a puppy. 'Do you? I mean – us playing in the garden – yours, I mean. You made the step for us – so we didn't have to …'

'Never forgotten it,' Lonnie spoke quietly again. His shyness reminded me of Rosie, and I hoped she had his kind nature. 'Until Linda disappeared, I'd never been happier than watching the two of you acting the giddy goat – the pair of you chattering on to those daft dolls.'

It was a nice memory but again, he didn't smile and just sat staring at his shoes. He still wore his white overalls from the shop. 'Did you ever think I had anything to do with her going missing?'

The question hit me like a football glancing off my head. 'No. Why would I?'

It had never occurred to me that Lonnie and Hazel would have expected me to suspect them of being involved with Linda's disappearance. I hadn't wanted Linda as a friend – perhaps they hadn't wanted her in their lives either. What nonsense! Had we all spent these years feeling guilty? But then I knew the truth about part of what happened that night. I was guilty.

The tension in Lonnie's thin body seeped away as he processed my question. 'Sure, why would you?' He glanced towards the kitchen and I saw Hazel in the doorway, stubbing her cigarette in the glass ashtray. She smiled at him with an 'I told you so' look on her face.

'Lonnie, when you were at the police station, how did you manage to get hold of the solicitor …?' I pretended I didn't know his name.

He shook his head, which I noticed still had its thick covering of curls, greyer now. 'No idea. I wasn't too surprised when I was taken away by that arrogant inspector – Jarvis ... piece of work he was. Even in the car he was trying to get me to say I knew where Linda had gone. I told him if I knew where she was, she'd be upstairs in her bedroom for the rest of her life for scaring the wits out of us.'

That sounded very much like what I'd read in the file. Could I blame Jarvis? If Lonnie was the abductor or murderer then the sooner he told everyone where Linda was hidden the better.

'Sure, after half an hour being questioned, I was certain the man was after tearing into me with his fists. And I knew the other officers in the room would have looked in the opposite direction and denied anything happened other than me taking a hard tumble onto the floor.'

Anyone else would have spoken more bitterly – not Lonnie. He must have seen the confounded expression on my face and twisted the side of his mouth into a half smile. 'I've had plenty of time to think about it, Janice – and honestly, if I'd been one of them and there was half a chance they had someone who could tell them where that little girl had gone – I'd have done the same.'

'Then the solicitor turned up ...?'

'No idea where he came from. I met him for all of five minutes when he confirmed Linda was Hazel's sister, I was Hazel's fella and we'd both been in bed asleep all night. Then he asked Jarvis and his mafia what evidence they had to hold me any longer. Big silence and shuffling of papers on the table, but not a thing forthcoming. "In that case, Detective Inspector, I shall leave with my client," he said and next thing I knew he was gone and I was waiting for a Black Maria to take me home.'

I could only imagine what Jarvis would have thought of that from a posh lawyer who had clearly never met Lonnie before in his life. 'So you left?'

'I did – with mixed feelings. I didn't want to be there as a suspect – but I wanted to be a part of the search for Linda. She must have been scared witless. But I could tell Jarvis didn't really think I had anything to do with her going missing – and he didn't want me anywhere near them, finding out they hadn't a clue where she'd gone.'

'I'm trying to find out what happened,' I said and hoped my shaky voice sounded full of emotion rather than trying to mask a guilty conscience. One day I needed to tell both Hazel and Lonnie about the night in the orchard, but I was nowhere near reaching the stage of showing that kind of courage.

Without speaking we both stood, and Lonnie glanced at his watch. Hazel appeared with a mug of coffee for him and he drank it down in two gulps.

The couple were still in love with each other, despite the testing challenge of Linda's true father and her disappearance. I'd never considered Lonnie as a suspect. How could I when my memory of him was never tarnished by unacceptable behaviour? He'd been a friendly but distant adult. His kind action of placing the box near the fence for Linda to play in my garden was probably because he wanted her out of his way while he worked on his vegetable patch.

He'd looked simply charming standing in the living room, holding the paper-wrapped lamb chops and looking bewildered when he saw me. He hadn't flinched like a man guilty of hiding a dreadful secret. It was cathartic for him to relate the events of his arrest and release as a suspect. His short story had told me so much about what I needed to know.

Someone had contacted the London solicitor to sort things out for Lonnie. A solicitor who wouldn't be intimidated by a detective like Jarvis, and eager to make a name for himself with an arrest. There could only be one possible source, but I couldn't share my thoughts just yet.

Hazel took the mug from Lonnie and squeezed his arm. 'Good. I'm glad it's you, Janice. I like seeing the old Sindy doll looking at me from your window. Sometimes, I like to think it's Linda, watching over us. You'll let us know … whatever you find … won't you?'

'Of course,' I whispered and left them in the room staring after me.

30

Taylors Villa

Jarvis was on a week's holiday with his family and I really needed to share my notes with him after my meeting with Hazel. I'd left her looking like a changed woman, her skin smoother and her face less tense after reliving her time with Keith Taylor and initially hiding Linda's birth from Lonnie. It hadn't brought Linda back, but I had promised her and Lonnie that we were closer to finding out the truth.

I had no idea how to track the Taylors in Spain. Hazel couldn't remember which part of the country they were in when she found out they were on holiday.

The orchard behind our houses had been sold in 1970 and after the land had been left in ruin for two years, a developer had built houses on it. Now, when I looked out of my bedroom window, no trace of any apple trees existed. Instead they were replaced by the red-tiled roofs of featureless homes.

I missed Detective Superintendent Jarvis when I stepped into his empty office after my two-day break. His desk was empty of files and paperwork, usually piled messily while he worked around them, jotting notes with his fountain pen.

It was tempting to nosey around his personal effects placed on the window ledge behind him. I knew the photos were of his three children at different ages, but I'd always been intrigued by the more glamorous picture of him shoved behind the other frames.

He looked smart in a black suit and black bow tie, half leaning towards his wife who wore a long emerald green gown and jewelled necklace. Her white-blonde hair was swept upwards into a French knot and her dazzling smile showed her pride in Jarvis, even though he'd grown a dreadful moustache.

Drawing closer to the window as though interested in the view outside I chuckled when I took a closer look at Mrs Jarvis. I knew her. I'd met her, sitting in our living room taking down notes in her pocketbook. Jarvis had married Alison Harper and from the photographs it was a happy marriage. Good for him, I thought.

Police officers needed a stable home life with a partner who understood the pressures of the job and the erratic hours, especially in CID. Not many officers, male or female, realised this and messed up their home lives with silly affairs. I was better off being single for the time being.

There was a clean mark on the dusty shelf and even an inexperienced detective like me could replace the frame without anyone knowing it had been moved and examined. I was tempted to wipe it of fingerprints and started to smile at my foolishness when something about the people sitting at the table in the background froze my hand on the frame.

After-dinner debris of discarded dessert dishes and half-empty glasses were scattered on the white tablecloth in front of two men talking to each other. The other two vacant chairs must have been occupied by their wives. The photo could only have been around three years old. Jarvis hadn't had a moustache during my time at the station.

I replaced the framed photo having given up on an irritating niggle at the back of my mind. The man sitting on the right of the table had turned his head towards the camera as the photo was snapped. He was frowning and the small mouth hidden in his bushy beard was taut and annoyed. It was his hairstyle that had caught my attention. Grey streaks ran through the dark brown layering of an expensive haircut. He looked familiar but he wasn't wearing a uniform and for the moment I couldn't recall where I had seen him before.

None of my snooping though was helping me find the Taylors' whereabouts in Spain. I needed to speak to another detective for advice on how to track them down and at least find an address.

Fortunately for me, Mick Carter was on duty and I caught him sitting back in his swivel chair, feet on the desk, reading the local paper.

'Cup of tea, Mick?'

Carter frowned at me over his paper and waved his mug in the air. 'What are you after?'

'Some advice – if you've got time.'

He swung his legs off the desk, stuck his leg out and with his foot dragged a nearby chair closer to his desk and laid the paper on it.

'Sit down, Miss Know It All. Watch and learn.'

My cheeks flamed with indignation and embarrassment. Not to call me WPC was an insult but to suggest I was being cocky was worse than any curt reprimand.

DC Mick Carter was well respected in the department despite his failure to progress upward to sergeant or inspector. To me, though, he'd always been grumpy and morose until the night he spent two hours making enquiries about Len Ward's cellmate. He was still going through AA and I'd heard from other detectives he'd been a difficult person when he drank. I wasn't sure whether a grumpy Carter was better than the man I knew.

I sat as close to him as I could bear. He always wore too much cologne and today it was Brut. Dare I suggest he try Paco Rabanne?

He turned over pages of the newspaper, pointing to articles and photographs.

'Villain and villain's wife.' The photo on the Anniversaries page was of a happy couple grinning at the camera with an expensive flower display framing the background. The man wore a dinner jacket that strained across his broad chest. His wife was over-dressed in a sparkly purple maxi dress with a diamond necklace, bracelet and earrings. She wore her jet-black hair piled on top of her head and with her dark suntan she sort of looked like Elizabeth Taylor.

Carter jabbed a finger at each of them in turn. 'He's claiming social and she works in the Bingo Hall.' He read a sentence from the article: '*Glynn and Vanessa Evans celebrated their Silver Wedding at The Moor Hall Hotel on Saturday ... with a hundred friends and family enjoying a 3-course meal and dancing to a live band ...*' He turned his flushed face towards me and waited expectantly.

My mouth opened and closed. I was expected to comment but I'd no idea who the Evans couple were – villains or not.

He frowned at my ineptitude. 'How did they afford a big posh do at the Moor Hall on a Saturday night – and who were the so-called one hundred friends and family?'

'They've been saving up?' I ventured.

'Their latest Jag cost a few grand and Moor Hall charges twenty-five quid a head for a dinner like that – that's a lot of savings on the money they bring in.'

My shoulders slumped. 'We should apply for access to their bank accounts?' I offered with a weak, hesitant smile.

'Already have – and a copy of the guest list is being

picked up from the hotel as we speak. The money had to come from somewhere and it could be legit. Or it might be from the run of Post Office robberies we've had.'

I leaned over the paper with more interest. 'I see what you're doing.' I flipped the page. 'What about him?' A deeply sun-tanned pensioner posed with a much younger woman wearing a smart white jacket, smiling at an elderly lady in a wheelchair. The pensioner looked familiar.

'What did you want to see me about, Janice?' My eyes flicked to the photo expectantly, but Carter folded the newspaper in half and shoved it to the corner of his desk. 'That's Hughie Green visiting a Cypress Care Home last week. Lesson over – what is it you want to know?'

I learned more from Mick Carter in twenty minutes than from hours poring over my training manuals. He was a mine of information and I understood why Jarvis used him as his right-hand man on most of his jobs. He was one of the old-school CID: knew everything and got results far quicker than the newer, qualified detective sergeants or DIs.

Checking Linda's file we found the telephone number that had been used to contact the Taylors at their Spanish villa after Linda disappeared. Carter typed it into the police computer for overseas addresses and we both watched the flickering screen for nearly ten minutes before an address appeared. Malaga. The villa was in Malaga.

'It doesn't mean they're still living there now. They could have moved – but I doubt it.'

'Why? New villas and hotels are being built all the time in Spain. Check with Judith Chalmers if you don't believe me.'

Carter ignored my suggestion. He'd probably never watched *Wish You Were Here* in his life.

'There's your reason. The Taylors fit a profile. Small-time business sold for far more money than they ever expected. Back in the 60s a lot of Brits were buying in Spain – Costa del Sol mainly. Costa del Crime we call it – more villains sipping Sangria on sunbeds around private pools than tourists.'

'You think the Taylors are crooks then?'

'Doubt it. I don't recognise the name. Nothing to suggest they're anything but an ordinary couple retiring to sun, sea and sand where their pound goes further in pesetas than it does in cold, wet England's decimal system. Their villa will be near vintage in Spanish terms. Bet you anything it's furnished exactly like their home over here. Same curtains and carpets – teapot and cups laid out in cupboards exactly the same as in their kitchen here. No point moving up in the world when they have to live on their savings.'

I was in awe of his knowledge until he confessed, 'I could be wrong, and Taylor is Mr Big in the slave trade.' His wink didn't help me relax.

'Every lead is worth following up. Good thing you weren't knocked back by Ray Bolton. Just don't expect too much from this. The Taylor couple were sailing across the Channel when the girl went missing.'

'How can we be sure about that?' We stared at each other and Carter waited for me to say more. He leaned his head on his hand and I fidgeted with my skirt, pleating the material in my fingers. When he'd tolerated me asking for his help with previous cell mates of Len Ward we didn't discuss anything other than the reports in Linda's file. Had Jarvis told his best mate what I'd confessed to him?

I lowered my voice, embarrassed by what I had to say. 'I was with Linda around 12.30am so it will be interesting to know which ferry the Taylors caught on that night – or early morning.'

Carter pursed his lips until he almost chewed his scraggy greying moustache. 'Any times in the file?' I shook my head. 'It's a long time ago but these ferry companies keep records going back decades. You might get lucky. Next question though is why a decent couple would kidnap a little girl – and why would she go with them?'

'Because they were her grandparents.' Carter was more interested. 'Linda didn't know they were related. Their son is her real father.'

'Bloody hell.' He almost sniffed the air like a dog scenting a rabbit. 'That *is* interesting.'

I told him about my arranged meeting with Thornton-Lea, but he advised me to cancel it. 'Without a warrant you can't expect him to tell you anything about a client and definitely not a name. You'll be wasting your time. Try the address in Malaga first. If you can't find anything about Linda, then we can re-open the file and put pressure on the solicitor.'

It was a chance I had to take and maybe it was time for Mum and me to take a holiday – a week in the sun – in Malaga. Carter helped to arrange leave for me, bypassing any objections due to short notice and leaving me to enquire about travel arrangements.

'Remember, you don't have any powers in Spain – not without authorisation and we can't apply for that yet.'

He dropped his head and peered up into my eyes. 'How are you doing? Healing nicely I hope.'

'Yes. Jarvis won't let me out of the station, though. Not until the hospital stop making appointments to change the dressing.'

'Are you scared of going outside again – on the beat – or with this lot, kicking down a few doors.'

I puffed disdainful air. 'Of course not. Make sure they know that – I don't need any special treatment.'

'Oh, that will soon stop. We've got short memories. You'll be paying for your own bacon sandwiches from next week.'

A uniformed probationer, WPC Cathy Newton, hovered in the doorway clutching an envelope as though it was dynamite. Carter cruelly left her standing there while we finished speaking and then gestured for her to enter the office, holding out his hand.

'Thanks, Mick. Good luck with the Evans' bank accounts.'

Carter's mouth drooped and he pointedly glanced at Newton. 'Discretion, Morton, discretion,' he mumbled, and I knew it was my cue to leave him.

31

Pat's Disaster

To my surprise it was David who took over booking the
flights and accommodation.

'Let's not bother with the Berni Inn for your birthday,'
he said when I told him I needed to go to Spain as soon as
possible. 'A friend of mine works for British Midland. I'll
call him and see what he can do. We could all go and have
a holiday at the same time.'

Mum was all for it. Judith Chalmers had worked her
magic again – Mum and I loved watching *Wish You Were
Here* and dreamed of places we'd love to visit for a holiday.
Spain was at the top of the list, with Benidorm as Mum's
first choice. Malaga would have to be a second best.

David's suggestion was a great idea for another reason.
I had no clue how to book scheduled flights and the tour
companies' package deals were fully booked for Spain.

He commandeered the telephone in the hall while I rifled
through my wardrobe and threw unsuitable clothes into the
suitcase Mum had bought me for my weeks of training at
Ryton. I used it when I went away on courses around the
country and it was starting to look shabby, with the white
cardboard showing through chipped red paint.

'What about Pat?' Mum appeared in the bedroom
doorway holding a pair of cream slacks. She reminded
me she'd been included in the restaurant booking and

would be disappointed if we didn't go. 'She's been looking forward to your birthday for weeks.'

That was news to me. I hadn't seen Pat for a while. Rob never called me as he promised and after coming to terms with that and being determined to find Linda with Hazel's help, there wasn't any need for me to keep in touch with Pat. The undercover job using Stephanie at her factory, although headed up by Jarvis, hadn't included me. I wasn't part of the operation – no doubt due to my tenuous connection through Pat herself.

With my head buzzing with plans for Spain, I dragged myself into the hallway to call her. I needed to find my birth certificate and head down to the Post Office to have my photo taken in the booth and then buy a 12-month visitor's passport. I didn't have time to listen to Pat's hyper chat.

In between his calls David sat on the telephone table's padded stool and scribbled notes in a small black book with a stubby pencil. I could see numbers and pound signs listed in a column and watched him nod and smile in satisfaction.

'Alright for me to phone Pat?' I asked and he walked into the living room to speak to Mum who was now fussing with a long 'to-do' list.

Pat finished at the factory around 4pm and as it was only 11.30am I prepared myself to leave a message with her mum. It was a surprise when Pat answered the phone in a shaky, tearful voice. Too late, I remembered she'd been seeing the plumber Danny and now it sounded as though they'd split up or something.

'That's OK, Jan,' she said without any trace of disappointment in her voice, 'I wouldn't have been able to come anyway. I've been sacked so I won't have any money.'

I so wanted to say it was a shame and I'd call her another time, but I knew it was heartless of me and I should at least find out why she'd been sacked. The intelligence could be useful to Jarvis even if they already knew from Stephanie.

Pat sniffled into the receiver. 'Jan, I don't know what I did wrong. Mr Sanjay called me into his office this morning after I'd had my tea break and told me I was talking too much and I was sacked. I've got a week's pay and that's it. That won't go far once I've paid Mum for my keep.'

'He sacked you for talking?' That was crazy.

'That's what he said – but I haven't been talking any more than usual and I've never even been told off about it before.'

'Did he think you were wasting time gossiping, Pat?' I had too much to do to stand in the hallway being sympathetic when I knew Pat so well.

'I never talk about anyone at work. I did it once when I first started there, and Millie Monroe was standing behind me with a face like thunder. I learned my lesson then. I know they get fed up of me going on about Cliff Richard but I wasn't doing that today ...'

I chewed a nail with impatience. 'It does seem strange, Pat ... You said you're one of the best seamstresses there ...'

'I am!' She wailed and sniffed. 'I was promoted to cutter last week to learn how to prepare the patterns. Dressmaking comes naturally to me.'

She continued to explain the importance of pattern cutting but Mum appeared in the doorway, so I mentally switched off from the conversation.

She spoke in a loud whisper: 'David said there's a good chance he can rent a villa in Malaga from his cousin. It's got four rooms so if Pat can get the time off work, she could come with us. The villa's free apart from the food and we'll pay her air fare.'

'What?'

Mum hesitated and winked, whispering she'd explain later.

My investigation into finding Linda was starting to look like its own package holiday. David was more than likely planning day trips for us all. But I needed time on my own in Malaga searching out the Taylors' villa without looking conspicuous. There could be some advantage to being nosey tourists.

Linda's potential kidnappers might be big-time crooks and without the official sanction from Jarvis and my superiors, the recce could turn nasty and land me in a lot of trouble.

I cut across Pat's snivelling. 'Pat, have you got a passport?'

'Yes, why?'

'You have?'

She gulped in air, curious about the change of subject. 'I've had one for years and Danny's booking us a week in Majorca in September. He was on holiday in Benidorm with the lads last year. He said it's lovely and in September it's not too …'

'Well, if you don't have to go to work come to Malaga with me the day after tomorrow. Mum's friend David is sorting out flights and a villa. Mum's paying for us as my birthday present. We'll celebrate when we're out there.'

I was ready to end the call and heard her voice, much stronger and excited. 'Ooh, Jan, that's lovely – better than the Berni Inn.'

'Good. You can look for another job when you get back.'

'I'm not going to look for another job. Danny's told me I should work for myself – as a dressmaker. He'll help me start up and put the word around his customers.'

This was a big surprise. I blinked as I tried to take in the news.

'That's great. Why are you so upset then?'

'Janice,' she practically screamed in my ear, 'I was SACKED. I don't deserve it.'

It really was time to end the call.

Nightmare #3

The cellar was dark, and water ran down the stone walls onto the stone-flagged, rubbish-strewn floor. The walls were high, and the only window was close to the ceiling. Two feet wide and narrow, it was partially open and freezing cold raindrops drifted into the cellar. Outside, only a half moon illuminated the small bundle of clothes in the corner.

It was Linda. I recognised her dressing gown and her blonde plaits.

She was hunched into a tight ball to keep warm.

Around my feet, hundreds of black objects scurried across the floor.

I had a choice: face the rats and walk over to Linda or leave her in the corner.

With a determined stance, I brandished the garden broom in my hands, sweeping the filthy creatures aside as I ploughed a path in front of me.

It was slow progress. So many of them, hundreds – or even thousands.

Linda watched me with impassive eyes, staring at the rats and not at me.

What was wrong with her? I was here to save her.

'Quickly,' I shouted. 'They'll be back any minute.' I didn't mean the rats, but I didn't know who the faceless 'they' were either. 'We have to get out of here. We can't wait any longer.'

Linda didn't move. Her dressing gown hung open at the front but not enough for me to see what she was wearing. All around her feet were carrier bags with half-eaten food and empty coca cola bottles. Linda stood in the middle of the heap as though she was an island in a sea of obnoxious debris.

At last the rats were cleared away. I'd reached Linda and could hold her hand.

'Come on, Linda. We can't wait here. They'll be back any minute.'

I scanned the wall with its open window.

'I'll help you reach the window. Stand on my shoulders and you can climb out. You'll be free. We can be friends again.'

There was no reaction. I tried to turn her body, ready to push her up the stone wall to freedom. It was like pushing a stone statue in the park. She didn't budge.

'Come on, Linda.'

'No.'

Her white face streaked with dirt contrasted with the yellow teeth in her open mouth. I couldn't see her eyes in their dark hollows, hidden by the shadowed darkness.

I tugged at her hand to shake her into action.

'They're coming,' I yelled. I didn't know how I knew – but I knew 'they' were close by.

'No.'

I pushed her but she only took one step back, determined not to move.

'Come with me,' I pleaded.

'No. No. I don't trust you, Janice. I'm staying here.'

She crumpled into a dishevelled heap amongst the rubbish bags and sank her face into her chest.

The rats were back, nibbling my feet.

All I could do was scream.

32

Revelations

I left a message for Jarvis with Mick Carter, giving him the full address of the villa David had rented and the telephone number, which I read out to him. He warned me to be careful and phone the office if there was anything interesting to report. He'd heard about Pat being sacked but I emphasised how strange it was that Mr Sanjay was prepared to lose such a good seamstress with a pathetic excuse. There was no response from him of course.

Pat was strangely quiet on the journey to Spain. I squeaked a little when we arrived at Luton Airport and bubbled over as the plane rumbled along the runway, but she sat silently with her head bowed. It was uncomfortable to see her behaving so out of character: nothing to say and watery eyes which leaked down her cheeks when she thought no one was looking.

David guided us through the checking-in process having already advised on which clothes we should take and removing anything we wouldn't need for a week in 28 degrees of heat and sunshine. He was invaluable with his help, speaking to the three of us without putting pressure on Pat to feel obliged to answer.

She and I sat together on the plane and after nodding when I asked if I could have her free peanuts, I knew I had to get to the bottom of her distress.

'Sorry, Pat, I hadn't realised what a shock it's been – losing your job.' She blew her nose on a crumpled tissue and added it to the others in her large yellow hessian bag. 'But you'll get another one – if the dressmaking idea doesn't work out.'

Nodding again, Pat fumbled in the seat pocket in front of her and held the paper sick bag to her chest, fidgeting with the edges to open it out, preparing it for use.

'Are you OK?'

There was a prolonged heavy breath. 'I will be. I hate flying. It's the take-off and landing I hate mostly but once we're well on our way I should be fine.'

'You've flown before?'

'My dad was in the war and he loved travelling. We go to Spain every year. Have done since I was about nine or ten. Torremolinos mainly – but last year we went to Benidorm. That's lovely, Jan. You'd like it there.' She stared ahead of her as she spoke, not turning her head to look at me or out of the window at my side.

There was so much I didn't know about Pat. She went to Spain every year and if she'd mentioned it at school – and she must have done – I didn't remember. No wonder she'd looked bored when David checked we had our passports and kept the boarding cards where he could see them. I thought she'd gone over the top when she produced a ten-year passport instead of the one-year one like mine.

'I'm sorry about your job. I know you loved it. I'd be devastated if I lost my job.' As the words left my mouth, I realised for the first time exactly how Pat must feel. Not only was she out of work but she'd been sacked from something she was good at. 'Thank goodness you've got Danny.' I stroked her arm, hoping nothing had happened between the two of them when he'd found out Pat was going on holiday with me for a week.

She turned her head and smiled as though a fishhook was caught in the corners. 'Oh Jan, he's been wonderful. I couldn't tell him until the day after it happened. He was busy and his mum was never in to take a message when I phoned. He called me the next morning before he started work and before I knew it, he was on the doorstep with a bunch of flowers from his garden and shoved a £5 note in my hand.'

I didn't have to pretend to be impressed. I was very impressed. The men I worked with every day were the least likely to show such sentiments over losing a job. Danny was turning out to be an exceptional young man.

'Is he still saving up for his own house?'

'A deposit? Yes. He's nearly there but he said we both need a holiday and we can get to know each other better,' she blushed and winked, 'and he won't cancel it either. He's really nice, Jan.'

'I'm glad.' How did it feel, I wondered, to like a guy and for him to like you back – and to make a fuss of you? It must be wonderful. It was less than wonderful to like a guy who only took any notice of me when I was under his nose. Out of sight I was out of Rob's mind and his life.

David's cousin's villa was a one-storey building, perched on the edge of a slope that once gave it clear views across the hillside to the sea in the near distance. Since it was built, other villas had sprung up around it, haphazardly scattered over the hills without obscuring the sea views completely.

It was small but comfortably furnished. There were four rooms: a kitchen and a large open lounge; a bathroom; and two bedrooms. Not quite the four bedrooms we'd expected. Pat and I shared a room with bunk beds. Mum had her own room with a small en-suite bathroom and David had to sleep on the bed settee which folded out into a single bed.

After we'd all admired the en-suite bathroom and thrown clothes from our suitcases into solid wooden wardrobes we dragged the sun loungers into the setting sun swirling the swimming pool with streaks of red and orange. David joined us with a jug of ruby wine he called sangria and poured it into glasses for us.

I had to keep reminding myself I wasn't on holiday. I was in Malaga for a purpose. I'd told David about Linda and the Taylor villa and he'd promised to find the address on his Michelin map and drive me past it in the morning. But for our first night he insisted that we walk into the town and have dinner in the main plaza, which he pronounced 'platza'. It wasn't far and we could always get a taxi back.

Pat gradually reverted to her usual chatty personality but still didn't have quite as much to say as usual. She and Mum talked Singer sewing machines and Mum offered to find her old one for her, hoping that Danny could fix whatever was wrong with it. She hadn't used it for years.

'Danny can sort that out,' Pat declared whenever Mum described a problem with it.

David and Pat disappeared into the villa to change for the evening, but Mum held my hand and asked me to stay with her. She had something she wanted to tell me. I'd noticed her fidgeting after the second glass of sangria and wondered if she was nervous about being in the villa with David. I still wasn't sure about their relationship. He was always very gentlemanly with her – pulling out a chair for her to sit in, interested in anything she talked about. He happily chatted about his work or listened to her talk about hers, cooking school meals and washing up afterwards.

He was never particularly affectionate when I was around. He helped her into her coat or summer jacket, opened doors for her but never openly touched her or sat with his arm around her. I hoped they weren't holding back for my sake.

It was nice to sit with Mum and I wanted her to relax and be happy. The sun had slipped into the sea, at first leaving a trail of fiery waves until a black darkness shrouded the view. Our only lighting was a string of coloured glass lanterns draped along the vine-covered pergola over the terrace. The faint sounds of classical music floated in the evening air from one of the other villas.

I prepared myself to accept any news about her and David becoming more serious than friends. We exchanged weary smiles and she held up her glass to chink it against mine even though it was empty.

'Happy 21st, Janice,' she said. Her hand shook. I couldn't see her face in the gloom, but her voice sounded tense despite the light-hearted toast. 'I know it's not until next week, but we can still celebrate here.'

She leaned closer towards me to stare into my eyes and squeezed my hand. The serious expression on her face scared me. Please God, I thought – not cancer.

My sandaled feet scrambled clumsily across the scrubby roadside towards the dancing lights of Malaga's town centre. My vision blurred through my tears and the drop in temperature pierced the exposed skin beneath my thin broderie anglaise blouse. Lethal prickly plants scratched my bare legs and toes as I hurtled along, desperate to escape from the villa and especially my traitorous mother.

Adrenaline propelled me forwards – my mind raced with a tumble dryer of thoughts trying to piece together what I'd just heard. None of it made any sense.

'Janice, I didn't want to tell you any of this until you were twenty-one. There didn't seem any point until you could have the money.'

Money?

'I've got to tell you the truth about your father.'

'What about him?

'He didn't die like I told you when you were a little girl.'

What did she mean, he didn't die? What did she mean? If he didn't die, then …

'He's alive?' I choked on the question, unable to process what Mum was saying. My experience of women who lied to their kids about their dad not being around usually meant they were doing 'time' in prison.

Mum explained quickly. 'He left us just before your second birthday. We agreed he wouldn't keep in touch because there was another woman he wanted to marry.'

If that piece of news wasn't shocking enough – there was still more to come.

I stared at Mum as though she had two heads. Earlier, I'd thought she looked chic with a pink cotton scarf covering her unruly hair, knotted at the back of her head, like Sophia Loren. With every word she spoke, revealing a side of my life I'd never known about, she grew more grotesque. She was a stranger to me.

'He's a good man, Janice; we married too young and when we were honest with each other we admitted we weren't in love – not enough to be proper husband and wife – and parents.'

'How does that make him a good man?' I'd asked in utter shock. Trembling with rage, I managed not to swear, even though I wanted to say all the worst words I heard every day at work.

'We would have stayed together and done our best. That's what you did when you got married. But then he won £50,000 on the football pools. It meant we could change our lives and not have to worry about money.'

'He left us with nothing?'

'No, like I said – he was a good man. When we heard about the win, we discussed what we would do. The Pools people helped us with everything. The money was split two ways and a trust fund arranged for you to have when you reached twenty-one.'

Trust fund? Was I rich?

'We found the house and paid for it, so you and I moved there. We didn't want anyone to know who we were, and it would be easier if I could tell people I was a widow bringing you up on my own. If anyone asked about the house, I could say there'd been some insurance money to buy it.'

I was incredulous. 'So we've always had money? All the time I was growing up and you worked at the school – we had thousands of pounds?'

'Well, I kept a few hundred pounds under my mattress to dip into if things became really hard – I used some of it to buy the car for you.'

'But it's on HP.'

She looked down at her hands. What a fool I was. 'It's not on HP, is it?'

Mum shook her head and tried to smile. She was clearly hurt when I spoke harshly and must have expected a more enthusiastic and excited reaction to her news. In the space of five minutes, I'd discovered my father wasn't dead and that I had a small fortune in the bank.

My mind whirled back to my childhood – hating the way we lived because we didn't have a lot of money. I could have had all the things I'd wanted – better clothes, shop-bought cakes and Sindy dolls. Lots of Sindy dolls like Linda had. She and I could have been friends on an equal footing. Maybe if we had been, I wouldn't have been spitefully envious of her.

My selfishness then wasn't my fault after all. Mum was to blame for hiding everything from me. I couldn't think about my dad, who'd walked away from me as a baby. I knew enough about men from my short career to know they could do much worse.

Shocked into anger I stood up and shouted at Mum. I don't know what I said but she knew I was furious with her. I couldn't face David or Pat and the last thing I wanted to do was to pretend to be happy sitting at a table with them eating goodness knew what the Spanish ate. Paella. That's what the Spanish ate. Why did everything in my life make me miserable?

We'd driven through the town centre on the way to the villa, so I was drawn towards it in the effort to walk off my black mood. I knew I should have been delighted to find out I had enough money now to give up my job and never work again. Mum said she couldn't touch the money unless it was to be used for my education or welfare. But she'd worked hard to avoid that.

My hands were screwed into tight fists. We could have lived so much more comfortably – maybe had holidays in Spain every year like Pat. Why on earth hadn't Mum told me years ago and left me with the choice of what I wanted to do with the money? And why had she been so scared to use some of it to decorate our house and have a more comfortable life instead of buying only what we 'needed'?

There wasn't enough emotion left inside me to think about the kind man who was my father. He sounded like a decent guy to do what he'd done but how could he walk away from us both and never once get in touch? I decided in the heat of my feelings that he must be dead. It would be easier to handle if he were dead.

Although it was dark when I reached the town it was still early. Lights in the plaza drew me into its centre and my pace slowed with weariness and unfamiliarity with the streets and side roads. The plaza itself was lined on four sides by pavement cafes filled with laughing tourists and locals, drinking and nibbling crisps and olives. Spanish guitar music filled the square from every cafe's competing cassette tapes.

How could everyone be so happy when I was utterly wretched? There was a ten-peseta note in the pocket of my shorts and I looked around for an empty table at one of the cafes. I didn't care about the scratches on my legs and small rips in my clothes. The cafes were ill lit with pretty, twinkling lights and fluttering candle flames on each table. I could hide my face in the dimness.

The heavy smell of garlic and baking dough mingling with fried potatoes reminded me I was very hungry.

Usually confident on my own territory, I felt uncertain about sitting down and ordering a drink in Spanish. How would I be understood? David had done all the talking earlier, fluent in the language. Couples or groups lounged at the occupied tables, relaxed and animated. No one sat alone.

Calming down, I walked around the square twice, trying to select a cafe that wasn't so busy thinking that maybe I could look as though I was meeting friends. There was every chance the others back at the villa would appear in a short while, looking for me and the real Spanish tortilla David and Pat promised Mum and me we would love.

The least-populated cafe was in a darkened corner of the square. Two small groups of Brits clustered at opposite corner tables. Their loud voices competed over each other to be heard. Raucous laughter let everyone know how much they were enjoying their own company.

One of the groups, an elderly couple, a middle-aged couple and a younger couple with a small child, looked like generations of the same family. They were heavily suntanned even though they spoke in English, switching to perfect Spanish to call the waiter. I sat a couple of tables away from them.

My mind settled into a more balanced state and I was glad to sit and be distracted by the family. The waiter ignored me, lounging against the door jamb of the cafe where I could see empty tables inside the brightly lit restaurant. The older woman, plump with her bare arms straining against a tight, poppy-flowered dress, caught my eye. She leaned across the table with its empty and half-filled wine bottles and prodded the middle-aged man.

When she spoke I recognised her Birmingham accent.

'Keith, love, help her out. You know what Juan's like with tourists.'

Keith?

Surely ... Surely not? Lots of English men who lived in Birmingham were called Keith.

This Keith turned towards me and the neon light from the indoor cafe illuminated his round face, black eyes framed with the pale outline from sunglasses. 'What are you after, love? Beer or sangria? The beer's cold and it's not too strong. Try a San Miguel.'

I was frozen like the cold clay of a statue. Behind his bulky frame, the young mother looked up and joined the family to stare at me with kind friendliness. I'd seen that expression before – a long time ago. Nearly twelve years ago. And even more recently, in a photo album.

I'd found Linda.

33

David and Linda

I called at the Taylors' villa the next morning. David drove me there as promised and waited while I went inside to speak to Linda. We hadn't spoken much during the short journey. He was adept at pouring oil on troubled waters and the previous evening had been the perfect opportunity to reconcile Mum and me.

They'd caught up with me at Tres Palomas, staring thoughtfully at my cold glass of beer and studying the beads of condensation dripping down the glass on to the round cardboard mat. The glass and the beer must have been kept in the fridge for it to be so cold. The evening was warmer in the plaza than it had been on the hilly walk. The outdoor seating was laid out under a canopy and as the tables filled up the cold beer was very welcome.

Even if I hadn't been trying to listen it was impossible not to hear the family banter at the Taylors' table. The little girl, with Rosie's features, entertained everyone and Linda was praised for having such a beautiful daughter. I already knew the first names of Mr and Mrs Taylor, so the only unknown was Keith's wife and the man who had to be the baby's father. I soon found out as the conversations overlapped.

Keith was married to a svelte Spanish woman he called Sofia and whenever the waiter was summoned the family all spoke in Spanish. The dark-haired and dark-skinned man with Linda who played with the baby was Paulo. He seemed to understand English but replied to questions in Spanish. It was a language I had never studied, but Pat assured me the only word I needed to know was 'helado' for ice cream.

Mum, Pat and David strolled past and spotted me at my table. I was too euphoric to dwell on the row with Mum. David and Pat must have heard me yelling at her, shouting my hurt anger at what I felt was her betrayal throughout my life. Every word I'd shouted must have hurt her and I'd left her in tears, weakly calling my name when I stomped off like a petulant teenager.

I acknowledged her with a brief hug and turned my head away when she tried to speak to me. David had glared at me for treating her badly, but I had other things on my mind. I'd have to deal with Mum and the shattering news she'd given to me another time.

There were other things to think about. Linda was alive. I'd always wanted her to be alive but pictured her living in squalor or being mistreated like the girl Tanya, who'd made up the story about being raped. Since the night she disappeared I'd had recurring nightmares in which I'd found her alone in a stinking, damp cellar and when I tried to drag her to freedom she'd resisted me with a distrustful wariness.

Now I could see she'd lived a safe and happy life I still had so many other questions. What exactly had happened that night I'd left her in the orchard?

The Taylors' villa was three times the size of the one David had rented for us. It sprawled into three separate homes around a large swimming pool with a smaller one next to

262

it. Built back from the main road it was reached by a small lane leading off it and away from passing traffic. It was private in every sense and even though two of the buildings were newer additions to the main one, the old style had been maintained. It was enchanting.

I forced myself not to compare it with my own home, a three-bedroomed mid-terrace with a paved garden so that we didn't have to waste time with lawnmowers and weeding.

'Are you ready for this?' David stared ahead and I knew he was still annoyed with my refusal to speak to Mum. He seemed to genuinely care about Mum and me – almost adopting us as his family. It didn't endear him to me, but I was grateful he'd turned out to be a decent guy. I wasn't going to apologise for running off the night before and he didn't mention it.

'No matter what happens in there, I'm a police officer and this is still a missing persons case.' My hand was on the door handle ready to press it down and escape from the furnace-like heat in the car.

Mumbling thanks, I searched for an encouraging sign from him, but his mouth stayed closed in a disapproving straight line. With one leg out of the car, I did a double take before leaping out completely. Something had jarred inside my head and the picture of Jarvis and his wife in the photograph flashed across my brain. David turned his head towards me, frowning and unusually without his friendly smile. He nodded curtly and pointed to a clump of trees further ahead.

I'd seen that look before – except he'd had a beard in the photo.

'How do you know Frank Jarvis?' I blurted out. Any possible doubt I might have had that I was wrong was allayed when I saw his eyes open wide with astonishment. A fraction of a second later his usual impassive, but cold expression masked his face.

'I'll wait over there for you – in the shade. No rush.'

Momentarily, I was torn between asking him more questions and seeing Linda. It wasn't really a serious dilemma. I'd waited nearly twelve years to find Linda and I couldn't wait to confront her. David would have to wait.

Before I could recall the faces of the men sitting at the table behind Jarvis and Alison, the car scrunched the gravel and slowly advanced towards the blissful shade.

My stomach felt as though it was full of undigested stale bread, heavy and uncomfortable. There wasn't time to dwell on David being upset with me. I approached the ornate metal gates set between stone pillars and pressed the intercom, hoping to be allowed in. After a brief reminder of meeting the family the previous night it was a relief when the gates opened smoothly.

Keith answered the front door of the middle villa, wearing tight denim shorts and plastic flip-flops that slapped on the terracotta tiles as he led me out onto the terrace.

'You caught me about to leave for the day,' he said as I followed him, walking across the light lounge carpet. 'I'm doing a painting job for a new development on the edge of the town. Sofia's doing some exterior touch-ups – plants and that kind of thing.'

He was friendly and relaxed, telling me how decorating contracts piled up and he was never short of work. 'The developer's asking a fortune for each apartment block, so it all needs to look very upmarket. Sofia's fantastic at that.'

We'd walked from the middle villa to a smaller one next to it where a smart young woman lounged at the wrought iron table, head back to enjoy the warm morning sunshine on her face. Matching white wrought iron chairs were scattered carelessly as though their occupants had recently finished breakfast and left.

Linda sat forward when she heard Keith's voice and our footsteps. She dunked a pastry into a wide bowl of hot chocolate and glanced at a Spanish newspaper which was in danger of blowing away in the breeze. Weighting it down with a jam-smeared plate, she wrinkled her tanned brow when she saw me standing behind Keith.

A short distance from us, inside one of the other villas, a woman's soothing voice mingled with a child's demanding wail. Neither Keith nor Linda seemed concerned.

'It's the lady we met last night,' Keith said and whipped the chocolate-tipped pastry from her fingers before walking away. 'She said she thinks she knows you.'

'Dad!' she wailed and reached for another pastry from a collection nestled in a napkin-lined basket.

There was the smile I remembered – friendly, trusting and a little puzzled. Linda dropped her head towards her left shoulder and frowned.

'Have we met before? Before last night …?' She struggled to remember and broke off a chunk of the plaited fried pastry to dunk in her bowl.

She pointed a dark brown hand at the chair next to her and I sat down. The padded cushion was warm, and the sun sparkled on the calm water in the pool. 'Are you hungry?'

I shook my head, but she rose slightly and called out in Spanish, '*Maria, otro chocolate por favor* …' Her accent was perfect. 'Have you tried churros and chocolate? It's my morning sin – I have to start the day with it, but I'm pretty good after this until supper.'

Even seated, she had a perfect figure, a flat stomach and straight back with firm shoulders.

'Linda,' I began and then sat back as a short, middle-aged woman appeared with another bowl of hot chocolate and placed it in front of me. It looked and smelt delicious, but I continued, 'My name is Janice – Janice Morton. I live next door to … Hazel and Lonnie.'

My words had been rehearsed throughout the night, just as I had rehearsed my interview with the police – Jarvis – after Linda disappeared. But I hadn't pictured this scene of stunning green hills heaped against each other with the sea in the distance, a cruise ship sailing slowly into port and this terrace with bougainvillea, palm trees and a late breakfast.

Nor could I have foreseen Linda's reaction. 'Janice. Morton. Hazel …' She spoke dreamily and hesitated with her mouth open as the thoughts tumbled into her head. The half-filled bowl was pushed away from her as though she wanted to rid herself of this inevitable conversation.

'Do you remember me, Linda?' I opened my leather bag and placed the Sindy doll on the table in front of her. 'We used to play together in the school holidays.'

Linda slumped against the padded cushion, propped up to soften the intricate iron carving on the chair. She wore a smart sleeveless blouse with a turned-up collar and matching shorts; the soft turquoise cotton emphasised her tanned arms and legs. Her long, sun-bleached hair was swept up into a loose ponytail that trailed over her right shoulder almost to her elbow.

She stared at the doll and slowly ran her finger, with its sparkling diamond engagement ring, over the cracked plastic mac. Her lips parted and she bit the side of her mouth as her fingertips traced along the red boots.

Looking up reluctantly, she studied me with sky-blue eyes and nodded slowly. She licked her lips where some of the churro's sugar lingered.

'Janice. *Madre de dias*. I can't believe it.' She shook her head slowly. 'You came looking for me – after all these years.'

'Yes – eventually. The police couldn't find you – so I decided to do it myself. They suspected a man caught for other child murders of killing you. I didn't want to believe you were dead ... but there was only one way to find out.'

Neither of us displayed any emotion. I wanted to grab her from her chair and shake her. The anger I felt against Mum, my past – and my present – bubbled up inside me again. I breathed heavily and forced myself to calm down.

'I've got so many questions.' I raised my arms to take in the terrace, the pool and the views and turned to face her. 'This isn't how I imagined I'd find you.'

Linda still looked puzzled, the familiar frown creasing the space between her eyebrows. 'No, I suppose not. I've never really thought about it. My dad tried to find out what was happening after we came to Spain, but the newspapers were nearly a week out of date by the time they arrived. When the reports stopped, we assumed everyone had given up looking for me.'

She picked up the doll and turned it over to stroke the mac where it still had its original shiny patina. 'When the inspector phoned, Nan and Grandad told him they were already here in the villa by the morning. Even though they expected someone to question them out here, no one ever came so we thought we were safe.'

'Did you know they were your family?'

Linda shook her head and relaxed into the cushion instead of perching upright. 'Never. I'd overheard my other grandmother talking to my other grandad about me one night. They were complaining I was getting too much for them as I got older and Hazel needed to take responsibility for her "own daughter". I didn't understand what she was talking about, but I knew they were talking about me. That's how I found out I was Hazel's daughter, not her sister.'

'You told me she was your mum. I swore to keep it a secret, so I never told the inspector – neither did Hazel or your grandparents.'

'We guessed they'd all kept it a secret. It made it so much easier to stay here with my other family – knowing I wasn't really missed at home. If I had been missed, they'd soon have told the police about my dad – Keith. They didn't though, did they?'

I examined the thick dark chocolate in my cup and took a sip. Politely, I tried not to recoil from its strength. Linda pushed the basket of churros towards me.

'Don't try and drink it. Dip the churro in the chocolate. Have you only just arrived in Spain?'

'Yes, first time. First time abroad. I had to buy a passport from the Post Office. I've never had one before.'

I bit into the chocolate-dipped churro and enjoyed the sensation of fried sweet pastry in my mouth. It was heaven.

'You're not the only one. I haven't been outside Spain since I arrived here in the back of Nan and Grandad's car.' She giggled and I remembered that innocent sense of fun Linda had when we were young. I'd thought she was just silly but now I appreciated there was more to her laughter.

'What happened, Linda? Oh wait …' I finished the churro, licked grease off my fingers and sat up straight in my chair, mentally pulling down an invisible uniform jacket, prepared to begin an interview. The polyester long-sleeved blouse I was wearing was only slightly less unbearable than my jacket would have been. Linda's outfit looked cool and I recognised the familiar twinge of envy I'd always felt when with her.

'What?'

'I should tell you that although I'm on a week's holiday with my mum and a couple of friends, I am a police officer and have been working on your file for a few months. Last night was an accident. I had no idea when I entered that restaurant that I would end up sitting just a few feet from you and your family. I had the address of this villa and I would have visited this morning to meet you for the first time.'

34

Linda's Story

I held out my warrant card and she took it from me, studying the photograph.

'Wow, Janice,' she whispered and handed it back, 'you're a policewoman. You've done well.' She sounded impressed and with the sweat gathering at the base of every hair follicle on my head, I felt some satisfaction.

Linda clasped her hands over her stomach to stop them from shaking. 'You're not going to arrest my family – and me, are you?'

I replaced my warrant card in my shoulder bag, but I knew I couldn't do anything without permission from Jarvis or someone of his rank. This was Spain and I wasn't sure how the English law worked out here.

'I don't have the authority to do that, but I will have to write up a report. You're an unsolved missing persons case from 1964. The police had to move on to other things when they couldn't find anything to work on to track you down, but no case is ever completely closed.'

'Oh. We're in trouble, aren't we?'

I guessed there must have been conversations in the family about the legal side of things if she remained in Spain.

'I just need you to tell me what happened that night.'

Linda nibbled the tanned skin on her index finger and abruptly stopped when she caught herself doing it. This was it, the moment when I could finally ask my questions.

'I've never stopped thinking about you,' I said in a low quiet voice. 'Did you try to find the secret door? It wasn't there in the morning, so you'd have been stranded.'

'I suppose it's been easier for me, Janice. It seems so strange to say your name again. I nearly named Rosita after you, but I've never forgotten my family in England and my mum's baby was so cute.'

'Your half-sister. Rosie is the image of you. I like her.'

Linda lifted her head to the sun and screwed her eyes tightly to shut out too many memories. She breathed in deeply and then met my eyes as she talked.

'When you ran off and left me – and I don't blame you for that by the way. I never have. I was used to having my own way and I wanted that peach. I didn't see why I shouldn't have it. Nan and Grandad gave me everything I wanted, to make sure I kept out of their way. I didn't realise it at the time.

'I was sure you'd come back after five minutes so I waited on the log. I tried to eat the peach, but it was horrible, so I threw it away.'

It all came back to me as vividly as though it had been just the previous evening. Despite the increasingly hot, stifling air I shivered a little, remembering the cold evening. 'I waited for you, Linda, by the secret door. Then I went up to my bedroom and looked out of the window to make sure you got back home OK. But I fell asleep and, in the morning, the secret door had gone.'

She smiled and bobbed her head up and down, like the brown suede nodding dog Mum used to have in the living room. 'Our very own Enid Blyton mystery, eh?'

We chuckled and I bobbed my head, copying her. 'I managed to work out what had happened – but not until ten years later when the detective inspector explained it to me!'

'And I thought you were the clever one.' The sun had moved around to hit the sunshade over the table, and I felt the heat penetrating my arms and into my bones. The chill had gone, thank goodness. Not that clever, I thought, when I was the one living in grey and miserable England and she'd been living like this all these years.

'My dad told me what had happened when I woke up the next day. I was scared after you ran off and left me and I tried to follow you but ended up walking in the wrong direction. There were lights on in the main house, so I knocked on the door and asked them to take me home.'

What a sensible thing to do! I wondered why none of us had thought of it before. Then I remembered that no one should have been in the house – the orchard owners were in Spain as far as the police were concerned.

'But …'

'Another two minutes and I would have missed them – Nan and Grandad. They were on their way to Dover when Nan thought she'd left the gas on under the kettle, so they decided to turn back. They were about to set off again when they saw me, crying and frightened.

'They're ever so kind, Janice. I told them my name and that I was staying with Hazel. That's when my life changed. Nan showed me a photo of my real dad and explained a few details of how they hadn't wanted me at first – but then they changed their minds. It was too late by then. It made sense to me. My other nan and grandad had accepted £500 to keep me and then changed their minds. It didn't seem so strange.'

'But you asked them to take you home to Hazel?' I asked, convinced the abduction had to have been against Linda's will.

'Nan asked me if I wanted to go to Spain with them and see my dad.'

I spat out dry air. 'Crikey, Linda, that was a hell of a risk. You could have been in great danger.'

'I know that now. If anything like that happened to Rosita, I'd kill the so-called grandparents. But I sort of knew them – I'd seen them passing the house in their car sometimes and once Grandad had smiled at me and waved. I was so tired and cold and the thought of a car journey to Spain seemed like a good idea. You must realise – I had no idea where Spain was – it could have been twenty minutes away and then I'd be back with Hazel and Lonnie.'

This sounded very reasonable. Had I understood much about geography at the same age? I thought of Pat, who'd been going on holiday to Spain since the early sixties.

'What did you do?'

'They lay me on the back seat under a blanket to sleep. I was exhausted and after I'd drunk some Ovaltine from their flask, I was dead to the world.'

I gasped a sharp breath at the expression, but Linda only smiled, tilting her head to one side.

'When I woke up next morning, we were driving through France. I asked what had happened to you and Grandad said he'd used some of the old fence panels to replace the secret door so no one would know it ever existed. No one except for you.'

It all sounded so simple as Linda told her story. Of course a secret door couldn't disappear overnight. Jarvis had investigated Linda's disappearance without needing to consider a secret door. He'd concentrated on the assumption that the little girl had been asleep in her bed at home and somehow ended up in the orchard. My guilty conscience thumped like a drum inside my head.

'They expected you to tell your mum and Hazel about the door and what had happened, so they had to reach Spain as quickly as possible before the English police sent out photos of me. Their idea was to take me to Spain. I'd meet Dad, live at the villa for a little while and then make up my mind if I wanted to go back to England.'

Linda gazed thoughtfully at the rippling water in the pool, causing the blue-tiled dolphin on the bottom to appear to move slowly. The sun steadily climbed higher and the temperature rose with it. The water looked so invitingly cool. I was a proficient swimmer after the lessons during my police training and could see myself cutting through the water as it cooled my head. Watching Linda, I tried to work out what she could be thinking.

'I didn't have to think very hard, Janice. I couldn't forget what my other nan had said about not wanting me. Hazel and Lonnie were besotted by Rosie and fussing around her after the doctor said she might have measles. I understand that, now I've got Rosita. I'm beside myself if her nose runs and she sneezes. And you didn't like me – my best friend.'

An invisible blow hit my stomach. Bile even rose into my mouth and I used an embroidered napkin to wipe my chin, feeling dribble running down my neck. There was no point denying it. I'd had to admit it myself after all. At least I had the courage to look Linda in the eye when I apologised.

'I'm so sorry, Linda. I was a jealous brat – you had everything I wanted ... But that was no excuse to be unkind to someone as nice as you.'

Linda's mouth opened and she frowned, ready to ask a question, but in the end, she didn't ask anything. Her next words were as effective as another blow.

'I didn't have a mum who loved me, Janice. Your mum was a real mum – telling you off and not giving into you like my nan and Hazel did. That's not love, Janice.'

No, it wasn't. Linda was right.

'My dad, Keith, lived out here. He'd dropped out of university and nearly had a breakdown, thinking about me apparently. Nan and Grandad were too embarrassed to tell anyone and sent him out here to recover. He'd never got over the decisions made for him.'

She looked smugly proud and I didn't blame her. I wondered if there was a man somewhere whose life had been ruined because he'd given me up. Where was my father living?

'He and a mate started a painting and decorating business in Benidorm. New hotels were being built so there was plenty of work. They did well but Nan and Grandad had bought this villa in Malaga for their retirement, so he and his mate split the business and he came here to work on his own. This place was much smaller in those days. Just the middle building at first but he built another so he and I could have more space. Rosita and I live in this one. Dad built this too.'

'It's lovely,' I admitted and choked back the old feelings of envy. What a wonderful life Linda had lived with family who provided her with so much security and love.

'When I told Nan I wanted to stay with them, and nothing about finding me was in the papers after a couple of months, she and Grandad sold the orchard and retired here to look after me while Dad was at work. I grew up speaking Spanish and English and went to a secretarial school in Malaga. I learnt a bit of bookkeeping from Dad's accountant and now I look after that side of the business for him.'

This development far exceeded anything I had imagined. The nightmare of Linda locked in a basement, surely had to fade from my restless nights.

'I met Paulo two years ago and we were engaged.' She paused and sighed. 'Then I fell pregnant last year. They don't like that kind of thing in Spain and he could have run off and ignored me.' She stirred the chocolate dregs with a cold churro, leaving it on the saucer and shaking powder from her fingers. 'We love each other, and we adore Rosita. We're getting married next month – nothing massive – town hall for the legal bit and then a party here.'

Her eyes brightened and she grinned at me. 'You'll have to come – and your mum – and your friends.'

'And Hazel, your mum …'

She must have expected that because she showed no surprise when I spoke. She sat very still staring at her folded hands in her lap.

'What's going to happen to me – and my family?'

'I have to find out. You haven't come to any harm so there won't be any charge on that count. But you were abducted as a minor without the maturity to make a big decision like staying here or going back to your family in England. Your dad will probably need to pay for a good lawyer.' A light bulb lit up inside my head, highlighting the last piece of the puzzle. 'Thornton-Lea perhaps?'

She shrugged her tanned shoulders without looking up. 'I've heard that name before. I think Grandad knows him.'

I smiled, seeing all the jigsaw pieces falling into place. Then I leaned forward to gently hold Linda's hands. It was the first time in our short friendship that I had ever done anything kind.

'Linda, I have to tell you. Hazel, your mum – she's falling apart. I've seen her a couple of times and although

I don't know much about mental breakdowns, I think she's having one. Rosie is the image of you when you were around the same age – when you disappeared. I think it's brought it all back to her. She needs to know you're alive. Will you speak to her?'

Tears rolled down Linda's cheeks like a leaking tap, gaining momentum. She grasped my hands tightly and let the tears fall, struggling to speak.

Eventually she whispered, 'I've missed her so much.'

35

Factory Raid

'Morton, I need you in uniform tonight.'

I looked up as I hung my hat on the coat stand, already staggering from its overload of winter coats, waiting for the season to change and to be reclaimed by their owners. It was my first day back after the holiday in Spain and I'd expected compliments for my lightly tanned face, not a command from Jarvis as soon as I walked through the door.

We'd spoken almost daily as I updated him from Malaga with the outcome of my visits to Linda and her family. The telephone in the villa was more reliable than I would have expected. The connection dropped now and then, but the calls were short enough for it not to be a problem. I had statements from Linda's grandparents and Keith to add to the one she and I had written after she'd told me her story.

Jarvis advised me that he would present the statements to the Director of Public Prosecutions with a recommendation that no charges be brought against the family. He couldn't guarantee though that Mr and Mrs Taylor wouldn't be charged for obstructing the course of justice in 1964 and therefore wasting police time and causing undue distress to Hazel and Lonnie.

I couldn't be certain he wasn't considering a similar charge against me for my part in obstructing the investigation. There had been plenty of time over ten years for me to at least have told Mum, who would have encouraged me to tell the truth to the police. It wouldn't have taken Jarvis long to suspect the possibility that someone else was in the orchard that night.

My nightmare about finding Linda holed up in a terrible cellar was replaced with the dread of having to stand up and listen to someone like DC Mick Carter cautioning me and leading me to the cells. I might have been successful in finding Linda, but I could easily lose my own job.

I hoped it wouldn't serve any purpose to charge the Taylors after twelve years, especially given the age of the couple and their well-meaning intentions, backed up by Linda herself and the evidence of her lifestyle as a result of the abduction. I could only wait for the outcome and I fished the handwritten statements from my briefcase to add to the file from my drawer.

The holiday had been a relaxing break despite my estrangement from Mum at the beginning. After the first four days of driving the hire car between the two villas I could truly admit to myself that for my part, 'Finding Linda Bateman' was now case closed. My guilty conscience, though still twinging slightly, was at peace. My fears about Linda's torture and death were allayed and now when I thought of her it was as a confident young woman, happy in her Spanish home with her family and daughter and planning her wedding to her fiancé.

After the constant sunshine and heat of Malaga I was irritated by the gloomy weather when it was so close to summer. The CID office smelt worse than usual of body odour, cigarette smoke and the crumpled chip papers which were piled up in my bin. Why my bin?

Jarvis reappeared in his doorway with Carter, holding a stiff sheet of paper. Unusually, he too was smoking and the shadows under his eyes were darker than ever. Looking around at the waiting detectives who were mumbling and dishevelled, I realised they must have all been working through the night. The atmosphere was tense and expectant.

'Alright everyone, gather round – you too, Morton.' He waved the paper outwards at shoulder height. 'Got it.' Everyone murmured and red-rimmed eyes brightened considerably. Carter, hands in his pockets, rocked on his downtrodden heels. Jarvis was about to continue when a spotty probationer blundered through the door, slamming it on its hinges against the partition. He carried a large cardboard box stacked with bulging paper bags. The smell of hot fried food surrounded him like a halo.

'My bacon and egg sandwich had better be in there,' Jarvis barked. When the probationer nodded, wide-eyed and I suspected with a couple of fingers crossed beneath the box, he gestured to him to lay it down on the nearest desk. 'Go on, grab your breakfast, lads. We've earned it. Now we've got the warrant we can all go home, get some sleep but be back here no later than 1800 hours for briefing.'

I sat at my desk, breathing in the more pleasant smell of bread and rolls with coffee in paper cups. The word 'Smiffys' was scrawled in red across each bag and we all knew there was nowhere better for a breakfast order. If only I'd arrived half an hour earlier, I could have ordered my favourite bacon and egg toastie with extra red sauce.

Bags were tossed over to whoever claimed each description shouted by DS Sean McIlroy: 'fried egg, hard yolk – that's you, Benton; crispy bacon, nearly burnt, fried egg, runny yolk, buttered white bread and brown sauce – that's got to be yours, boss …'

Jarvis grabbed his bag and a coffee from the cardboard carrying holder and told me to join him in his office. I picked up Linda's file and followed him, my stomach rumbling as the smell of his food wafted over me.

It grew worse when I had to watch him take a large bite from the sandwich, runny egg oozing over its sides to be captured by his tongue. He talked with his mouth full, wiping it between bites with the pathetic paper napkin.

'I need you back here tonight, Morton – same as the others, six sharp. You'll be with the other uniforms to go in first and then me and the lads will follow once you've all secured the place. Don't touch a thing. If you see anything suspicious, stand next to it and alert Inspector Paulson. You know the drill.'

'Yes, sir,' I said feebly. 'Where are we going?' As well as the onslaught of pungent bacon and egg, I was aware he'd called me 'Morton' twice when usually he said Janice if we were in the office. Did this mean I was now part of the team? He always called the guys by their surnames and now it was my turn. I wasn't sure I liked it.

I placed Linda's file on his desk but sensed from his body language that he wasn't in the mood to discuss it. No need, when we'd spoken so often about it in the past week. My eyes widened in shock when he tossed his half-eaten sandwich onto the cover, ignoring dribbles of runny egg congealing immediately against the faded green card.

'Your shift finishes at four, right?'

It seemed appropriate to stand to attention, hearing the formality in his tone. My uniform was freshly laundered and my shirt starched and pressed like new. I had no worries about presenting a smart appearance.

'Well, you'll have to wait here and put in for some overtime.' He pursed his lips when he looked at me, then finished his breakfast in two bites, leaving me to stand waiting for further information. Something wasn't right between us. Something had shifted. Gazing behind him I noticed that the photo of him and Alison had gone.

'Everyone will be briefed tonight. We're raiding ...' He stopped as a scruffily dressed man in his mid-thirties appeared in the doorway. It was Detective Superintendent Thomson, last seen in the hospital after I was stabbed and, before that, messing about with a halter neck dress.

Before Jarvis could continue, the two men locked eyes and I became invisible. 'I need to speak to you, Frank – now!' He stepped aside, indicating I should leave the room immediately. His ripped brown leather jacket stunk badly as I brushed past him. Whatever was bothering him stopped him from acknowledging me and the door slammed shut as soon as I left.

For some reason I couldn't fathom, my heart thumped as though I had just run a mile. Even my ears were ringing. Was I being paranoid? Was this what it was like after being away from the office for a week? I was scared I wasn't going to continue in CID, maybe because of my involvement with Linda's disappearance and because of the police time wasted on the case.

Was Jarvis embarrassed because he should have solved Linda's disappearance in 1964?

In less than three minutes I was put out of my misery when Jarvis slammed his door open and shouted, 'Morton, get in here.'

The rest of the team had left, with just a couple of stragglers chatting. They quickly vacated the office, not wanting to become the focus of Jarvis's anger. Only Carter remained and as I quickly ran into the boss's office, he followed me uninvited. Jarvis hesitated when he saw him, but flickered his eyes, allowing him to stay.

The drug squad officer, with his untidy tawny hair and Jason King sideburns, leaned against the office partition, glowering at me as though I was his number one enemy. It turned out I was exactly that.

Jarvis too was furious and breathed heavily through his nose, controlling his temper before speaking. My heart thudded so loud I thought it would escape in two pieces through each ear. What the hell …?

'Anything you'd like to tell me, Constable Morton?' Jarvis spoke louder than usual and leaned forward with each hand on the middle of the desk. 'Anything at all? Constable to detective superintendent? Any. Thing. To. Report?'

Bloody hell. This was serious. I felt Carter stiffen behind me and suck in his breath. Scared and terrified, I calmed myself a little. If this was a drugs issue, then there had been a mistake. A big mistake.

I tried to speak but my mouth was as dry as blown sand. 'Sir,' I wobbled, feeling tears prick my eyes and my face flood bright red. 'I … I d-don't understand …'

'Don't you? Don't you really?' He thrust his contorted face closer towards me and when I flinched, he rocked back to stand upright at his desk. Without turning, he held his open left hand behind him. 'Thomson.'

The drug's officer passed him an A4 colour photograph and, without looking at it, Jarvis slammed it on the desk, letting me study it.

'I'll ask you again,' he snarled. 'Police Constable Morton, DO YOU HAVE ANYTHING TO REPORT TO YOUR DETECTIVE SUPERINTENDENT?'

Now I was shaking uncontrollably, staring down at the photograph of two people sitting in a Spanish cafe, drinking wine and laughing. What was the problem? There had to be a stupid mistake. I looked from Jarvis to Thomson in turn, puzzled and indignant.

My mouth was still dry, my lips taut, but I answered him with a steady voice, 'I still don't understand, sir.' I shook my head as I spoke.

Thomson swallowed a snarl. 'Get it sorted, Frank,' he growled, keeping his malevolent eyes fixed on me.

Jarvis watched me closely. 'That is you in the photograph?'

'Yes, sir.' I was genuinely puzzled. He must have seen that because his voice was calmer this time.

'What I want to know, Constable Morton, is why you are sitting – quite happily – in a Spanish restaurant, drinking wine – with Cameron Talbot – the man not only hired to kill you but who is also up to his ears in the drug smuggling at the clothes factory where your friend works?'

36

The Truth about a Tally

Carter, standing close behind me in the small room, must have sensed my shock. I felt his hand on the middle of my back, preventing me from falling backwards.

'His name's Rob,' I whispered. 'That's not ... it can't be a Tally ...' My voice trailed off. I had never known Rob's last name. I'd never asked him because I didn't want to tell him my own surname. Images of us together flashed through my numbed brain.

In the silence, Thomson slammed the palm of his hand against the partition. 'Frank. We don't have much time.'

Jarvis rubbed his unshaven chin and looked up at me from his seat. 'Start from the beginning. How and when did you meet ... *Rob*? And why didn't you tell me you'd met him?'

Why ... why ... why would I tell Jarvis about anyone I met at a nightclub?

'I met him at Cassandra's, the club in town, last year. We only spoke for about half an hour before the club closed. I didn't know I was supposed to report ...'

Ignoring me, Jarvis spun around to face Thomson who was watching me intently. 'Your boys are in there aren't they? Have they said anything?'

Thomson shook his head very slowly, deep in thought.

'Even though there was a death threat against my officer?'

The mood was shifting slightly. Was Jarvis back in my corner?

'When did you see him next?'

'A couple of months later. I'd had a burger with Pat in her lunch break – my friend who worked at the factory. There's a burger van on the industrial site and ...'

Again, Jarvis spun his chair to face Thomson. 'We know that don't we, Doug?'

'She's saying this happened before one of the UCs took over the burger van.' He looked at me. 'What was Tally doing there?'

'He wasn't at the site. He was driving past when he spotted me walking home. We arranged to meet at Cassandra's two weeks later. He said he had some business at the site – he's a chef in his parents' restaurant in Spain. He wants to open a place of his own in the centre of Birmingham.'

Thomson mumbled into the room, 'Spain – that's where he sails from. Fabric is exported from Pakistan through Europe and then your boyfriend sails here to unload it on to a canal barge from Liverpool and then it's driven to the factory. What did you tell him you did for a living?'

Jarvis shot him a warning glance. I reported to him – not to the drug squad.

'He's never asked me about my job. He talks about himself most of the time – like most blokes you meet in nightclubs.' I couldn't resist the smart remark. They'd definitely mistaken Rob for a Tally boy. 'He only knows me as Jan. I pretended I'm a secretary. I never said who I worked for.'

Jarvis leaned forward and jabbed at the incriminating photograph. Tears pricked the back of my eyes again. I looked really pretty for once, wearing a white, high-collared blouse that Linda had given to me. My face was studying Rob as we talked, so happy to be with him after our chance meeting in Malaga town centre.

'And this was also a coincidence was it? Did you tell him you were going to Spain?'

The questions were thrown at me like spears from a hostile native. But his tone was softer now. 'I hadn't seen or spoken to him since the last time at Cassandra's. I hadn't been back to the club while I worked on the Linda Bateman file. The next time was just last Friday in Malaga, when I saw him sitting in that restaurant. He said he'd lost my phone number and didn't know where I lived.'

Thomson folded his arms and sniggered, studying his charity shop trainers with mismatched laces. I noticed the skin on the left side of his nose was puckered from a small scar. 'Of course he had.'

Jarvis stared thoughtfully at Carter who had stepped a little closer to my side. 'So you met this bloke in the nightclub. You liked him?' I nodded, smelling the sausage and brown sauce on his breath.

My cheeks were blazing now. I was grateful Carter spoke more pleasantly to me. Was this the good cop, bad cop routine? 'Yes, I liked him. But he obviously didn't want to see me. He never made any effort to ask more about me ...'

'He doesn't need to ask. This man, known for being violent, already knows everything about you – especially where you work. Especially where you live!' Thomson was playing the even worse bad cop.

My shoulders slumped but I wasn't ready to give in. 'Are you sure this is the same guy you know as Cameron Talbot? It could just be someone who looks like him.'

Thomson, the same rank as Jarvis, was too much of a professional to be swayed by a mere constable, a female constable. 'We're sure. And if he suspects there's a stakeout at the factory, we'll be wasting our time tonight.'

Jarvis tensed his shoulders. 'What about your friend who works there? Does this Rob know about her?'

I thought about that carefully. 'I don't think so. He's only met Pat briefly twice and when he saw me in his car, I'd walked a good distance from the site. He couldn't connect me with the factory unless he saw her working there – but she would look very different to how she dresses for a night out.'

'And Malaga? She was with you out there, wasn't she?'

My eyes glanced down at the photo and I shook my head. 'Not that night. She was missing her boyfriend all week. She stayed at the villa most of the time to get a good suntan. She'd eaten a dodgy prawn the night before, so she wasn't well. Besides, Pat was sacked from the place just before we went away …'

Thomson's head shot up with fresh interest. 'Why?'

I understood his point. 'A stupid reason that didn't make sense. She was talking too much, her boss said – but she's always talked too much, that's how I suspected there was something dodgy going on there. We can't understand why she was sacked. But it's common in that trade – another good dressmaker starts for less money, so they get rid of the ones who earn more.'

Carter breathed normally and laid his hand on my arm. 'You heard enough, boss? I suggest WPC Morton stays here until we've finished tonight. No access to a phone and without permission to leave until you say so. I can arrange for one of the other lads to be in the office at all times to keep an eye on her.'

'Yes.' Jarvis tapped his front teeth with a biro he'd been twirling on his desk. Thomson had left his spot guarding the partition and moved closer to the other superintendent. 'Do that. No need to cancel is there, Doug?'

Jarvis swivelled his chair to face Thomson who bent towards him. I was invisible again as they talked in their own code to each other. Short sentences that meant nothing to me. I was still in too much shock over what had just happened to take anything in. Was Rob really related to the Tallys? Surely if he'd been hired to kill me, he could have done it anytime in the past twelve months.

My blood froze when Thomson whispered loudly, 'You can trust her if you want, but I don't.' It was followed by a more urgent quiet discussion. From nowhere my head buzzed with Linda's proclamation in 1964: 'Lonnie said he wouldn't trust you as far as he could throw you.' But it wasn't true – not anymore.

The whispering stopped. Thomson pushed past me and left without acknowledging either me or Carter. Jarvis was on his feet, grabbing his briefcase. He picked up Linda's file and threw it in his pending tray.

'I'm going home. You should as well, Mick. We need to be fresh for tonight.' He glared at me. 'You won't be needed. You should have mentioned this, Morton – I should have known about anyone you met like this Rob. But I admit, I never suggested you did – so that's on me.

'You heard what Carter said – do not touch the phone. The one on your desk will be removed and do not speak to anyone outside of this office. And I have a job for you to do.'

Thank goodness for that. I hoped I could get back in his good books and keep my job, which now seemed to hang in the balance. I didn't care if I had to leave the CID attachment and walk the beat for the rest of my life, it would be the end of my world if I was kicked off the force. I pictured myself handing over my warrant card and being escorted from the station.

'Using your "so-called" skills,' Jarvis snarled, 'which I now hold in severe doubt ever existed, look up all males in the county matching the description of the man you know as "Rob". When you've finished, I want all the results ready to go over with me tomorrow. It's up to you to prove that our finest, senior, professional drug squad and undercover officers are wrong.'

I opened my mouth to reply but after a nod to Carter and reminding him to get himself home as soon as possible Jarvis was gone. The fury and disappointment he felt towards me lingered in the room like a polluted cloud.

37

Steph

It's amazing how kind people can be when you're in trouble. When I returned to my seat there were three food bags on my desk, each with a cold half sandwich for me to eat as I hadn't been part of the breakfast order. The handful of detectives not involved in the raid on the garment factory vied with each other to relate occasions when Jarvis had gone ballistic with them and boasted about who had been yelled at more often. If I'd managed not to cry in front of Jarvis and the arrogant pig Doug Thomson, this show of support threatened to break me.

I'd stayed strong throughout my career so far. During training at Ryton, a woman police sergeant had chatted to me in the bar one night while the guys crowded round the darts board. 'A word of advice, Janice: never, ever cry in front of any other police officers. It's professional suicide. You could apprehend the biggest crook in the country, and someone will ask if you're the woman who cried on duty ten years earlier.'

There'd been a few circumstances of exceptional emotional challenge, when I'd felt tears fill my eyes and noticed a male officer in the same situation. It was an unspoken understanding to separate and walk away while we dealt with our feelings. I couldn't break down now.

Steph Grainger was the first to appear in the office early in the afternoon. She was formally dressed in an expensive linen suit which fitted her neat, slim frame perfectly. Her brown suede boots matched the earthy colours in the material and the cream blouse looked like silk to me. With freshly washed hair and a broad grin she approached my desk, looking triumphant until she spotted my drooping shoulders and hooded eyes.

'Don't be daft, Potter,' she called over her shoulder to an older detective who'd sat with me all day and mumbled something as she passed him. 'I know better than to take freebies from a place I'm checking out. Just like you do.' DC Potter found something more interesting to look at on his desk. 'What's up, Janice? All this kicking off tonight is down to you – you know that don't you?'

Yes, I did know that. And single-handed I could have ruined everything.

Checking file photographs for a match with Rob's features had almost been a waste of time. With the Spanish photo next to my left elbow, showing his face, I had scrutinised every detail of the Tally twins. The resemblance was undeniable. Rob's tan almost camouflaged his freckles but, stepbrother or not, the likeness was too strong to ignore. I double checked by measuring the distance between their eyebrows and the bridge of their noses. It was the same for all three.

This wasn't enough evidence to present in a court case, but it was enough to confirm what Thomson inferred. The love of my life was a man known as Cameron Talbot.

'Oh, Steph, I've really messed up.' I didn't expect any sympathy. Steph was a career detective, focused on her work, and rarely had much patience when things went wrong. She kept herself detached from the idiotic, racist and profane banter in the office. I wanted to be like her but knew my own failings too well to realise that ambition.

When she frowned and opened her eyes wider, I pushed Rob's photo towards her. 'This is Rob, the man I've met a few times and I like – liked – very much.' I followed it with a printout of the Tally twins' arrest photos. 'His half-brothers. Tally One and Tally Two: Chaz and Dave.'

Steph examined each photo in turn and then again – and again. 'Are you sure? They're all fair-haired, good-looking in a rough kind of way – noses could be similar – but …' She tossed them back over to me. 'I know a couple of guys who look like this … Rob?'

'Cameron Talbot.'

She was shocked when I said the name and she grabbed the Spanish photo again. 'You're kidding. I've never seen a photograph of him.' She peered closer, then looked at me. 'Are you sure?'

Where was Steph when I needed her at 8.30 this morning?

'Yes. I've had all day to prove Detective Superintendent Thomson wrong. His officers have been following this guy for a couple of weeks after they found out he's a part owner of Cassandra's – where I met him last year. They were pretty sure he's the guy the twins are paying to kill me.'

Steph repeated the 'F' word seven times as though she was reciting poetry.

'So how does your Rob threaten tonight's plan?'

I shook my head. Trawling through microfiche records of reports on the Tally twins and their stepfather's family, including his known to be violent son, Cameron Talbot, I hadn't discovered any evidence of a link between him and the garment factory.

'The drug squad are sure he's the European contact, importing rolls of fabric from Pakistan via Spain into Liverpool – and then by different routes to Birmingham, including the canal. The raid will prove if there are drugs hidden somewhere within the fabrics.'

Steph whistled. 'So they put all that together from my reports?'

'Those and the halter neck dress you bought.'

'How?'

I had to grudgingly admit that the day Thomson turned up in Jarvis's office with the Customs officer, they hadn't been messing about after all.

'Thomson and a Customs officer smelt cannabis very faintly on the material. If someone had smoked it near the dress it would have been stronger. But if it had been stored close to the material in bags ...'

Steph whistled. 'I wondered if there was a good reason why the fabrics were kept in a locked storage room after delivery. And they were only ever unpacked during the night shift, when most of us had gone home. Sanjay's family turned up at the premises after our shifts finished. I don't think I've ever seen this guy at the factory, though.' She held up the photograph and squinted at it.

'No, I'm sure of it. But then if he's involved on the overseas side he wouldn't need to be on site.' She was deep in thought and I wished my head held as much information as hers to help me piece some of the puzzle together.

Before he left in the morning Jarvis had sanctioned access for me to some of the Operation Mini Skirt reports, which outlined the months of surveillance by the drug squad, and Steph's undercover work. The last day's report had involved myself and was uncomfortable reading when I saw my name in print, along with the words 'stupid WPC' and 'not to be trusted' sprinkled with unsavoury adjectives not found in my old school dictionary.

How could I blame them for the suspicion?

My desolate mood worsened as I read more and more about Rob. It became obvious he was Cameron Talbot. His birth certificate, possibly the only genuine thing about him, started a trail that led through his school years and trips to Spain to his name on the deeds of ownership of Cassandra's club. Customs confirmed his passport was stamped last Friday for entry into Spain via Malaga.

When I'd spotted him, head down, sitting at a table in Tres Palomas I'd been stunned. I'd called out his name softly to be certain and, at first, he didn't hear me. Now, I wondered if in fact he hadn't expected to be called Rob. How many other aliases did he have? He'd been reading something in a letter when I drew closer to his table and hastily tucked it away in his trouser pocket when I repeated his name.

'Bloody hell. Jan? Jan? Is it you?' His head had swivelled around searching for other companions. 'You look fantastic. Sit down and I'll get the waiter to bring another glass for the rioja.' He disappeared inside the restaurant for ten minutes and then returned with a clean tumbler.

No one could be that good an actor. He'd been genuinely surprised to see me – and not all that pleased at first. When I explained I was in Malaga with Mum, David and Pat he'd smiled while his eyes blinked frantically. He only had fifteen minutes left and then had to leave. He'd wanted to know where I'd been during the week and mentioned a beach we should have visited.

The short time passed quickly and before the bottle of cheap wine had even half emptied, I waved to him as he sped off in a noisy sports car. Had the drug squad officer, tailing him, written that in his report? He must have done. But Thomson preferred the drama of sullying my reputation.

Whoever it was must have found out my name and, by the time his report and the photo hit Thomson's desk – wherever that might be, he'd recognised who I was. I couldn't blame him for marching straight to Jarvis, convinced I'd jeopardised the whole operation.

'Don't worry, Jan. We've all made mistakes.' I'd heard that claim a few times during the day, but it was difficult to believe the perfect Stephanie had ever slipped up. 'You should have been told to check out anyone you met before committing to a relationship with them.'

'But we've never been in a relationship. We've spoken for less than a total of two hours since we first met. If he'd asked me on a date, then I probably would have checked his details. But he's never done that.'

Steph gave a little snort of a laugh. 'You like him, don't you?' I nodded, blushing, and examined my fingernails. Even though he was a bastard Tally, my heart still bounced like a rubber ball every time I looked at his photo. I wondered if I could keep a copy. 'And he's supposed to be paid to kill you – or harm you, or maybe your mother?' Oh dear, the rubber ball had melted like a Dali painting into cold vomit lying in the pit of my stomach.

'It's hard to believe that,' I mumbled.

'It is hard to believe that. He could have arranged to meet you after that first night and pushed you under a bus. He could have spiked your drink and raped you in his car, tossing you out in a country lane, with no memory of what happened. But he hasn't done a thing. He likes you as well.'

I looked up at her, tears swimming in my eyes. Steph was serious. 'When these petty criminals are paid to do a job, they do it, otherwise they don't get paid. This Rob/Cameron may be involved with drug smuggling – and it looks as though he is involved – but he still needs to follow orders from someone above him.'

Steph didn't waste her breath saying anything meaningless. Her words comforted my bruised heart and ego. There was something else I needed to ask her.

'Why was Pat sacked?' I expected her to frown and ask for a description. There must be around thirty women sewing in the factory. 'She's a friend of mine.'

Without any hesitation Steph answered me. 'That was down to me.' She hushed my shocked squeal. 'I needed her out of the place before things started to move. My observations were too suspicious to ignore and after tonight, Janice, there won't be any factory. There'll be yellow DO NOT ENTER tape across every door. The workforce won't have jobs – and neither will they be paid. At least your friend had a week's pay to buy enough tissues to mop up her tears. I did the wages and I made sure of that.'

My brain hurt and I was emotionally tired after the long day. Steph left me to find two cups of tea for us both. She'd known Pat was my friend and how, from her gossip and chatter, I'd suspected something was amiss and that had prompted the undercover operation now in progress. Her actions were meant for the best. Pat would never know she should be thankful for losing her job – but I knew, and I would never forget what Steph had done for both of us.

I was too embarrassed to face the next shift of officers in the station. I'd heard the police dogs whining softly along with the shuffle of boots running up and down stairs. The first stage of the raid had started, and my misery deepened. Putting Rob's betrayal aside, my beloved job was compromised, and I was missing out on the thrill of taking part in a potentially successful drugs seizure.

Standing back from the window to see below without being seen, I watched as men and women checked jackets and pockets for equipment. The raid was too serious for light-hearted banter and no one wanted to be responsible for slipping up. The yard lights illuminated the organised bustle of plain clothes and uniformed officers. Two dog vans were parked with their doors open and patient canines observed the excitement from behind their cages.

Nick Watson, promoted to sergeant while I was on holiday, stood tall and composed in the middle of a group of his shift officers. He patted the shoulders of the female probationer, Newton, and I felt a stir of jealous frustration. If I hadn't been so stupid that could have been me down there with him and the others.

Jarvis hurried around the yard like a bumble bee gathering pollen. He had a word or an order for each person who listened closely and nodded, sometimes directing him towards someone else. I wondered if he was armed like on the night we'd encountered the Tally twins. No one would know if he concealed the weapon under his jacket. His arms moved around, up and down, emphasising a point until he was sure it was understood. It was easy to spot the probationers: they half-heartedly saluted him, uncertain of the protocol.

The marked and unmarked cars, police vans and a motorbike started revving engines. Doors slammed and eventually Jarvis, satisfied everyone involved in the raid was ready to leave, sat in the back of his own vehicle next to Carter. A WPC I didn't recognise was at the wheel. The yard gates were wide open and one by one, at timed intervals, the vehicles and police motorcyclist left as quietly as possible.

Down in the yard I watched a probationer close the gates and as the last bolt slid into place, the lights were switched off plunging it into blackness.

'You bastards,' I heard the probationer roar. 'I can't see an effing thing.'

The raid had begun, and I was alone in the office, excluded from the real work of a police officer. Never had I felt more like a secretary than at that miserable moment.

In the quiet and the solitude and despite all the thoughts running around in my head, another niggle kept rising to the surface. Why was Rob in Malaga last Friday? And why had he been in such a hurry to get away from me?

38

After the Raid

The raid was a success, apart from not finding anything to tie Cameron Talbot in with the drug smuggling. Very little paperwork was found at the factory or at any of the owners' homes and nothing that involved him. None of the Pakistani family admitted to even knowing Rob/Cameron. Jarvis and Thomson were highly commended when a cool half million pounds' worth of cannabis was found inside the folds of rolls of fabric, quickly sniffed out by the excited dogs. The trained animals continued to search every nook and cranny of the factory and apart from a small quantity of weed in a locker, the rest of the place was clean.

Carter called in briefly to tell me to go home. It was late and his clothes were dusty and grubby, but he still looked awake and lively, thrilled with the outcome of the raid. He carried a half-full plastic bin bag with bulging contents.

'Cash,' he announced, 'thousands of pounds. Hidden all over the place. Can you help me count it and then I can log it in the overnight safe? There's still more to come, but Jarvis can sort that.'

Thankful to be deemed useful and trustworthy, I cleared my desk of photos and together we checked the money. It was all in tens, twenties and fifty-pound notes which made it easier to shuffle into piles of thousands. We had to concentrate hard and didn't speak about the raid.

Eventually, we agreed on the total and stacked it in a large cardboard box for the walk-in safe in the custody office.

He hesitated before he left the room and waited while I slipped on my thin cotton jacket. Holding the box with both hands, he clumsily reached out one of them to tap my arm.

'Don't worry, Janice. Frank's in a much better mood. He's been a nightmare planning this ever since Doug smelt cannabis on that dress. They trust each other but it was still a long shot we'd find the drugs.'

He lifted the box higher to his chest. 'This cash is a huge bonus.'

I could only grunt miserably, although I'd pulled a sour expression when he mentioned Doug Thomson.

'Don't let Doug get to you. He was at Ryton with me and Frank so the three of us go way back. Jarvis likes you, so Doug can shout all he likes, but Frank will always stick up for you.'

'It didn't feel like it,' I mumbled.

'Let me tell you this. While the dogs were sniffing around Sanjay, Doug grabbed the lapels on his jacket and threatened to tell his wife about his mistress unless he called off the contract on you.'

My head shot back with shock. Pat's boss had used Rob to threaten my life. How was this possible?

'I thought it was the twins?' I began, floundering with increasing tiredness, numbing my disbelieving brain.

'Sanjay used them to pass the order to their step-brother. The dog handler gave a sign to the dog to start snarling. It didn't take long for Sanjay to tell Doug what he wanted to hear.' He grinned with smug delight at the memory.

'Good.' I still mumbled but I was relieved that Mum and I were safe. I followed Mick down the stairs, with even greater relief to leave the building at last.

The small reception area was empty and I hesitated before opening the door. 'Mick?'

He turned, giving the box another heave against his chest. Banknotes were extremely heavy.

'Do you think I'm a person you can trust?' I dreaded his answer, but his puzzled expression gave me hope.

'If we thought you couldn't be trusted you wouldn't be sitting in the CID office – and don't forget Jarvis had included you in tonight's shindig. Go home.'

'Goodnight, Mick.'

Carter continued walking down a corridor and called over his shoulder. 'Jarvis wants us all in tomorrow around midday – to make up for the late shift. You as well, Morton.'

Morton. Back to Morton. I grinned and breathed a happy sigh as the cold night air hit me. So far, so good.

When I finally arrived home after Carter told me to leave and get some sleep, I broke down in floods of tears. It was nearly midnight. I hadn't eaten anything since breakfast due to nerves and I was emotionally and mentally exhausted after the worst-ever day I'd had at work. My temporary euphoria from hearing Carter's encouraging words had dissipated while I drove home in pouring rain.

All I could see in my head was Jarvis's furious face when he left. Whatever Mick Carter might think, it was Jarvis who was the decision maker. I still didn't know if I would be disciplined for seeing Rob and not reporting it to my senior officer. When I walked in and switched on the living room light, the bulb flashed and popped, plunging me back into darkness.

It had been the last straw and I could only stand howling until Mum ran down the stairs to hug me. My uniform was crumpled and I was smelly from a day in the office. My blue shirt was greasy around the collar and cuffs. I cried like a five-year-old and it was a relief when Mum held me in the warmth of our kitchen.

'It sounds terrible, Janice,' her voice was calm and soothing. 'Jarvis is usually so nice to you – and you were the one who found Linda when he failed. I know you said there's more to it than that but see it from my point of view. You're a really good police officer. It's obvious.'

I'd sobbed out the story of Rob – which she'd half guessed anyway after being banned from answering the phone whenever I was home.

As she warmed some milk to pour into my cocoa, I noticed her mouth twitch slightly and she pinched her nose as though stifling a sneeze.

'What's funny?' I didn't snap out the question. I was too intrigued to find out what could possibly be funny.

'Oh nothing.' She was an expert on knowing the exact moment when the gas should be switched off before the boiling milk foamed over the side of the saucepan into a burnt mess on the stove. She lifted the pan and poured frothy milk into two mugs.

'It's just that ... well, who would have thought you'd fall for the one person paid to do you in? It could only happen to you, Janice, love.'

Neither of us laughed but we both smiled weakly. There had been too much gloom for one day. I finished two bowls of Sugar Puffs and was still hungry. We didn't have churros but Mum had bought ring doughnuts to dip into the hot chocolate and to me it was just as heavenly as sitting on the Spanish terrace in the sunshine.

The memory of that first day in Malaga brought back another unpleasant memory, as stark as the fluorescent overhead kitchen light. I'd done my best to shove it to the back of my mind to discuss after I'd sorted out the Linda file. But now I wasn't sure that would even happen. I pictured again the congealed egg stain left by Jarvis's sandwich on the cover.

Dipping the firm sugary chunk of ring doughnut into the hot chocolate, I reached out my hand to hold Mum's fingers. It was her left hand and I touched the scratched, cheap gold ring she'd always worn.

'Mum, I'm really sorry I was so ungrateful about what you and my dad did for me.'

'I know, love. You said.'

'But I mean it. I was horrible to you on holiday.'

'Let's forget it. You should have some fun thinking about what you want to do with the money. You could buy your own house now.' She turned away to pour cold water into the empty saucepan.

'Oh, I won't do that.' She turned back with another weak smile. 'I know which side my bread's buttered: clothes washed and ironed, shopping done and my meals on the table for me. I'll never leave home unless you run off to Gretna Green and marry David.'

My shoulders relaxed and I leaned back on the faux leather corner seat around our kitchen table. I meant it as well. Home was comfortable and I felt safe here with Mum.

I had another thought. 'You can stop working now. You don't have to keep your job in the school kitchen.'

'You could stop working as well. You don't have to put up with men like Jarvis treating you like a naughty schoolgirl.'

We both shook our heads. 'No, Janice. I like my little job. Don't forget your dad gave me a nice tidy amount of money as well. It's my nest egg and I try not to touch it. I like the school – I like the ladies and I like the kids. I'll give it up to look after your first baby.'

Tears welled in my eyes but I refused to let them fall into my mug. My stomach clenched when I thought of my feelings for Rob. His betrayal hurt me so much. Why couldn't he have been a normal bloke like Danny, instead of being mixed up with drugs and a dodgy nightclub? I didn't believe the Rob I knew would have harmed me ... I wouldn't believe it.

'Don't hold your breath waiting for me to have babies and a Happy Ever After. The men I like are either psychopaths or destined to be chief constable one day, ordering me on traffic duty or washing the patrol cars.'

I managed to smile at her to prove I was joking and not taking myself seriously.

She was really smiling properly, in the way that crinkled her eyes, and a small dimple formed a hole in her right cheek. I wanted the awful day to melt away from me. I'd have a bath before bed, throw every bit of my uniform into the laundry basket and hope the next day would be an improvement. At least the raid had gone well – I knew that much.

I was dunking the second slightly stale doughnut into my cooling chocolate and pushed thoughts of Rob out of my mind. I'd been thinking of my father and my trust fund during my long and boring day and seeing a gaping black hole of unemployment in front of me. I should appreciate what I had and not regret what I'd missed.

'Tell me about my dad.'

It was so late, and Mum looked as tired as I felt. We were both enjoying this rare moment of talking without having to look at the clock. I remembered that Mum needed to be at the school by ten o'clock in the morning, but she didn't seem bothered.

'He was a good man. You remind me of him: clever, sharp and committed to your job. He worked in the car factory but wanted to be a carpenter. He loved wood. He was very artistic – could draw anything and turn it into a sculpture.'

I thought of the tools we used to have in the shed until Mum gave them to Lonnie, who helped us turn it into a summer house.

'The money we won meant he could do what he wanted with his life without abandoning me penniless. I liked him for being so decent, but I knew I didn't love him. If the pools win hadn't happened, we might have ended up arguing all the time and divorced, fighting over you and … any other children we had. I'll tell you more about him another time.'

I had to agree with the last part. I'd seen the damage an unhappy marriage could inflict on parents and children. I'd been lucky. Could I have ended up living like Tanya?

'I've been thinking,' I said as I swallowed down a morsel of dry doughnut. Linda would not have been impressed at our makeshift churros. Mum sat next to me and picked off the tiniest crumb of doughnut to chew. 'I'm going to see if I can help Pat set up her business. She makes beautiful clothes and fashion will never … well, go out of fashion.'

'I think she's sorted on that.' Mum shrugged. 'Her boyfriend is determined to help her out. He sounds like a nice young man. She told me in Spain about their plans – ambitious but impressive.'

'But if it delays them getting a house of their own it could be better for me to be a partner or something – an investor maybe. Then if my job doesn't work out …' I pushed the dreadful thought out of my head. 'Then at least I might have some income from Pat's business.'

Ready for the hot bath and my bed, I stumbled into the hallway just as the phone rang. I still hoped every call would be Rob. Could it be him this time? Would he protest everything I'd heard was lies and he'd be in Jarvis's office first thing in the morning to prove it.

'Janice? That was quick. I thought you'd be asleep.'

I yawned into the phone, not caring about the whole senior officer thing anymore. 'I'm just about to go to bed.' Then my conscience got the better of me. 'Sir.'

His gravelly voice was almost lost in a babble of noise in the background. Someone was shouting for an interpreter and a scuffle seemed to be breaking out behind Jarvis. I heard him cup his hands around the receiver.

'It's been a good night. I'll make sure your name is included in the report – for the intelligence in the first place. We're all taking tomorrow morning off so be in the office by two at the latest. We'll need you to catalogue the evidence with the others when you come in. There's a lot of it.' The scuffle grew louder, and I heard heavy boots running into the room before the line went dead.

39

Photographs

I wasn't sacked from the force and I wasn't suspended.

Jarvis was promoted to Detective Chief Superintendent and moved to take command of a division in Manchester after the factory raid. Despite my uncertainty about him, I was mortified when I heard the gossip in the CID office and hoped it wasn't true. I'd become used to him being my boss and hadn't thought the situation could only be temporary.

Mick Carter confirmed it. 'He was brought up in Manchester until he joined the force and moved down to Ryton,' he said. 'His dad's not in good health so he and Ali thought they could move back with the kids before they get too choosy about schools.'

I tried not to appear glum. 'I was surprised when I found out he married WPC Alison Harper.'

Mick became guarded. He hadn't given away information that wasn't necessary or for any purpose. We were in the canteen in the early afternoon and it was empty, with only the noise from the cooks wiping the floor and closing the shutter.

'They were an unofficial item for years. It's not the done thing to date colleagues.' His lips disappeared into his moustache and he opened his eyes wide as a silent warning. I thought of Nick Watson and then banished him from my mind. We were friends. Just friends.

'Then one day he was in a meeting with the chief superintendent when a buzz went around the station that Ali had been knocked into the canal by a thief she'd recognised. She'd banged her head on the side but a couple walking by had fished her out and ran off to call an ambulance. When Frank heard she was in hospital he walked out of the meeting, commandeered a police car and drove off with lights flashing and siren blasting.'

'He could have been sacked.' I was shocked.

Mick nodded. 'He could have been kicked out before he parked the car across the entrance to the hospital and nearly got a parking fine.'

Fancy Frank Jarvis being so cavalier with his job. If I was shocked before, I was astounded at this information. Mick stood up and we left the canteen together. 'It took him a while to be promoted to chief inspector thanks to that stunt. Ali resigned after she left hospital and they were married six months later.'

I wanted to 'tut' but kept silent. Any stories I heard like this one, always ended with the WPC leaving the job. It would never happen to me. I'd clung on to my own position by the skin of my teeth and had no intention of doing anything stupid and jeopardising my career ever again.

At the beginning of June, I finally completed my two year probationary period. I achieved top marks in my final exams and was proud to be a Woman Police Constable in the West Midlands Police Service. There had been moments in my career when I'd feared I wouldn't make it, so it was a relief to enter the next phase. Mum was excited and proud and at the passing-out parade I made sure she stood in the right place to watch me salute as I marched past the chief constable. She looked smart in a purple tweed suit and black leather gloves.

Before Jarvis left, he made time to speak to me in his office. After the excitement of the raid and all the preparations to take Sanjay and his gang to court, we'd barely seen each other. Apparently, Customs weren't too happy that the raid had taken place against Adam Byrne's advice. The drug squad had seized the drugs and the supplier but Byrne wanted the syndicate behind the organisation. Consequently, Thomson, Jarvis and Byrne were often in heated discussions with each other and everyone in CID kept out of their way.

Jarvis packed his personal possessions into old cardboard boxes. All the photographs from his shelf were gone. After telling me to sit down, he stopped packing and sat at the desk as though he was interviewing me.

At first, I dreaded he was giving me a verbal warning but instead he sternly advised me to keep studying.

'Some police officers do a great job as constables all their lives. They're a support to their colleagues and they amass a ton of invaluable knowledge and experience. But that's not for you, Janice. You've already shown you've got something that's vital for the job – curiosity and observation. There's a lot the force can add to that – if you're willing.'

I murmured my agreement and wished the manual wasn't so thick and my brain was more capable of memorising the endless procedures and the law.

He ignored my feeble excuses. 'You've done well in your time so far. Finding Linda Bateman is over now.' He handed me the dog-eared file; the egg stain stared me in the face, but I had no wish to look at it again. 'The DPP has agreed it's not in anyone's interests to pursue any prosecutions. The file will need to go to Registry.'

It was the best news he could have given me. Linda and Paulo were married now, and it would be a relief to her and the family. Rosie had made a beaming bridesmaid with a proud Hazel and Lonnie enjoying a holiday in the sunshine. Mum and I could have been there but under the circumstances I didn't want to take any more time away from work.

'Sir, can I ask you something?'

He frowned and nodded.

'How do you know David Brown? He sees a lot of my mum.'

He half turned to the window and then remembered the photo was tucked inside one of his boxes. Irritated, he leaned forwards with his hands together on the desk. I waited to hear something interesting.

'Janice, I've just said you have an excellent and enquiring mind. But there are some questions you don't need to ask – and there are answers you don't need to know. Is that understood.'

It was a puzzle. How could I say I understood? I didn't understand. He must know the man called David Brown. Why couldn't he tell me. As for 'questions I didn't need to ask', it only made me more determined to find out David's connection to a senior police officers' dinner.

Jarvis didn't dismiss me, so I fidgeted with the file and waited for him to continue.

'That business with the Tally brother.'

I stiffened but Jarvis waved his hand as though swatting a fly. 'What was said in this room on the morning of the raid stays within these four walls.'

What a relief. 'What about Detective Superintendent Thomson, sir?' That man hated me. I was sure of it.

Jarvis grinned and shuffled papers on his desk. It was his sign he wanted me out of his office. 'Don't worry about him. If he wants to make a fuss – and he doesn't – I can remind him of the time he threw a dangerous prisoner into the back of the prison van and then forgot to lock it. Now get on with your work and remember what I said about studying.'

I wanted to salute him, but he was sitting down at the desk and he wasn't in uniform. He'd helped me a lot and I was sorry he was leaving.

I no longer suffered from the overwhelming guilt over abandoning Linda. Rob was a mysterious figure somewhere in Spain and if he knew what was good for him, he'd stay there. Interpol and the UK Customs investigators had his details and he should lie low unless he wanted an undercover copper to recognise him.

I tried hard to forget him. Neither Pat nor I would be spending Saturday nights in Cassandra's ever again. Danny had missed her while she was away for all of seven days. When she returned, he gave her a narrow gold band with diamond chips all around it. He called it an eternity ring and asked her to 'go steady' with him. I was pleased for them both.

Steph was right: the factory staff all lost their jobs. The factory was sealed up until the case was completed and the outcome of any convictions known. Then it would be for sale and if no one bought it, the contents and furniture were to be auctioned off. I'd let Pat know when that happened so she could bid for anything she could use for her new business.

A month after the raid I was on study leave, sitting at home trying to concentrate on my training manuals for the sergeant's exam. Having survived a terrifying crisis that threatened my future, I was determined to be more focused.

It was a stifling hot summer's day and my bedroom window was as wide open as it could be to let in an occasional breeze. Taking a break, I leaned my head outside only to cook in the Mediterranean-like heat. The garden looked pretty, and our fence had been painted white after the ivy was killed off and cleared away.

The sight of Rosie standing on her soap box peering over the hedge at our back door was a welcome distraction. I called to her from the window and told her to wait for me to come round and we'd have some cake. She held up a photo album with a big grin on her face – wedding photos. I hoped there weren't too many.

Mum had baked a Victoria sponge and home-made strawberry jam oozed from the middle. David's mother had shown her how to make the sponges rise to a depth that made the Lyons version look flat and uninteresting.

'Take some home with you for Hazel and Lonnie,' I said, wrapping a couple of slices in greaseproof paper. We escaped with our plates to my bedroom. The kitchen was being updated and everywhere downstairs smelt of paint and plaster. It was nicer in my bedroom despite the sizzling sun streaming through the window.

Once our cake was eaten and fingers were licked clean, we sat on my bed flicking through the album.

'You look lovely,' I said for the fiftieth time at the fiftieth photograph of Rosie with Linda, Rosie with Lonnie, Rosie with Hazel, Rosie with just about everyone. She looked happy with all the attention and clutched her squirming niece. I swished the yellow chiffon-capped sleeves on her dress. She'd insisted on wearing it to show me. It was stained with pizza sauce and smeared with chocolate, but the photographs were evidence of its original charm.

She was thirteen now and growing tall, with the lovely nature her sister possessed. We enjoyed each other's company and as far as I knew she hadn't changed her mind about joining the police force. The thought of it inspired me to study harder. I could help her in the future if I achieved a sergeant's or inspector's rank.

After we finished the cake and a discussion about Spain and weddings, I lay back on my bed feeling sleepy. I heard Rosie tinkering with the lotions and potions and jewellery on my dressing table. When I could no longer hear her twittering to herself, I opened my eyes.

'Rosie, where are you? You mustn't go into Aunty Evelyn's room. She doesn't like people to go in there.'

Too late. I popped my head around the door expecting Rosie to join me straight away. She lay on the floor reaching beneath Mum's bed.

'You mustn't do that, Rosie,' I began and stopped as I watched her pull out an old leather photograph album. 'What's that?'

'My mum keeps hers under the bed. She looks at it before she goes to sleep.'

Rosie was guileless about digging around in someone else's belongings. She was going to make an excellent police officer if she carried on that way, I thought.

Ignoring any qualms of doing something wrong, she sat cross-legged on the floor and opened the album across her lap. I decided to join her. It was my baby photos from the first year I was born, and I now understood why there were some gaps. Mum had said they were loose photos that dropped out and were lost. I guessed they may have been of my dad, proving he hadn't died shortly after I was born.

It had been years since I'd looked through the album. I'd never been photogenic, unlike most babies, so I was never bothered about looking at myself. Over the years my opinion hadn't changed. Rob had made me feel special for the first time ...

Don't go down that path, Janice. Concentrate on the badly focused photos.

There I was in my pram, dressed head to foot in a black and white monstrosity of knitwear from woolly hat to mittens and booties. I must have been about eight months old, grinning uncertainly at the camera. It was a familiar expression of mine. A mixture of curiosity and suspicion. Rosie roared with laughter and I nudged her in playful chagrin.

'I'll remember this when you join the force and I'm your sergeant. I'll give you all the horrible jobs to do.'

She pored over each photograph, amused at the old-fashioned pram and plastic rattle. Both of us thought my bewildered expressions were hilarious. Rosie carefully turned over the waxed sheet which separated each page of photographs, ready to torment me with the next horror story of my terrible twos.

Abruptly, I held her arm. 'Not yet,' I whispered, unable to trust my voice not to crack.

In my work, whenever I spotted a distinctive facial feature in either a suspect or a victim, my blood momentarily froze, and goose bumps rippled along my arms. The same thing was happening as I looked at the once-amusing photographs. They were all similar, taken on the same day with the same leaf-shedding tree in the background. A suited figure bent down next to the duckpond, his face turned away from the camera.

I wasn't looking at the man in the background.

First photograph: Pram. Baby. Smiling. Two small teeth showing at the front of my open mouth.

Second photograph: Pram. Baby. Smiling. Only one tooth on show at the front of my open mouth.

It was impossible. I wouldn't lose – or gain – a tooth in the matter of a few minutes.

Rosie was quiet and we both studied the photographs. She pointed at the second photo.

'Janice, that baby isn't you.'

Of course it was me.

'Of course it's me.'

'That baby girl is you. You can see the two teeth in all the other photos. But that one …'

The babies were identical. If one of them was me, then who was the other?

Read more about Janice Morton, promoted to sergeant in Book 2: The Search for Susan (with Sergeant Janice Morton)

Acknowledgements

Writing this book gave me a great deal of pleasure. I wanted to set it in Birmingham at a time that I remember while I was growing up. Janice's house is my house and the orchard existed until it was developed into a small housing estate. The characters though are completely fictional. Although, some of the names may have been borrowed from past friends.

Janice is a year older than me. When I was almost at the end of the final editing, I discovered from an ex-WPC with the West Midlands Police that recruits could only be accepted at Ryton from the age of nineteen. I had originally wanted her to be eighteen and had to make the necessary revisions. Penny Talbot wrote about her career in *Policewoman, Wiltshire Constabulary (1970s)* and when I contacted her by email, she was very helpful with my research. I have always been grateful to people who have written about their lives from diaries and experiences and published them. Penny's husband, Michael also published his memoir in *A Peeler in the Family (West Midlands Police 1974 – 2004)*.

Another book that has become almost a bible for me is *Drug War* by Peter Walsh which outlines the war on drugs in Britain since the 1950s fought by Customs and the Police. It was extremely informative in describing drugs transported from Liverpool to Birmingham along the canal system. This has helped with future novels featuring Janice Morton as she is promoted in her job.

For every writer there are many friends and family members who give great support and encouragement. My husband Steve is the first on the list, especially for putting up with me tapping away at the laptop every night and singing along to disco music with headphones in my ears. There are two more books to edit and a fourth to be completed so his patience will have to be never ending. Appreciation too must be given to my sister-in-law Yvonne Harris and mother-in-law Fay Harris, as well as my nephew, the intrepid traveller and new father, Martin Phillips.

Hopefully, I won't leave out any of my friends who have had to listen to me talking about my ideas or reading drafts of the book. Hopefully, they will understand how valuable it is to be asked, 'How is the book?' just so that I can talk over the latest developments. Thank you to Mitzi Bales, Rosemary Butler, Thelma Fisher, Robi Brown, Gail Atherton, Alison Eaves, Maggie McKenzie, Rena Crutchfield, Sue Hogg, Tracey Lawrence, Susan Dear, Emma Russon, Janet Wurstlin, Lesley Bowden and I'm sure, many more.

Principally though, it is the members of the *Tring Writers' Circle* who must be acknowledged for listening to each chapter read out at our bi-weekly meetings. Their constructive feedback helped me to stand back and re-think themes and story outline. A memorable remark was 'How is this moving the story on?' from Abby Fermont. Thank you also to Davina Smith, Helen Garton, Sandra Hill, Jules Wake, Liz Manning and Nicky Bull. Nicky also edited the final draft and helped me to review my work once again. These ladies have encouraged me since 2012 and are themselves brilliant writers.

It's a privilege to have imagination and creativity. I hope all who read this first novel in the Janice Morton series enjoys it.

Julie Harris
February 2021